Praise for *The Wrong Family*

"*The Wrong Family* is your new obsession... You've never read anything like this."
—**Colleen Hoover, #1 *New York Times* bestselling author**

"It's not just a stunning thriller—it's a force of reflection, as full of empathy and truth as it is shocking twists and turns."
—**Megan Angelo, author of *Followers***

"Tarryn Fisher's latest thriller is like riding a roller coaster in the dark... You won't devour this book. It will devour you."
—**Tess Callahan, author of *April and Oliver***

"No one writes as authentically as Tarryn Fisher. She is truly a once in a generation writer and *The Wrong Family* proves that, yet again."
—***New York Times* bestselling author Anna Todd**

Praise for *The Wives*

"You'll have whiplash until the very end. *The Wives* will leave the most sure-footed reader uneasy until the last word is read."
—**#1 *New York Times* bestselling author Colleen Hoover**

"I couldn't put it down... Nail-biting, heart-clenchingly good from the start, with characters that you both root and cringe for. I loved every word."
—***New York Times* bestselling author Alessandra Torre**

Fans of Gillian Flynn's *Gone Girl* will revel in *The Wives*... Will keep readers on their toes until the final page."
—***USA TODAY***

"A fantastic thriller...filled with twists and turns you won't see coming."
—***PopSugar***

"[An] engrossing psychological thriller... Suspense fans will be rewarded."
—***Publishers Weekly***

"Fisher is a writer to watch."
—***Kirkus Reviews***

Also available from Tarryn Fisher
and Graydon House

The Wives

For more about Tarryn Fisher, visit www.tarrynfisher.com.

THE
WRONG
FAMILY

TARRYN FISHER

GRAYDON
HOUSE

**GRAYDON
HOUSE®**

Recycling programs
for this product may
not exist in your area.

ISBN-13: 978-1-525-81000-8

The Wrong Family

This edition published by arrangement with Harlequin Books S.A.

Graydon House
22 Adelaide St. West, 40th Floor
Toronto, Ontario M5H 4E3, Canada
www.GraydonHouseBooks.com
www.BookClubbish.com

Printed in U.S.A.

For Traci "Face" Finlay
and Aunty Marlene

THE

WRONG

FAMILY

PART ONE

1

JUNO

Juno was hungry. But before she could eat, she had to make it to the fridge without cutting herself.

She eyed a safe-ish route through the largest shards of glass that led past the island. She wore only thin socks, and as she stepped gingerly from a black tile to a white, it felt like she was playing a human game of chess. She'd heard the fight, but now she was seeing it in white porcelain shards that lay like teeth across the floor. She couldn't disturb them, and she definitely couldn't cut herself. When she rounded the island, she saw a green wine bottle lying on its side, a U-shaped crack spilling wine in a river that flowed beneath the stove.

Juno eyed all of this with mild curiosity as she arrived at her destination. The old GE hummed as she opened it, the condiments rattling in the door. The shelves were mostly empty—clean, but empty, Juno noted, the essence of this house and everything in it. *Except today*, she thought, looking back at the slaughtered dinnerware. She pressed two fingers to her lips and sighed into the fridge. They hadn't been to the market. She tried to remember the last time they'd come home with bags of groceries, Winnie's reusable sacks sagging as badly as Juno's tits. *They'll go soon*, she told herself. They had a child to feed, Samuel, and thirteen-year-olds ate a lot. But she was still worried. She pulled the only two Tupperware containers from the shelf, holding them up to the light. Spaghetti, three days old. It looked dried out and clumpy: they'd toss it tonight. She set that one on the counter. The other contained leftover fried rice. Juno held this one longer; she had smelled it cooking last night from her bed, her stomach grumbling. She'd tried to name the ingredients just by their smell: basil, onions, garlic, the tender green pepper Winnie grew in the garden.

Prying the lid off the container, she sniffed at its contents. She could just take a little, skim off the top. She ate it cold, sitting at the tiny dinette that looked out over the back garden. They'd been fighting about the house, and then money, and then Winnie had slammed the casserole dish on something—presumably not Nigel's head, since he was alive and well as of this morning. The wine had been knocked over seconds later.

The clock above the doorway read ten seventeen. Juno's sigh was deep. She'd run over-schedule, and that meant no time for a shower today. She ate faster, hurrying to wash her fork and dry it, then she tiptoed around the deceased casserole dish, making a face at the mess. She'd started a book a few days ago, and she wanted to get back to it. At sixty-seven there were few pleasures in life, but Juno considered reading one of them.

She glanced back once more to check the state of the kitchen, wondering who was going to clean up the mess. She liked the checkered black-and-white floor that Nigel was eager to trade for fabricated wood. The olive green fridge would have been impressive once on the Sears sales floor, and it made her heart flutter every time she walked into the kitchen. It was a *lived-in* kitchen, none of that sterile modernism you typically found in subdivisions named after trees. And she was lucky to be here. Greenlake was the type of neighborhood people were willing to pay exorbitant amounts of money to live in. She knew that, and so the last thing she wanted to do was upset her standing with the Crouches. She flicked the light off and stepped into the hallway, leaving their business to themselves. That wine was going to be a mess to clean up.

To Juno's left and down six feet of hallway were the foyer and formal living room. The foyer was a depressing little alcove with stained-glass windows looking out over the park. It used to be paneled in dark wood, but Winnie had it painted white, which only moderately improved the overall feel of it. And then there were the family photos: studio portraits of Sam through the years as his teeth jutted from his gums like Chiclets. There were a couple of Nigel and Winnie, too, doing wedding things: Nigel in black tie and Winnie in a simple slip dress that was no doubt inspired by Carolyn Bessette's on the day she married John Kennedy Jr. But despite the desperate attempt at cheerfulness, the foyer was doomed to look like a vestry. Juno had heard Winnie commenting on the gloominess and hinting endlessly at Nigel to do something about it. "We could have that tree outside the front door cut down. That would open up the room to so much light..." But her earnest suggestions fell on a man too distracted to hear them.

Winnie had settled for keeping the light above the front door on at all times. Juno quietly sided with Winnie on this issue. The entryway *was* gloomy. But beyond the front doors, past a smallish, unfenced yard and then a busy street, was Greenlake Park. And that was the best thing about the house. Greenlake, a neighborhood in Seattle, was urban-suburban in feel, and its center was the lake and park after which it was named. Looping around the lake was a 2.8-mile nature trail. You could be homeless or a millionaire; on that trail it didn't matter—people came, and walked, and shared the space.

Juno trudged right instead toward the rear of the house, and the hallway opened up to the family's dining room on one end and a great room on the other. When she'd first moved in, she'd been startled by the clash of color and pattern that jumbled across the room.

Nudging a fallen throw pillow out of her way, Juno walked slowly to the bookshelves, flinching at the pain in her hips. She was limping today, and she felt every bit of year sixty-seven. The bookshelves were just a dozen feet away, but she paused at the halfway mark, standing still and closing her eyes until the pain passed. She'd get there eventually; she always did. When the throbbing passed, she shuffled forward, her joints crying out. It was a bad day; she was having more and more of those lately. If she could just make it to the bookcase...

It had been that way for quite some time, the disease raking its way across her joints. Her symptoms had felt flu-like initially, steadfast aches hanging on to her bones in meaty tendrils. But now it didn't just merely hurt to move, her joints were on fire—the pain often so intense Juno wanted to die. Her extremities were always swollen, her fingers tinged blue like Violet Beauregarde's face in *Willy Wonka and the Chocolate Factory*. To make matters worse, she was hit with five to six dizzy spells a day, and every time she fell it hurt worse, being that there was less and less of her to cushion the fall. She didn't have a computer of her own, so she'd used the Crouches' computer to Google the best diet for her condition, asking the big robot in the sky what foods she should and should not be eating. The big robot said to eat things like fish, beans and to drink a lot of milk. Juno had been eating a can of beans a day since, though she could do without the fish, and when she was especially angry with Winnie, she'd drink milk straight from the carton standing at the fridge.

There was a slight incline from the living room to the book nook; it was there that Juno failed to lift her toe in time due to an untimely dizzy spell. She stumbled sideways as top became bottom and bottom became top, and her thigh slammed into the sharp edge of a side table. Clear, sharp pain flared as she opened her mouth to cry out her surprise, but the only sound she made was a strangled gurgling before she fell. The last thing she saw was the spine of the book she was reading.

Juno sat up slowly. Her mouth was dry, and it hurt to open her eyes. She was embarrassed even though there was no one around to see her. What was that about? She rubbed the spot on her thigh, wincing; there'd be a plum-sized bruise by tomorrow. For the first time in years she found herself wanting a drink—a strong one. If she was going to topple around like a drunkard, she might as well be one. It was all talk, though. She'd given up drinking ages ago, if only to prolong her life, and the stuff that Nigel kept in the house made the roof of Juno's mouth ache. *Enough with the pity party, old girl,* she thought, *it's time to get up.* She shifted so that her legs were folded beneath her and then dropped forward until she was on her hands and knees.

Last week she'd fallen in the bathroom and got a nasty cut when her forehead met the corner of the basin. She hadn't passed out that time; she'd just been dizzy, but it had been enough to send her keeling over.

The cut throbbed now as she crawled like a dog, head down, her knees singing painfully, her hands and feet swollen and puffy like unbaked dough. When she reached the chaise longue, she hauled herself up using the last of her energy. She hurt, every last inch of her; she'd be paying for this fall for days.

"Ha!" she said, staring resentfully at the books.

She found her novel, sliding it from between the stacks and tucking it under her arm as she made her way to the nearest armchair. She hated sitting in the chaise longue; it made her feel too much like Winnie. But she made it through only one page before the exhaustion of the morning caught up to her.

Juno woke with a start. A male purple martin sat on a branch near the window, chortling. *Tchew-wew, pew pew, choo, cher!* She hadn't seen one since before they'd all left before winter. As she sucked back the saliva that pooled in the corners of her mouth, her bottom lip quivered. She was drowsy, her limbs sleep soaked. It was her damn circulation again. She slapped her thighs with mottled hands, trying to get the feeling back. She was exhausted with a capital *E*.

As she pushed forward out of her chair, her book thudded to the rug, landing on its belly, pages crushed and folded like origami. She looked with alarm first at the book and then at the shadows, which were all wrong. Her head jerked in the direction of the window, which faced east toward the back garden. To the rear of the garden was a gate that led to an alley. Nigel Crouch often came home through that door, but the gate was closed, the latch still in place.

The clock—what did the clock say? Her eyes found the time on the cable box. She registered the numbers in disbelief; it was suddenly becoming hard to pull in air. Stumbling toward the stairs, Juno forgot the book that had tumbled from her lap moments before. The very last thing she wanted was a run-in with one of the Crouches today.

She was just in time: Nigel had come home from work earlier than usual today. There was the clatter of keys on the table, and then the hall closet opened as he dumped his work bag inside. From there she heard him go straight to the kitchen, probably for a beer. From where Juno lay under her covers, dreading having to hear another blowout fight, she heard him swear loudly. Her index finger found the place behind her ear where her skull curved into her jaw, tracing the spot with the pad of her finger, a childhood comfort she still relied on. Neither of them had been willing to put aside their pride to get out the mop and clean the mess from the fight. Juno bet he was wishing he hadn't chosen today to come home early. She heard him walking directly over the casserole dish, the heels of his shoes grinding the porcelain to sand.

The fridge opened, followed by a loud "Dammit!" His beer shelf was empty. She heard him head over to the pantry instead, where Juno knew he kept a bottle of Jack Daniel's hidden behind the condiments. Over the course of months, Juno had gleaned that Winnie hated smelling alcohol on his breath. Her father had been killed by a very wealthy drunk driver, and she claimed the smell triggered her. The settlement from the lawsuit had been huge; Winnie and her siblings had been handsomely paid for the loss of their father. Because of that, Winnie didn't allow Nigel to drink anything stronger than beer or wine.

From where Juno lay, she imagined that he was glancing over the mess of angrily spilled wine as he drank straight from the bottle. He had a lot to be aggravated about, in her opinion. Two days ago, Winnie had taped a husband to-do list to the side of the fridge. Juno had paused to read it, flinching at the tone. It wasn't directly addressed to him, of course; it never was, but there was an underlying assumption that these were his jobs. The top of the notepad said Projects, underlined three times:

-Fix the doorbell.

-Stain the back deck before it rains.

-Remove wallpaper from bedroom near stairs.

-Dig up the plum tree. It's dead!

-Clean the gutters.

She heard a cabinet open and close. Juno knew it was the one under the sink by the sound the loose hinge made; he was grabbing a rag. Then the sound of running water and the rustling of a sturdy black garbage bag being shaken open. And then, listening to Third Eye Blind on full blast, Nigel began to clean the mess his wife had made the night before. It took him fifteen minutes, and at one point she heard the vacuum going. When he was finished, she heard him lingering near the front door, probably considering if he should give the doorbell another go.

There was nothing *wrong* with the doorbell; it worked perfectly fine. Juno was of the strong opinion that Winnie was spoiled.

"It's too loud," Winnie had complained. "Every time someone rings it, I feel as if we're being robbed at gunpoint."

Juno wasn't sure what chimes had to do with being robbed at gunpoint, but the lady of the house wanted the bell switched to something "more soothing."

By now, Juno knew a thing or two about this family. For one: Winnie was a too-much girl. There was always too much spice on her food, too much mustard on her sandwich, too much cologne on Nigel. If Nigel tried to do things his own way, Winnie would watch him like a hawk, waiting for him to mess up. And he did—he always did. If someone were waiting for you to mess up, well then of course you would. She was like a door-to-door salesman, the way she demanded everyone conform to her whims: once her spiel started, you were screwed into listening.

And for two: Nigel hated color—hated it. His den was decorated in defiance of Winnie's garish collection of designer decor, which was sprinkled across the house, meant to look unassuming and missing by a long shot. Mr. Crouch did most things passive-aggressively. Juno had a great deal of respect for the passive-aggressive. They got things done, in their own way, though if it went unchecked, it led to trouble. She'd seen it in the couples who'd dragged each other into her office, demanding that she fix their spouse. "You can't fix it if you don't know it's broke," she'd tell them. And Nigel didn't know. The rules by which he lived were the result of being an only child and being an only child to a single mother. Winnie was his priority—he had an innate need to take care of women, and specifically *his* woman—but he was bitter about it. Maybe he hadn't been in the beginning, but he was now.

The box at the door (which Nigel had ordered) said the new bell played "Twinkle, Twinkle, Little Star." Winnie had squealed excitedly when she saw it, and Juno had smiled knowingly into her elbow. Juno knew that Nigel had been snide in his choice, yet his bubbling blond bride was pleased as pudding.

She heard him linger for a moment longer before he moved on. There would be no doorbell installation tonight.

2

WINNIE

It was 6:47 p.m. when Winnie's car pulled past Mr. Nevins's ancient Tahoe and into her own driveway. As soon as her car was in park, she cast an irritated glance in her rearview mirror. The Tahoe, a rusty beige thing festooned in bumper stickers, was parked on the street directly outside her living room window. It had been there for the last three weeks, and Winnie was tired of looking at the yellow rectangle that said *You Mad Bro?* that Mr. Nevins had slapped drunkenly on the back passenger-side window. Yes, she was mad, and she didn't need that sticker calling her out every time she happened to look that way. But tonight was not the night to be angry at the neighbors; tonight was a celebration.

She checked her makeup in the visor mirror, having freshly

applied it at work before she left. It looked like she was wearing little to no makeup, of course. That's how Winnie rolled: she liked to make things look easy when really everything she did had a lot of sweat behind it.

Stepping into the drive, Winnie tiptoed across the gravel, being careful not to sink her heels into the dirt. Her bag under her arm, she opened the side gate, hearing Nigel moving around the kitchen before she could see him. She felt bad about last night; she'd overreacted. She knew that now. Her plan was to apologize right away, get it out of the way so that they could enjoy the rest of their kid-free night. She hadn't meant for things to get as heated as they had, but lately Winnie had felt off balance emotionally. It was her own fault; sometimes she looked for things to be upset about, as if a lack of problems was its own problem in her mind. Nigel would rather pretend that nothing was wrong, though he hadn't always been like that. Her husband hated confrontation, and that comforted Winnie. The kitchen window came into view, and Winnie saw that Nigel had left the back door open.

She breathed a sigh of relief when she stepped into what she thought of as the belly of the house. It was clean, the spills from last night mopped and cleared away—not a speck of her Pyrex on the floor. She felt more positive than she had even five seconds ago. Nigel was a good man; he'd cleaned everything up so she wouldn't have to, even though she'd been the one to pick the fight.

As she closed the door quietly behind her, Nigel stood with his back to her, examining the contents of the fridge. Winnie took a moment to admire him; he hadn't heard her come in on account of the music he was playing, "Dreams" by Fleetwood Mac. She didn't want to startle him, so she waited, her hip leaning against the lip of the counter. It felt like such a strange thing to do, being that they'd been married for over a decade, but sometimes Winnie had no clue how to act around her husband.

For the most part, Nigel was charming, funny, easy to talk to—*check, check, check.* The one thing people never seemed to pick up on was the fact that he refused to talk about himself. If you asked him a question, he'd deflect, lead the conversation back to you. For this reason, Winnie felt like she couldn't really know her husband; he simply didn't want to be known. She was content to be part of him, however shallow that made her.

When he turned around, she had her best smile ready.

Nigel jumped. "Je—sh—you scared me."

"Sorry. I was actually trying not to."

Nigel didn't smile back; he was distracted. Winnie cocked her head, trying to read his face. He was wearing his feelings tonight. Nigel became still when he was troubled—his face, his body, everything frozen in sagging, bent defeat.

She skipped over, wrapping her arms around him. He smelled so good, and not because of cologne or aftershave— *Nigel* smelled good. When they'd first started dating, he'd accepted her enthusiastic affection with the amusement an owner would have for a new puppy. And Winnie had loved being Nigel's new puppy; the joy her personality seemed to bring him gave Winnie's every day meaning. He'd given her the nickname Bear, a Winnie-the-Pooh joke.

But then the bad thing had happened.

After that, it was as if the rosy illumination with which he viewed her had been replaced with harsh, supermarket lighting. She wasn't Bear anymore. Now she was just plain old Winnie. But it wasn't like she still had hearts in her eyes every time she looked at him, either. They were settled into their arrangement, whatever that was, and though Winnie loved her husband very much, she saw him through human eyes now.

"Nothing for dinner," he said. Lifting his hands to her back, he looked over his shoulder, staring dully into the fridge. Winnie thought he was joking. She smiled, wanting him to get on with it and tell her where they were going.

But then he pointed to the plastic containers stacked on the otherwise bare shelf: spaghetti and fried rice. "The spaghetti is old," he announced, and then held up the Tupperware container of rice. "There's barely enough for one person. I could have sworn there was more left over."

She screwed up her face, the two of them examining the Tupperware, Winnie trying not to cry. He'd forgotten their anniversary. He'd forgotten once before, in the beginning, and he'd felt really bad about it. Winnie didn't think he'd feel bad about it this time.

"Eggs," Nigel said suddenly, jarring her. "We have a box of powdered eggs that came with that survival kit your brother got us."

"For our wedding?" Winnie gaped. She was hoping the word *wedding* would spark some recognition in her husband, but Nigel didn't answer—he was in the pantry moving things around.

"Why can't we just get takeout…?"

There was no answer. When he emerged from the pantry, the box of powdered eggs in his hand, her heart shriveled a little. This was for real, this was serious: they were going to eat fifteen-year-old powdered eggs for dinner. Winnie opened her mouth, the words poised on the tip of her tongue, ready to fly, but then she noticed a dark curl resting across her husband's forehead. He looked like a little boy—like Samuel. She didn't really know why in that moment she lost her voice, or why she'd lost it a hundred other times. She loved this man something terrible; she just wasn't sure if he loved her anymore. Today was their fifteenth wedding anniversary, and they were having powdered eggs for dinner.

While they ate, Nigel talked about a book. Usually Winnie was better at listening, but today she was furious that he'd forgotten their anniversary and now was talking about something that didn't interest her in the least. Had he thought she'd read it? It was Stephen King, for God's sake. The only feelings Winnie could pull when she thought of those brick-sized books *were* misery and desperation. All puns intended.

She watched as he ungracefully spooned neon eggs into his mouth, oblivious to her discomfort. He was so hungry; why was he so hungry? The ketchup, she noted, made their anniversary dinner look like a crime scene. Picking up her glass of water, she drank deeply, trying to open her ever-constricting throat. The kitchen was cold. Winnie wanted to get up and close the door, but she was too tired. Nigel's voice was a dull drum, and she listened to the beat rather than the words. She wondered if she should give him the present she'd bought him; it would make him feel bad, but she'd been so excited about it. In the end, she said nothing, pushing her fake eggs around her plate until eventually she dumped it all down the disposal. She didn't want to upset Nigel; she needed him in the mood.

Winnie wanted one last shot at getting pregnant again before her ovaries went into retirement. Her friends thought she was crazy—she had a perfectly healthy thirteen-year-old son, why in the world would she want to start all over? As she stacked the plates into the dishwasher, she tried to list the reasons: because she hadn't gotten to enjoy it the first time, because she felt like she owed Samuel a connection in life other than her and Nigel, and because she wanted someone to love her unconditionally.

But by the time Winnie's dainty blue dinner plates were tucked into the dishwasher, her attitude was limp and her tear ducts were straining. Nigel was still sitting at the table, scrolling through his phone with glassy eyes. She didn't like the way he was sitting, with one ankle balanced on a knee so casually. Winnie stood in front of the fridge to hide the tears now rolling down her cheeks.

One, four, eight and fifteen: those had been the hardest years of their marriage. Sometimes it had been her who'd caused the trouble and sometimes it had been Nigel. A lot could happen in fifteen years. But no matter how Nigel messed up, no matter what trouble he brought into their marriage, it would never be as bad as what Winnie had done. She knew that and he knew that.

The very thing that kept them together was also the thing that kept them apart.

3

WINNIE

Her first date with Nigel had been a setup by Winnie's cousin Amber, who "knew a guy."

The guy she knew was Nigel Angus Crouch, and if Winnie had heard his full name before she agreed to the date, she would have said "Hard no." Fortunately, her cousin kept his full name to herself during the matchmaking. Amber had just moved to Washington from New York the year before. She already knew more people than Winnie, who'd grown up there.

"What guy? How do you know him?"

"Kevin knows him. He's starting over."

"Starting over? What does that mean?" Winnie hadn't exactly trusted Amber's taste in men; her last boyfriend had kept pet snakes. She shuddered, remembering the time he'd made Winnie *wear* one. A scaly scarf wrapped around her neck with a lethal heaviness. Amber's answer came three seconds late because she was taking a drag of her cigarette.

"He was engaged. I think it was a bad breakup." Her lips formed a cartoonish "O" as she blew the smoke out. Winnie waved it away. "His fiancée didn't want kids. Look, he's nice…maybe a little weird…good-looking, the way you like 'em."

Whatever that meant. Winnie had agreed in the moment because she hadn't had a date in six months and was starting to feel dried out. Amber set up the date via text while sitting sideways on a lawn chair, blowing smoke away from Winnie this time. The guy had agreed right away; Winnie guessed he felt dried up, too. Dinner would be at a restaurant downtown, Winnie was to meet him there, and if things went well, they could grab a drink at Von's after. But when the day rolled around, she hadn't wanted to go. Her friends were going to Marymoore Park for a concert and someone had backed out, leaving a spare ticket. She was about to text her date and cancel, but he texted her first.

I've stalked you on social media and still can't decide if a distressed leather jacket or a suit jacket would impress you more.

Winnie, who had been lying on her back in bed, sat up suddenly, having a strong opinion on the matter. Winnie was very protective of animals; she had a theory that one day they'd get angry enough to take the world back from people. The ones who would be spared were definitely the vegetarians, more props to the vegans. She did not eat, wear, or put animals in cages for this reason.

27

Faux leather or real? She'd texted back. She'd been wearing a Nirvana hoodie with a yellow smiling face and she wound the string around her finger as she waited for his answer.

I'm about as faux as they get, he replied. She'd liked his dry humor and she liked that he'd admitted to looking at her social media; she'd tried to do the same but his was set to private and the only photo visible was of a group of five men. Winnie had no idea which one he was.

She texted her friends to let them know she wouldn't be coming, after all, and got ready for dinner instead.

Nigel, as it turned out, was the opposite of what Winnie pictured. He was small, though well put together—symmetrical, like a gymnast, with thick black hair swept stylishly away from his face. When he greeted Winnie in the lobby of the restaurant, wearing dark denim and a white T-shirt, she'd immediately felt disappointed. She imagined he'd be more dapper, but there he was—his face unremarkable, his eyes the most boring brown. Winnie was in the process of fixing him—adding a beard, dressing him in colors more suited to his skin tone—when she lost track of her thoughts. Nigel was smiling. The transformation was so stunning that she'd suddenly felt shy. And he wasn't wearing just any jeans, she saw now, they were designer. She reached up to secure her hair at the nape of her neck and then ran her hand down the length of it until it sprang free of her fist. Nigel's eyes watched all of this like someone observing a dancing poodle, good-natured amusement on his face.

"Faux nervousness or real?" His sensual mouth curved around the question, pulling into a lazy smile.

Winnie had butterflies. She wasn't even embarrassed that he'd picked up on it; it made him seem older, sexy.

"Ask me again after we've had a drink," she'd said decidedly.

By the time dinner came, Winnie was on her third cocktail and she was more focused on Nigel's hand slowly climbing up her knee than she was on his boring face. She didn't think he was boring anymore. In fact, she'd never felt more electric. They had sexual chemistry, but it wasn't just that. Where Nigel seemed subpar in the looks department, until he smiled, he was extraordinary in every other department. He never moved his eyes from her face, not the entire night; not even when their server in her slinky dress tried to make eye contact with him. They would often drift down to her lips while she was talking, which made Winnie squirm in her seat. And he asked her intelligent questions; questions that were so intense Winnie felt both sad and relieved to be talking about it at the same time: "How did your father's death affect the way you viewed your mother?"

Before Nigel, Winnie had only dated athletes, and a variety of them, too. There had been a rugby player, a tennis player, a quarterback, and a professional fisherman. Winnie had often wondered why she was attracted to Nigel, who wasn't even remotely her type. She found him sexy because he assumed that he was her type. His confidence was so audacious, so misplaced on the dull features and short stature, that Winnie had been fascinated—and oddly enough, turned on. Their date had led to another the following night, and then another. Within a month Winnie had moved into Nigel's apartment (it was closer to the city than hers), and in six short months they were engaged. And maybe he had been on a bender after his previous relationship, but here they were fifteen years later, living in Winnie's dream house.

Even her friends bought into it now. Though they still occasionally made comments about Nigel's lack of enthusiasm for their nice things. It was, Winnie thought, funny how they'd brag about their boats, and extravagant trips to Europe while Nigel's face would look…bored. "Can't you at least pretend to be interested?" she'd chide him after.

"They're such phonies, Winnie. Isn't it enough that I accept them as phonies? Can't we call it a day with that?" She'd laughed, and then they'd made love. Nigel was clever and Winnie was beautiful. She'd cultivated the perfect life, but it couldn't erase the past.

If it weren't for the house, Nigel might have been happy. *Rephrase that*, Winnie thought: if it weren't for the house, Nigel might be happy with *her*. He'd made jokes about it being cursed, but she knew he believed it. Her husband was superstitious, a gift from his mother, and he blamed the house for most of their troubles. No matter how much Nigel hated it, Winnie loved their house on Turlin Street. It had chosen them, in a way. It was a little rough around the edges— harder to love in some rooms than others—but it was a very good house. And, most importantly, her friends were jealous. *A house on Greenlake! Why, that's almost as good as a house on Lake Washington!* They'd all said so, which had brought a deep flush of pleasure to Winnie. Of course, that was fifteen years ago, and most of them had three kids and houses on actual Lake Washington by now.

She stepped into the tub and closed her eyes as the water climbed over her shoulders. So much for getting Nigel in the mood. At least she could enjoy a hot bath on her anniversary.

Winnie had a tendency to just go for it when she wanted something, and if she were honest with herself, that was probably where the trouble started. She'd wanted the Turlin Street home, and they'd paid a huge amount of money to live in a house he hated. Winnie knew that if it weren't for her, Nigel would be living in a place downtown, something new in one of those buildings that reflected the sky and had a Starbucks and a gym attached. Nigel hadn't grown up like Winnie, in a large rambler with her twin brother and three sisters. His mom had been of the single variety, hardworking and bone tired. They'd rented rather than bought, always something small and modern.

The house had almost seemed to fall into their laps—or perhaps Winnie's lap. After months of bidding wars, failed inspections, and schlepping from one model home to another, Winnie had gone for a run around Greenlake, without Nigel, to clear her head. They'd been fighting about houses non-stop. She'd been parking her car along the curb as the owner drove the spikes of the For Sale sign into the front lawn. She'd hopped out of the still-running car and ninja-sprinted across the lawn in her New Balance sneakers.

"I'll buy it," she'd said, barely out of breath. "Your house. It's sold."

And as the former owner recounted later, Winnie had pulled the sign out of the ground and put it in the trunk of her BMW. They'd closed three months later.

Winnie's memories of those twelve weeks were hazy. There had been a lot of back and forth until finally the offer was accepted, and then all of a sudden, they were owners of a very old, very large house. Prime location. "Seriously, Nigel. Who doesn't want to live on Greenlake." Winnie had said those words as they walked arm in arm toward their new home, just twenty minutes after the closing. Her eyes were as wide as the day Nigel had proposed.

They'd lived in the house for less than a year when the roof sprung a serious leak. Nigel had to cash out his 401k to replace it. Then, right after they brought Samuel home, they'd discovered the attic had black mold and had to be gutted. They lived in a hotel for a month with their new baby while the repairs were made. Years later, Nigel had wanted to add an apartment that could be locked off from the main house by a door in his den.

"But why does it need its own entrance?" she'd countered. He was growing impatient with her; if she dug her heels in it would cause a fight.

"We can rent it out if we ever run into trouble with money—which, frankly, after all we've sunk into this house, might be soon," Nigel had explained, even as the color drained from his wife's face. And then he'd added, "It will also increase the value of the property." Like Winnie cared. Her insides pinched together at the mention of money. Her only relationship with it was to spend it.

"I've taken a look at our finances and—"

"Just do it," Winnie said. "I'm sure you know what you're doing." She called Amber right away.

"He's right."

Winnie heard a car door slam on Amber's end. She was a real estate agent now, probably arriving at a house for a showing.

"It will add value to the property, and yeah, you could also put it on Airbnb. Earth to Winnie, it's a thing now."

"Not a thing I'm comfortable with," Winnie snapped.

But she let Nigel win that round. And she supposed it *was* a good business decision. It's not like he was aching to let a stranger move in, but there it was—the option.

When Winnie got out of the bath, Nigel was downstairs unpacking groceries from two recyclable bags. She looked through his purchases, hoping to find a card or a box of candy, but there was nothing exciting except for a new can opener. She suddenly felt disappointed in herself. What had she been hoping for? Fireworks and champagne? Nigel was a good man who loved her; she was content with that. She threw a smile his way as she helped him put everything away. Later, when they were in bed and he reached for her, she didn't stiffen up, even though part of her wanted to—she'd already given up on the evening. She let him, and he innocently fell asleep minutes after, oblivious to the crying Winnie did well into the night.

Because now, all these years later after the horrible thing that had occurred inside this very house on Turlin Street, she didn't know if anything would ever be enough.

4

JUNO

Juno had moved to Seattle from Albuquerque, New Mexico, four years ago. She'd lived one life there and another in Washington, the two starkly different. New Mexico Juno had a career and a family, a husband and two little boys. She was plump and full breasted, and she wore paisley as a fashion statement. Her practice had started in a storefront she shared with two therapist friends. Five years into their little triad of mental health, Juno had enough clients to warrant her own building. She bought an old Burger King on the outskirts of town that had gone belly-up and converted it into *Sessions*, a family counseling facility. That was before she more or less burned her life down and ended up in Washington.

She'd heard that the weather didn't try to kill you with

heat or cold, and that was just fine for her. The most damage Seattle could do was a misty rain that made you feel a damp sort of sleepiness. Juno hadn't taken much with her when she'd left Albuquerque, only what she could carry in her thrifted suitcase. Just a handful of memories, among them Kregger's reading glasses, which she occasionally used.

She ended up moving into the Turlin Street house fifteen years after Winnie and Nigel purchased it. By then, all the renovations had been finished and the downstairs had a small apartment with its own entrance. The first time she saw the house—red brick in front of a backdrop of purple-gray clouds, like some sort of painting—she'd sighed. She wasn't there to see about a place to live, just to admire the house in its Gothic beauty. But then the opportunity had presented itself, and Juno had taken it. She was in deep need of change, and the house on Turlin had beckoned her. Juno had stood rooted to the sidewalk as someone drove by blasting music. She took the first steps toward her new home as the singer sang "I knew that it was now or never..."

Their son, a lean bean with sandy hair and blond eyelashes, seemed equally as puzzled by his parents as Juno was. She often spotted him shaking his head at them when they weren't looking, like he couldn't believe the stupidity. She suspected that Samuel scored high on the Wechsler, higher probably than both Winnie and Nigel combined. Juno had seen it many times over the years, parents bringing their children in for Juno to fix like they were appliances instead of complex individuals. You couldn't fix a child—they didn't need fixing right out of the box. Kids just needed a healthy example of love to thrive beneath. He found her sitting on a bench by the water just yesterday, and they'd had the biggest and best of heart-to-hearts. She was certain that she was the only person with whom Sam could discuss his interests, as disturbing as they may have been to anyone besides Juno. And she had told him that as they sat next to the lake—the lake that she had described as "Calm as rice."

"Calm as rice?" he had laughed, grasping at his abdomen and rocking his head side to side.

"That's right," Juno said. "Calm as rice."

"I've never heard that before."

When he had sat down next to her, his eyebrows were drawn. He looked more like an unsure child and less like the opinionated boy she'd grown to know.

"You know some of the most famous serial killers of all time are from Washington?"

Juno had leaned back on the bench, frowning up at the yellowing sky. "Let me think," she said. "Ted Bundy!" She looked at Sam, who nodded enthusiastically.

"The Green River killer...what was that fellow's name? Gary something..."

"Ridgeway," Sam finished.

"Yes. That's right." Juno nodded.

"Yates, and um...yes, there was that one man who was truly evil. Targeting children—just disgusting. Dodd," she ended with a smack of her lips.

"My parents freak out when they see me looking at that stuff online."

"Well, do you blame them? If your mom was obsessed with watching violent car crashes every night before bed, wouldn't you be concerned?"

"My mom is obsessed with a lot of things that concern me." His face was blank, but she saw the humor in his eyes.

Juno couldn't help but smile. The kid had a sort of wry adult sense of humor.

"Moms are obsessed with mom things. Kids are obsessed with kid things. Nothing wrong with having different interests and loving each other the same."

Juno was surprised at how easily she slipped into the counseling role after all these years. She was also surprised at how flat her words sounded.

"Sometimes I feel like I'm not even their kid."

"Maybe you're not," Juno said it casually, her tone light. Wasn't there a time in every adolescent's life when they convinced themselves they were adopted?

Sam is a special boy, Juno thought to herself now as she stood in the doorway to the bathroom, her gaze sliding over the bottles of perfume and lotion that sat on the subway tile next to the bathtub. She completely avoided her own reflection, already knowing what she would see and not wanting to see it—the raw, red butterfly mark across her nose and cheeks. She would see the puffy, jaundiced eyes, and she would see skin mottled like a duck egg.

She slipped the light switch on and stepped inside. She shuffled through the door, her back still stiff from the way she'd slept last night, to the sink where glass bottles were arranged around a silver tray. Eucalyptus, tea tree oil, jasmine. Juno chose from the rows and carried them over to the tub. This was her favorite part of the day, when she had time to let the water ease the pain from her body. She let the water rise as high as it could, and then, lowering herself into the water, she made the sounds a very old, very tired woman made. She tried not to look down at herself as she sank to the bottom of the tub, though she caught flashes of bony thighs, the skin so vellum-thin she averted her eyes.

She'd enjoyed her chat with Sam at the park yesterday. But now, lying in this tub and recollecting the moments she spent

37

with him, she found that the therapist she had retired years ago was stirring inside her again.

Sometimes I feel like I'm not even their kid, he'd said.

It means nothing, she told herself. *Just enjoy your bath.*

Juno opened her eyes. There was no clock in the bathroom, but she knew what time it was by the light reflected on the wall. It was time to get out and move on to the next thing.

It was late afternoon, and Juno's hair had dried to a springy gray halo—erratic curls that would shoot up instead of down. She tugged on one as she made tea, another nervous habit that had accompanied her from childhood. Her hair had been red once, but that was a long time ago, when she drank gin martinis and smoked clove cigarettes. Another life and another woman. Everyone had wanted to touch it: fat red curls that fell to her waist. Old women often stopped Juno on the sidewalk to comment on the color and tell her they used to pay for color like that. And now Juno was the old woman. The corner of her mouth lifted in half amusement as she sipped her tea. She was less funny-looking now that she was older, or maybe her eyes were the problem. The tea was strong and sweet. Juno drank it fast, thinking of her pain pills downstairs in the haven she'd made for herself. She was running out; she'd counted six last time she'd looked. She'd have to count on the Crouches to bring more. Juno's mood turned sour; the tea suddenly tasted wrong in her mouth. She hated relying on people. She dumped the rest of her tea down the sink and went about cleaning her mess, a new worry ticking at her brain.

At four o'clock, Mr. Nevins from next door parked his Tahoe right outside the living room window, and Juno poured herself a finger of Nigel's whiskey even though she didn't like the stuff and had pretty much given up drinking. She carried it upstairs to the sitting area that looked down at the park. She always felt prickly at this time of day, knowing they'd be home soon. They filled up the house with tension: often sexual, other times just the naked, ugly kind.

The second floor sitting area was the best part of the house, the view somehow both hectic and peaceful. The house sat on one of the busier streets surrounding Greenlake Park, one that fed to and from I-5. Juno sank into a rocker, letting the whiskey do its job, watching the commuter traffic begin its slow crawl. Nowadays this was her window to the outside, where she rarely stepped any longer. But she knew the sounds and smells well enough to use her imagination. Two women paused on their walk to take a selfie as a Maltese dog sniffed the grass around them, and a man in tight neon yellow running shorts almost collided with them. He jumped to the side at the last minute, narrowly dodging them and almost landing on the Maltese. The women straightened up from their selfie, none the wiser.

Over the grass and in the park, a family with three teenagers gathered in a little huddle, holding Starbucks cups and laughing. They looked cold. Sam wouldn't be home for another few hours from practice, but she liked when he was home because a light spot developed between his parents, easing the mood of the house. She knew each of them by their steps, and Sam's were the clumsy *clomp clomp clomp* of a loose-gaited boy. A baby giraffe, skidding and bumping corners. It was so cute; she remembered it from her boys. The sun was coming down over the lake now; it dashed right through the windows where she was sitting. Leaning back in her chair, she let the sun touch her all over.

It was time to go downstairs.

Near the front door, pushed in a rush toward the wall, were the remnants of Nigel's attempt at the doorbell. Juno looked over the mess, touching her tongue to an infected molar on the right side—wires, coils, and screws scattered over the wood, failed DIY confetti—and then she stepped over it.

5

WINNIE

"Hold on." Nigel was forcing himself to stay calm. She heard him switch the phone from one ear to the other. When he came back on, his voice sounded strained. "Did you say your brother is staying with us?"

As Winnie launched into a quick recap of Dakota's latest scheme, her stomach sank lower. She watched as Carmen stepped off the elevator, a white paper bag clutched under her arm. She raised a hand as she passed Winnie's desk, but Winnie didn't give her the cursory smile she normally did.

"He took his paycheck to the racetrack and bet it all on a trifecta. Manda kicked him out."

"As she should," Nigel said. "But Dakota needs to—"

"It's just for a bit," Winnie said cautiously, and then into the receiver she hissed, "Shelly took him in last time, it's technically our turn."

Winnie was glad her husband couldn't see her face; she could see it in the reflection of her computer monitor and it was pale and afraid. Shelly was the oldest of the Straub sisters. Nigel hated her—had from the moment her eyes had met his and she'd said, "My sister didn't do a very good job of describing you." He'd assumed she'd meant it as an insult since she'd ended her statement with a little laugh and then looked away like he wasn't important. That had been his account of it anyway. Shelly never made much of their first meeting, which Winnie supposed was like her sister. She was rarely impressed, and if she was, it had something to do with money.

Despite Shelly's poorly hidden disdain for her sister's husband, Winnie deferred to everything Shelly said—all the siblings did. After their father died, their mother seemed to forget how to parent beyond smothering them in weepy affection. It was Shelly who had raised her siblings, making them dinner, getting them to bed, and occasionally forging their mother's signature on school forms. If Shelly told Winnie it was her turn to take Dakota, Winnie would accept her lot without complaint; he was her twin, after all, though sharing a womb together didn't make living with him easier. Nigel, on the other hand, wanted to complain, she knew that. In fact, he wanted to speak to the manager, but the manager was a five-foot general who wore practical chinos, a sharp bob, and didn't give a shit about what Nigel or Winnie thought. Shelly, the oldest, lord of the Straubs.

Winnie pulled in a deep breath, ready with her list of defenses and justifications. Hadn't she put up with his mother for years? The mother of an only child can be clingy, especially when she was still single and relied on said only child for practically everything. She'd prepared a list of all the times that dealing with his mother had been hard for her—pathetic, she knew, but the guilt angle was all she had to work with.

"Do you really think that's a good idea with Samuel in the house? He was really upset last time Dakota stayed with us."

Her heart sank. The Samuel angle knocked every justification out of her mouth.

Two years ago, Manda had kicked her husband out for sexting with a coworker. When she confronted him, Dakota had thrown every dish they had onto the kitchen floor in a rage, then proceeded to slip and cut himself on a piece of dinner plate. He'd blamed Manda for his fall, saying she'd upset him, and then schlepped off to the hospital to get four stitches in his forearm. He'd ended up at Shelly's that time. Winnie distinctly remembered her saying "So what, right? He didn't even have sex with her…" And Shelly had moved their beloved brother into the spare room.

"Yeah, but Shelly, if Mike did that—" Winnie had protested.

"Ha! He knows better. And besides," she'd said out of the corner of her mouth, "Manda has really let herself go."

The next time Manda kicked him out it was for a tiny pouch of white powder she found in his wallet. They'd taken him that time—her and Nigel. It had been Chelsea's turn, technically, but she was in Hawaii for her tenth wedding anniversary with her wife, Mary. Dakota had hidden in the spare room for a week, and then one night, he'd gotten high and drunk while Winnie was cooking dinner and had stumbled into the living room wearing only his tighty-whiteys while Samuel was watching TV. As Samuel watched wide-eyed from the sofa, his uncle threw up on the PlayStation and then shat himself.

Manda had always fought with him for—wait for it—drinking too much in front of their kids and acting erratic.

Instead, he came to drink in front of Winnie's kid, which of course had caused a fight with Nigel of epic proportions.

Winnie paused for a long moment, and then she swore. "Shit. Dammit. How could I forget about that? I can have Samuel stay with my mom for the weekend. We'll reassess on Sunday." All the sisters were the same way about Dakota—they babied him. Except he wasn't a baby, and Winnie had a sinking feeling that this time Manda wasn't going to forgive him.

"Maybe Dakota and Manda will work things out by then, anyway—they usually do," she said. She stared at her screen saver: a photo of her and Nigel and Samuel standing on a beach during their vacation to the Dominican Republic last year.

"It's never been this bad before. Manda might not be so willing to take him back this time. He's been a college kid on a bender for the last ten years, Winnie."

She sighed deeply. Dakota's emotional outbursts as a child were frequent; Winnie remembered him as being sulky and demanding. Their father's death seemed to tip him over the edge; he navigated through his grief with fists and one suicide attempt when he was seventeen. But he'd always been angry; at what Winnie didn't know. He seemed to pick and choose his triggers. At their joint tenth birthday party, Dakota was so furious that he had to share a party with her that he'd picked up the sheet cake that their mother had paid three hundred dollars for and dumped it into the pool. Winnie could still picture him standing in his camo swim trunks with the neon orange trim, the cake a large sheet with a photo of their faces airbrushed across the top. He made eye contact with her the second before he launched their smiling faces into the deep end. He hadn't been punished, of course; their parents had laughed it off to their friends.

For their thirteenth birthday, they'd both been given little glass bowls with betta fish from their aunt Shea. A week later Dakota found that his betta had gone to the ocean in the sky. He'd stormed into the bedroom she shared with Chelsea and snatched the bowl from her desk. Winnie had tried to stop him, but he was already a foot taller than her and he held the bowl above his head, sloshing water on her face as she reached for it. He'd darted to the bathroom, then flushed Winnie's very alive fish down the toilet along with his dead one as she wailed in protest. "Fair's fair," he'd said, pulling the lever. He'd felt bad as soon as he'd done it and had burst into tears. Winnie had forgiven him, of course, but sometimes all these memories came together in a very uncomfortable way. If he'd been like that with his twin sister, what was he like now with his wife, Manda?

Nigel was waiting for her to say something. She pushed her thoughts away. "I know—jeez—I know. He never recovered from Dad's death. But he's family, so we'll just have to work this out. Be patient with him. Everyone can chip in." Her voice was falsely positive. She sounded like a drunk cheerleader. And he wasn't just family, he was her twin. There was extra responsibility that came with that.

After fifteen years of marriage, Winnie knew his stance without him having to say it—Nigel disagreed. He did not think Dakota and Manda were going to work it out. This was not his problem, nor was this his brother, nor did he believe in the twin bond. He didn't want to chip in. *There were perks to being an only child*, Winnie assumed bitterly, and while Dakota moving in with them may have been a completely normal thing to Winnie, she knew that to Nigel, it felt like an extreme breach of privacy. Dakota lacked the respect of a good houseguest: he was a slob. He left dirty dishes all over the house, the remnants of frozen burritos congealing in red

45

lumps, empty beer cans stacked on counters—and the tissues. Oh, God, every time he stayed with them there was so much crying. Nigel called them snotflakes—little hardened wads of white that made their house look like it was decorated for Christmas. Then there was the drinking problem, which had led to the horrifying moment for Samuel.

"Well, he'll be there when you get home," Winnie said. "He stopped by for the key. He can stay in the blue bedroom."

"Uh-huh."

"Are you mad? You sound mad."

"I'm mad," he said. "But it doesn't make a difference because you already moved him in without talking to me about it."

Winnie said nothing.

"If he so much as looks at me the wrong way, Winnie..."

"I know, I know," she said. Her breath exhaled in a whoosh. She could picture his chin dipped, eyes narrowed, pressing his tongue up against his front teeth. "I warned him," she said. "I swear it'll be okay. He's in a bad place, but he'll behave."

When Winnie got home thirty minutes later, she found Dakota on his knees installing the doorbell Nigel himself had failed to install for some weeks. It was a peace offering. She watched him for a few seconds, dreading the whole night ahead of her; she'd get a decent serving of guilt from Nigel, and Samuel would turn his moodiness inward. Her concern for her son was already consuming her, and this was only going to make it worse. Why Winnie had said yes to this she did not know. Actually, she did know: her sister was a bully and Winnie was about as easy to manipulate as a hungry dog. Dakota had music playing as he worked, a whiny country song. She heard him humming along to it and her heart softened. She still saw her brother as a little boy.

"Hey, you." Her brother jumped at the sound of her voice. He was still wearing his uniform—Nigel always said he looked like a baked potato in his courier uniform. Dakota stood up, suddenly reminding Winnie of how tall he was. He resembled their father, six-four and beefy. Winnie had to bend her head back a little to look into her brother's face, which was contrite. His red-rimmed eyes wouldn't meet hers when he said, "I'm really appreciative you all are letting me stay. Manda…"

At the sound of his wife's name on his own tongue, the six-foot-four-inch brute of a man burst into tears. And that was the moment Nigel pulled into the driveway.

Winnie seated Dakota at the dinette, and Nigel made tea for the three of them. It was something his mother did when someone was upset. She watched as he handled the little bags of tea and the cubes of sugar. He poured a few beats of whiskey into his and Winnie's mugs, noticeably skipping Dakota's, and Winnie held her tongue. She knew better than to give Nigel a hard time about drinking, especially after forcing Dakota on him. She felt she'd need the alcohol herself. Dakota took the mug gratefully.

Winnie sucked the warm liquid between her teeth and eyed Dakota over the rim of her mug. Her sisters still crooned about how handsome he was, but she was starting to see the emergence of a much scruffier man. He'd had a six-pack through high school and college, and despite living in a cold, rainy state, he'd spent much of his adolescence shirtless to let everyone know. Sitting close to him now, Winnie could see that his hair was thinning and his nose was starting to take on the bulbous appearance of a seasoned alcoholic.

"You should shower, dude, shave. You'll feel better." Nigel was eyeing Dakota with much less tact than she had. She meant to give Nigel a look to say he'd crossed a line, but Dakota nodded solemnly.

"I lost my job today."

Nigel's mug landed on the table with a hard thud. Winnie squeezed her eyes closed. *No, no, no.*

"Why?" That strangled word was all she could manage.

"Got in a fight with some guy."

Nigel leaned forward, disbelieving. "'Got in a fight with some guy'? What? At work?"

Dakota nodded. "He had it coming." He said this very seriously. Winnie saw her husband's fist clench. *Oh boy, here it comes*, she thought.

"Are you kidding me, Dakota? Your marriage is hanging by a thread, you gambled your mortgage payment, and now you got yourself fired because you wanted to play street fighter on the job?" This time it was she who said it, and both her husband and brother looked at her in surprise. Winnie could play bad guy, too.

Dakota started to cry again, his big head drooping over his almost empty mug. She could see the scar on the bridge of his nose, the one he got from fighting with Nicholas Bowcamp when he was in the tenth grade. The fight was over a comment Nicholas had made about their recently deceased father. Dakota shoved Nick, and he rebounded with a right hook that broke Dakota's nose. Winnie remembered watching the whole thing go down from the stairs in front of the school, her stomach in her throat as she watched her twin beat Nicholas Bowcamp into the pavement. If it happened today, there would be dozens of videos all over the internet, but the most people did that day was watch and cheer. The boys were technically off school property. Nicholas Bowcamp spent two days in the hospital with a concussion. "He's just lost his father," their mother told the police officer who had come by the house. "He's not usually like this." The Bowcamps, who were devout Catholics, conferred with their priest and decided

48

against pressing charges so long as Dakota sought counseling. The counseling had seemed to work for a while, and Dakota had attended youth group at a nondenominational church and gone on a mission trip to Mexico. He spouted Bible verses all summer and volunteered at the local animal shelter. Winnie remembered him always smelling of wet dog during that time. It was all fine and dandy until his senior year when he seemed to change overnight, shrugging off his religion and replacing it with a deep melancholy. He started smoking cigarettes and was suspended twice in one quarter for fighting.

Winnie was about to comfort him when she heard the front door open. A few seconds later, Samuel came bounding into the kitchen, a soccer ball tucked under his arm. He had what Winnie called the "hungry lion" look on his face. He headed straight for the fridge with barely a glance at the table where his uncle and father sat.

"Samuel," Nigel said. "Say hello to your uncle."

Samuel turned around with a start, a Gatorade bottle at his lips. "Hello, Uncle," he parroted. "Are you crying?"

Dakota launched into a fresh flurry of tears, sobbing into his hand. Samuel raised his eyebrows at his father and quietly exited the room without so much as acknowledging Winnie.

"Go to your room, Dakota," Nigel said firmly. "And cry in the fucking shower."

In an effort to redeem herself, she took Samuel to dinner that night, even though it was late, just the two of them. Nigel had opted to stay home and keep an eye on Dakota, but Winnie knew that what he really wanted was to find his bottle of Jack and coat his anger with it. The realization was there, right in front of her, and she still didn't want to deal with it. They walked through the park, cutting across to the row of restaurants that all had Vegan Friendly signs in their windows.

Samuel had been quiet for most of their walk, kicking at stray rocks and sighing deeply whenever she said something.

"What are you hungry for?" she asked, her voice bright and falsely cheery. If Samuel hadn't pointed to Quarter Deck at exactly that moment, she would have burst into tears. Okay, fine, that was something; at least he was giving opinions. She followed him to the host stand where he politely asked for a table for two. The thorny thoughts she'd been having washed away. He was a good boy; he did the right thing, even if he grumbled about it. And honestly, what teenager didn't get a little growly? She felt better when they sat down at the table, water and menus in front of them. Winnie watched a woman and a boy a few years older than Samuel tuck into their food. They were talking animatedly to one another, the boy making gestures above his head while she watched him with her mouth ajar. The woman was one of those bohemian types. As Winnie watched, she lifted her burger to her mouth with fingers that were decorated in turquoise rings. They traded burgers after the first bite, nodding in approval as they swapped back again. She turned toward Samuel. "So, should we share a salad and a grilled cheese? You pick the salad."

"I don't want a salad."

"Okay…then what about a quinoa bowl?"

Samuel was cracking his knuckles, watching the TV over the bar.

"Hey! I'm talking to you." She saw him stiffen; he looked like a kid ready to bolt. Winnie saw a couple of heads turn their way; maybe that had come out wrong. She offered an apologetic smile. *Backtrack, backtrack, backtrack…*

"I'm hungry. I want to order!" she said in a more cheerful voice. She pushed his menu toward him, aware that the mother-son duo across the way were now watching them.

He looked at her through his lashes for a minute before seeming to accept the apology.

"I was thinking about getting a burger." He didn't look at her when he said it, but Winnie was glad. A little smile had crept onto her lips. He'd noticed the mother and son across the way, too; she'd seen him looking. A burger was a great idea.

"Good idea," she said, glancing at the menu. "I will, too." When the server came by, Winnie order two Impossible burgers with chips. She eyed the salads wistfully but shut her menu with a snap that blew her hair up around her face. That was what parenting was all about—the sacrifices. She would eat fake red meat if it meant bonding with her son.

The chips cut into the roof of her mouth. Winnie only flinched when Samuel wasn't looking. She hated feeling judged by a thirteen-year-old. He ate them like they were as soft as cheese; she watched in amazement as their sharp little ridges folded like paper behind his teeth. She felt victimized, her mouth tender. She reached for her veggie burger instead. Samuel hadn't touched his; he was too busy grinding up those vicious little chips. She was trying hard not to say anything; instead, she bit into her own with enthusiasm.

"Try your burger. It's delicious."

"I don't think anything pretending to be something else can be delicious."

Winnie set her sandwich down, frowning. She blotted at the ketchup in the corners of her mouth. "What are you talking about? I thought you wanted a burger."

He looked up at her, his chin tilted in a challenging way. He reminded Winnie of a bull in that moment.

"I wanted a real burger."

"Samuel!" she said, exasperated. "Come on. Now you're just being ridiculous. You've had a hundred veggie burgers."

"And I've never liked them."

She replaced her sandwich on the plate and stared at him. "So you're just not going to eat them anymore?"

"I'm not," he said. "I'm going to eat meat from now on because I'm not a vegetarian."

The food she'd already ingested rolled in her belly. Winnie felt sick. She'd spent thirteen years raising this boy in what she thought was the best way, and now he was dismissing their way of life so casually, like it didn't mean anything.

"We'll talk about it later. If you're not hungry that's fine, but your dad—"

"I am hungry. I ate all the chips and I'm still hungry."

She knew that if she told him to eat his veggie burger the argument would continue and spoil what was left of the evening.

Samuel was scrolling through his phone now, and she noticed that he was reading an article in the *Seattle Times* about the homeless.

"Do you want dessert?" she asked, pushing her burger aside. His only response was to raise a curious eyebrow like he was being pranked. She lifted a finger to call the server over, her eyes never leaving his face.

"Can we have one of every dessert on the menu, to share?" she said, glancing at Samuel. His face was incredulous. "So long as they don't have meat in them."

He cracked a small smile. *Truce!* Winnie thought.

"Don't you want to see the menu...?" the server asked. Winnie's smile broke for a brief second. Hadn't this stupid girl heard her? She was trying to be the cool mom. "Just one of everything," she snapped. The girl nodded and walked away. Her expression said *It's on your dime, salty bitch.*

"What are you reading?" Winnie asked.

"Nothing. Something for school." He immediately closed the browser on his phone and set it face down on the table.

"You know, I used to work with the homeless, for my job, before you were born." She expected him to ignore her, or— cue her personal least favorite—roll his eyes, but instead, he looked at her with interest.

"In what capacity?"

Capacity! Winnie almost snickered, but she knew how much that would offend Samuel. When she was his age, she certainly wasn't saying words like *capacity*. Besides, she was used to his large vocabulary. She kept her face neutral.

"Well, I was a case manager for people with mental health issues. Some of my cases were…well…homeless."

"Really? How old were they?"

Now that she had his attention, she didn't plan on losing it. She shrugged as nonchalantly as possible. "All different ages, some as young as you, all the way up to people Granny's age."

"Why were they homeless?"

Winnie searched her mind for a good answer, one that would interest him.

"I had one guy, his name was Adam. He came up to Seattle when he was twenty-four, right after getting out of jail. He beat a guy up, that's why he was in jail," Winnie said, seeing the question on Samuel's face. "He'd gone to school to be an engineer—before the fight and the jail time. But by the time he got out, his mom had disowned him, and he had no other family in the area."

"So, nowhere to go," Samuel concluded.

"That's right. He came to Seattle because he heard he could get work up here, but the job didn't pan out, and so he was homeless." There was a long pause during which Winnie thought he was done discussing the topic, but then he propped his birdlike elbows on the table and rested his chin in his hand. "Did he have a mental illness?"

"That's none of your business," Winnie said firmly. She

could tell that switching to the mom role had cost her Samuel, because he looked away. She felt immediate regret. Should she have told him that Adam was diagnosed with schizophrenia and that on his twenty-sixth birthday he'd gone missing? The police hadn't bothered to look for a homeless man, though they'd written up the report for Winnie and then told her to have a nice day.

"They have a very hard time, Samuel," she offered gently. "Discussing their medical history is highly inappropriate." But he was giving her that look that made her feel stupid.

"That was like fifteen years ago," he said. "But it's fine."

"Thirteen," Winnie corrected with a frown. "Don't age me." Samuel glanced up to check her face and seemed to relax at the joke. Winnie was sweating beneath her shirt. She hadn't realized how hard this would be—parenting. People, for some reason, chose only to highlight the good parts: the cute chubby cheeks and cute little socks—not the temper tantrums and lollipop bribery it took to get them in the socks. Winnie tried to relax, softening her voice. "And you're right. Adam was mentally ill. He also had PTSD from an incident in prison—" Winnie didn't tell Samuel how violent the *incident* had actually been "—and he had a personality disorder and a bunch of other stuff."

"Why did you stop working there?"

"I had you, silly. I wanted to be a mom."

"Why couldn't you have done both?" He almost sounded accusatory. She tried to bat the feeling away. She was projecting her own feelings onto her son.

"I…well…I didn't want to. You remember that Bible story about Hannah you learned in religious studies a few years ago?"

"Yeah, the one where she begs God for a baby because she's barren and his other wife is having all the kids."

Barren, Winnie thought. *What a word.* "Yeah, that one. I felt like Hannah, I guess. I'd been waiting for a baby for so long, praying for one, and then I got you." Her own simplistic answer irritated her, like things were ever that easy; but Samuel seemed to accept it.

"You could go back," he said.

Winnie managed a thin smile. She hated talking about Illuminations. She had no feelings of nostalgia when it came to her former workplace. It had been full on relief when she left, and not just because of what had gone down. Counselors at mental health facilities were overworked and underpaid. The thought of taking Samuel's suggestion made her want to throw up. She remembered running into one of the other case workers, Dan Repper, shortly after she quit. She'd been browsing the stands at the farmers' market when she'd seen him approach her out the corner of her eye. Winnie had immediately tried to extract herself from the berry-buying, shoving a twenty into the seller's hand just as Dan's nasal voice called out to her.

They started speaking just as Winnie propped the crate of blueberries on her hip, and she felt like she moved it from right hip to left at least a dozen times before the conversation was over. Dan told her he'd taken over half of her caseload when she left, split it with Dee since Illuminations was short on counselors. He'd sounded accusatory so Winnie had apologized immediately; she would have sung the apology if it meant getting out of there. But Dan had more to say.

"There's a woman coming around the office asking for you. She says you were her counselor but won't give us her name."

"What does she want?" Winnie tried to keep her voice neutral, smiling at a golden retriever as it paused to sniff the crate she was balancing.

"Your home address." Dan's words sank into her brain with

55

cold teeth. Winnie was so shaken she felt like she was shivering in the mid-August heat, and he was going to notice.

"Anyway, Beula at the desk—you remember Beula?" He didn't wait for her to reply. "She told her that under no circumstances could we give out counselors' home addresses. The woman said she'd find you herself and walked out."

Now, Winnie mentally shook herself before answering Samuel's question. "I have a job, silly—being a mom."

Samuel shrugged. "It would be cool to help people."

"Well, I help them now," she said quickly. "Just in a different way." She hated the defensiveness in her voice, hated that Samuel heard it, too.

"Chill out, Mom, I get it. You plan parties now, right? To raise money for the homeless."

"Well, no," Winnie said tightly. "I sometimes help with the charity events, but now I manage the people who…manage the people. If that makes sense."

The server unloaded five plates onto the table in quick succession, and in the face of imminent sugar, Samuel stopped asking questions. He was still a kid and she could control some situations, but how long would it be before he started asking questions about why his dad never really looked his wife in the eye?

6

JUNO

For one brief and awful year, Juno and Kregger had lived in Alaska. It was the seventies, and in America, lust was on the menu for the decade. Juno and Kregger were wet for adventure, hard for travel. They sold everything in their little studio apartment, gave their parrots and cacti away to friends, and bought two one-way tickets to Anchorage. The pull was the Wild West, and they were young enough to still want to play. When Juno remembered the cold and isolation she experienced that year, she would shiver. But back then, back in grand ol' 1977 when they arrived at the meager airport, the Trans-Alaska Pipeline had just been completed and oil was flowing. Kregger planned to work the oil, and Juno planned on getting a job wherever they'd have her. She was working on her thesis, and Anchorage had seemed like the place to buckle down and get it done. So while Kregger worked those grueling hours, Juno shriveled in the Alaskan winter like a cock in the cold. It wasn't at all what she'd pictured; Anchorage was a muddy little place with gambling dens, drug houses, and street walkers, as Juno's nan called them. Half wild and half civilized. Late at night, men would shoot guns into the sky to blow off steam. She'd be so afraid on the nights Kregger was gone that she'd carry her blanket and pillow to the closet and sleep on the floor under the sweeping hems of their clothes. When summer came, things got moderately better. She was able to walk to the city center without fear of losing her nose to the cold and got a part-time job at the Piggly Wiggly.

The tired little grocery store was on Spenard Road where massage parlors lined the street all in a row like little duckies. Juno had suspected Kregger stopped by once or twice, but she never asked and felt better not knowing. Other than getting your wang wanked, there was little to do. Squalid little bars, adult bookstores, and houses of worship all shared a street just like Jesus would have preferred. There was a drive-in theater, they'd been excited to discover. They went twice in that year: the first time it had been winter and the exhaust fumes from the cars rose into the air until it was impossible to make out the actors' faces on the screen. And they'd gone in the summer when the days were endless and night never fully arrived and found they couldn't see a damn thing on the screen because it was too bright. They'd laughed all the way home that time.

The memories would often come with a strong mixture of revulsion and nostalgia. The Fancy Moose on Friday nights, and Club Paris for special occasions, lying alone on a ratty brown sofa for days while the snow caked itself around the tin box they called a house. Juno had begged Kregger to take her home, home to civilization and chain fast food. Home to the glamorous hot squalor of New Mexico. They'd stuck it out for the year—due process, as Kregger called it. The last time she had felt truly claustrophobic was in Anchorage, Alaska, from 1977 to 1978.

And then there was now.

The brother being in the house was bad—bad for everyone, but mostly bad for Juno, who had taken to hiding. She didn't like him; she could agree with Nigel on that. For one thing, he never left the house—lurking in the family room and downstairs in Nigel's den until late, keeping Juno up with his drunk laughter. He pretended to leave the house in the mornings under the guise of *"beating the pavement to look for work"* but he really snuck back in shortly after the family left. Since Dakota had arrived, they'd taken to leaving the alarm off during the day, which was less of a hassle for her to come and go, she supposed.

Dakota only cried now when he got off the phone with his wife. And with tears like that, she was fairly certain Manda wasn't taking him back. She'd seen him passed out on the sofa once, a dozen mini bottles scattered around the remote like confetti. He must have cleaned it all up by the time Nigel got home because she didn't hear explosive yelling. He was taking advantage of their charity and making no attempt at all to find a job, despite what he told his sister and brother-in-law. And Juno found herself claustrophobic, desperate to get away and breathe fresh air. He was imposing but stupid. A giant, looming dummy. When Winnie conversed with him she crooned, and when Nigel spoke to him he bit down and spoke through his teeth. Sam avoided his uncle altogether. From what Juno pieced together, there'd been a fight a couple years ago, well before she'd moved in. Sam had witnessed the whole thing. Nigel had taken flak from the family, being that Dakota was a guest in his house at the time, though an unwelcome one even then, and Winnie had sided with them, staying with her sister for a week and taking Sam with her.

Juno found it a bit maddening—why marry a man and then serve loyalty to the family you'd left for that man? As far as Juno was concerned, when you got married you started a new family with the person of your choosing: leave and cleave. You had to fight it out together, figure it out as a team. And when the extended family tried to get involved, as they usually did, you were to tell them to mind their stinking business. Either way, she was forced to share a house with the big buffoon, and she wasn't happy about it.

She was lying with her head nestled on her favorite blanket and eating stale Cheez-Its when she heard a familiar suction of air followed by the boom of the front door closing. Sitting up in bed, Juno listen for any further noises but heard none. Good, he was gone. Maybe today he'd actually find that job. First things first, she thought, winding her hair into a bun—she had to pee.

After relieving herself, she stood at the sink, brushing her teeth vigorously for several minutes. Juno could still remember the days of her own deep depression, when she would go for days without bathing or eating a thing. She'd lost near a hundred pounds and never put it back. If only Kregger could see her now, thin and lithe. She let out a little whoop of laughter, looking at her body in the mirror. Kregger had never been attracted to thin women; he'd probably tell her to eat a stick of butter.

It was when she looked at her face that the laughter was snatched from her throat. The right stuff was all there: nose, eyes, chin, mouth—but the way her skin hung was unfamiliar. She regretted looking in the mirror; she always managed to avoid it; what happened this time? As she headed down to the kitchen, she made a vow never to look in the mirror again.

Dakota had at least stocked the fridge with lunch meat and bread, so she made herself a giant sandwich. She did something really risky in fishing the last pickle from the jar and setting it on her plate with a decided, vinegary plop; then she emptied the pickle juice down the drain and put the jar in the recycling before going to eat her lunch at the dinette. The meat was slimy and cloyingly sweet as it stuck to the roof of her mouth with the foamy bread. She took a long sip of Dr Pepper, enjoying lunch on Dakota's dime, though it wouldn't be long until it was on Nigel and Winnie's dime. Juno felt bad for Nigel about the whole Dakota thing.

Throughout the entirety of her lunch, she stared at the rogue hangnail on her thumb. Time for a clipping, she thought as she cleaned up after her meal. She'd seen a pair of nail clippers lying around, but she knew how it went—things were never around when you wanted them. So she began her hunt for the nail clippers.

Juno stepped into Winnie and Nigel's bedroom. The rattan fan whirred soundlessly above the bed, stirring the smells of the room. She was tempted to turn it off, but she knew better. Instead, she walked on the balls of her feet toward the nightstand. She'd start there first. Juno slid the first drawer open. Everything was unbearably tidy: three squat jars of lotion stood in a neat line. Next to them was a woman's devotional, a tube of Carmex, three unused notebooks with floral covers, and a tampon. But no nail clippers.

The next drawer had much of the same, the organized clutter of an uninteresting woman: a box of truffles, two expensive-looking pens, more floral notebooks, these with Winnie's handwriting on the inside. Juno sat lightly on the edge of the bed and flipped open the cover of the first one.

Was it a diary of some sort? She squinted down at Winnie's spiky handwriting, trying to make out the words. They were...thoughts. Dated, and one per page. That it wasn't necessarily a diary made Juno feel less guilty about reading it. Pacifying her conscience with that, she looked to the first one. It read: *Day after day it eats me. I am tired, but not tired enough to kill myself.*

Juno frowned. Had she read that right? Little Miss Perfect Winnie Crouch had days where she just didn't want to live?

She turned the page, thinking she'd opened it to a bad day—even people like Winnie had those once in a while, she supposed, but the next entry was similar: *I tore the pages out of my favorite book, one by one...*

Juno was more than shocked. Winnie wasn't a darkness and gloom girl; she had subscriptions to *Harper's Bazaar*, *Esquire*, *Food & Family*, and *Marie Claire*, the kind of person who considered herself an artist because of her beautifully curated Instagram account. Juno wasn't making fun; it was just a fact—Winnie wasn't drinking from a deep pool. Or at least Juno had thought so, until now. Abruptly she flipped the notebook closed and put it back where she found it. She really needed nail clippers.

She checked Nigel's side of the bed and the bathroom drawers. She pushed junk around the junk drawer. The Crouches had an endless supply of matches; Juno pocketed several boxes and moved to a different drawer where she found an unopened package of LED tap lights. She held them for several minutes, considering. Winnie had probably forgotten they were there. She stuck the package in the waistband of her pants. Then she decided to check Sam's room for the clippers.

She didn't like snooping in Sam's room, and she didn't do it often, being that Sam was the person she liked the most in the house. Sometimes, when she had extra time, she'd wander up there to see what he was reading or what little project he was working on. Without turning on the light, her eyes scanned the silhouettes of furniture. She found everything tidy and put away. No pieces of metal lay scattered across his desk, either.

Generally, tiny remnants were strewn about his room as he built model airplanes or put together a tiny wooden T. rex with parts so small Juno could barely pick them up with her fingers. But today, something was off. Looking around, she noticed an absence of the usual stuffed animals that sat on his bed. The posters of superheroes were gone, too, fresh navy paint on his walls to replace the light blue wallpaper. Juno harrumphed. He'd gone and grown himself up overnight.

She remembered their conversations in the park, and suddenly the nail clippers were forgotten. She found herself nudging the mouse to his desktop, and the screen sprang to life. Having raised two sons, Juno knew the types of things boys got up to online; for that reason, she avoided his open internet browser and looked beyond that, at his desktop. He was working on something; it looked like the back end of a website. Sam-Side.

She slumped into his chair, not taking her eyes from the screen. Had he designed this? She'd hired people to do this for her when the internet became a thing, for the business. Kregger had reassured her when she was intimidated by all the buttons and screens—and then when all the buttons disappeared, and it was just screens. Her website had been amateur compared to this, and it had cost her a whopping twelve hundred dollars in the early 2000s. But here he was, a thirteen-year-old boy building his first website. They made them different nowadays, and she suspected he was tired of building toys— at least the ones they made for boys. She tried to understand what she was reading. It was a blog. She could see several blog titles in the box that said DRAFTS, all of them yet to be published.

"You've been busy," she heard herself say out loud. Snooping was wrong, but what was the harm in taking a little peek—it wasn't like she was some stranger off the street. Once upon a time, she'd been a bona fide psychologist, for God's sake. She felt a wave of excitement that didn't have anything to do with being a psychologist. It was a familiar feeling; she'd spent thirty years digging and plowing through people's brains—learning their secrets and hearing the ugliest desires of their hearts. She may be retired, but her lust for knowledge had never gone away.

The first draft Juno clicked on was titled: *Pretty Sure I'm Adopted*.

Sam had said this to her in the park, too, and she'd responded lightly. In a clinical setting, Juno would brush this off, too; adolescents went through a period where they felt disconnected from everything, even the people who loved them most. Juno compared it to a young lion learning to roar, picking fights, feeling insecure but acting volatile.

But this particular blog entry had never made it past one sentence. Sam, new to adult words, had described his feelings in one staggering fritz of emotion: *Wolves know when they're being raised by bears.*

She stared at the words. Rolled them around in her head, where they gelled together with his cryptic phrases at the park, the words in Winnie's journal. *"Day after day, it eats me."*

7

WINNIE

The dinner was tradition. Last year it was at Don and Malay's, the year before that it was at the Parklands', and this year it was the Crouches' turn. Vicky Parkland called to confirm on Monday evening just as Winnie was getting home from work.

"Friendsgiving. You didn't forget, did you? You did."

"I didn't," Winnie said confidently. "This is me we're talking about."

She had forgotten.

"Yeah, you do live for a party," Vicky agreed. "I just hadn't heard anything and—"

Winnie rolled her eyes. Vicky was calling because she heard about Dakota. Today, Winnie was the tea.

"Things have just been…there's been drama…"

She could hear Vicky walking into her bedroom and clos-ing the door. Mack must be home, she thought. Vicky never gossiped in front of Mack, who thought it was crass. Win-nie walked into her own bedroom; Nigel wasn't home yet. She loved the way the room smelled: a mixture of wood polish, orange blossom, and her and Nigel. But today, as she stepped inside, she smelled something else—something she wasn't used to smelling in their space. She hesitated on the threshold, looking around uncertainly. She'd made their bed this morning, arranging the throw pillows the way she liked them; now one of them was lying on the floor next to the nightstand. She walked over and picked it up. Could it have just fallen off?

And then she smelled that smell again. Yes, she definitely smelled something…musky. That was it, the distinct smell of sour body. Had Dakota come up here for something before he left? She clutched the pillow to her chest, sniffing the air like a beagle on the hunt. Winnie would ask him later; in the meantime, she opened one of her drawers, pulling out a dainty glass bottle, and squirted it four times into the air. The sweaty smell was gone, replaced by orange blossom. The cheap stuff never lingered in the air like the good stuff did. Call her a snob, everyone else did. The same went for this house. Nigel had wanted one of those crappy, cheaply built model homes, but Winnie had put her foot down; it was her money, after all. Now she lived in her dream home with her dream man.

"Okay, spill," Vicky was saying. Winnie didn't want to spill; she didn't like when the tea was about her, but she'd for-gotten Friendsgiving, and telling Vicky about Dakota would distract her from that.

She launched into the story after an eager "Spare nothing!" from Vicky. Hosting the damn thing *had* seemed like a good idea a year ago. Now Nigel was going to resent her even more.

By the time Winnie sat down at her desk, Vicky was in full advice mode. She half listened to Vicky's story about her delinquent sister-in-law who always placed the blame on her brother Tommy when they fought. "...so really, Winnie, we don't know the story, and Manda is probably overreacting."

"You're probably right," she said.

During college, Vicky had a horrendous crush on Dakota, who was a freshman to her junior. She'd wanted to marry him "So we can be sisters!" When Dakota deflected her advances, Vicky had moved on to his roommate: Mack.

Winnie held the phone between her shoulder and ear and typed her password into her computer. She was thinking about the joints in the back of her underwear drawer, the ones that Dakota had got for her. She wasn't usually a weed smoker, but lately, she was so stressed she felt like she was losing her mind.

"Have to go, V, I have a million things to do before tomorrow."

"Okay, text me the deets."

"Sure." Winnie hated when Vicky said "deets." She also hated that Vicky insisted on calling their gathering Friendsgiving just because Taylor Swift did it.

After she hung up with Vicky, she called Nigel straightaway. When he picked up, it felt like a great fist had grabbed her stomach and squeezed.

"Are you serious, Winnie? We just moved Dakota in. No."

"Nigel, they planned their trips to visit family around this. We've literally had these plans for a year. We can't just cancel on them!"

"We can, because things happen. They'll get over it."

"I can't believe you're being so dismissive about this."

There was a long pause before he spoke again.

"Okay...okay."

Winnie felt the hands loosen on her stomach a little. "Okay...?"

"Yeah. I don't want to fight about it. Just okay."

Nigel was in a surprisingly good mood on the day of Friendsgiving. She was suspicious; was he holding back his irritation? Winnie had to remind herself that she was being negative with no real basis for that feeling. When she needed supplies from the store he volunteered to go: "What my baby wants, my baby gets!" he called on his way out the door.

His errand gave Winnie time to get herself ready. She shot upstairs to do her makeup and slip into a dress she'd bought online for the occasion. She had always wanted to be the most interesting person in any room. She'd gone to great lengths as a child to stand out; once, at thirteen, she'd chopped off her waist-length hair during one of her parents' dinner parties, announcing to a room of her father's coworkers that she was done with blatant sexism. A few years later, during her emo phase, she'd fed right back into that blatant sexism and paid one of her brother's friends to tattoo the words *Sweet Girl* on her upper thigh. And late into her teenage years, Winnie had decided that sex wasn't a big deal at all and freely slept with whomever she felt she had a connection with, all this during her self-professed "hippie stage." Now that she was a grown-up, Winnie felt like she was still playing a role—a more grounded and responsible one. She recycled voraciously; grew her own organic vegetables that she fed to her perfect child and smart husband; had gay friends, Black friends, West Indian friends, and—more recently—a trans friend. Winnie volunteered, always kept spare dollars in her purse for the homeless, and kept her tight-knit group together by being the peacemaker. When Winnie came downstairs, Nigel had come back, and he was whistling.

"You can make your risotto, right?" Winnie asked. "The one everyone loves?"

"Yep."

"And pick up a case of wine from the—"

"Got it," he said.

Nigel did make his risotto. It was on the stove when the first of their guests rang the newly installed "Twinkle, Twinkle, Little Star" doorbell. Don and Malay, who arrived wrapped in scarves and toting a bottle of Bordeaux, were exclaiming about a museum opening like it was the second coming of Christ when Nigel walked into the living room. Despite their being Winnie's friends from grad school, and that they were horrendously pretentious, they loved Nigel.

Winnie knew her friends, and they weren't as nice as they pretended to be. Nigel had been taken on as a sort of pet to the group: the kid with the single mom who grew up eating Hungry-Man dinners and went to community college. They fed him pieces of their intellect and humored his lower-middle-class mentality with stories of their own artistic and ostentatious upbringings. Nigel always acted like this was a real treat, but after they were gone, he and Winnie would laugh about all the obnoxious things her friends had said. It became part of their marriage, what made them a team: "We're laughing because you're all the same." Nigel had stolen the line from Kurt Cobain, but that made it even better to Winnie.

Don's dad owned racehorses and Malay's mother had been an international supermodel in the eighties. When Malay saw Nigel, she spread her arms wide and he stepped into her hug without reluctance. Winnie watched in amusement as her husband became entangled in Malay's scarves, his watch snagging a piece of the silk. Don stepped in to help.

"Just another man trying to snag my wife away from me!" Don winked conspiratorially at Winnie, who smiled weakly in return. He was dressed in a brown leather jacket and skintight black jeans. It might have worked if his body weren't shaped like a rectangle. Once Don had them free, Nigel offered to take his jacket.

"It's part of my outfit," he said, placing an offended hand over the right pocket of said jacket. Winnie smothered a giggle and tried to catch Nigel's eye. But he wasn't looking at her, he was too distracted to care about their friends' idiosyncrasies.

"Still driving that Subaru, I see." Don smirked over his little round glasses.

"It won't die." Nigel shrugged. This was part of the routine, the talk of the neonish green station wagon, which all of Winnie's friends detested. Nigel and Winnie had this argument frequently.

"I happen to like the alien shit color of my car. What I don't like is defending it to these buffoons every time they come over," Nigel always said.

Sam came barreling down the stairs in a flurry of awkward arms and legs, and Nigel veered for the kitchen. Despite his earlier good mood, he didn't want to be here, and Winnie was starting to realize that she agreed with him. The doorbell rang. She knew it would be either the Parklands or the Fromlics, and when she swung open the door, she was right on both accounts. The four of them, having arrived at the same time, stepped inside, complaining about the weather and lack of parking in tandem: Desiree and Uri, Vicky and Mack—Winnie had been roommates with Desiree as well as Vicky in college, and their husbands were mostly boring additions Winnie chose not to know well.

She'd confessed that to Nigel once, and he'd patted her on the knee and said, "I'm not sure their wives want to know them, either."

Winnie chose that moment to laugh at Nigel's years-old

joke and suddenly felt like she missed her husband, even though he was just in the kitchen.

"Where's Nigel?" Desiree shrugged out of her jacket. "Did he make the risotto?"

"Yeah!" Winnie wiggled her eyebrows up and down, congratulating herself on being the fakest person on the planet.

"Lemme go grab him," she said through lips that felt stiff. She accepted the bottle of wine Uri proffered just as Dakota walked in the front door. He looked surprised that everyone was there, and Winnie realized that she'd failed to tell him about Friendsgiving.

He accepted a couple of high fives from her friends and the childish slapping of palms made her flinch as she gripped the chilled bottle, pretending to study the label.

"This is great," she lied. Dakota was in a good mood, playing things off like he knew about the party all along. A gust of relief rushed from her lips as she arranged them into a smile. She had the sudden urge to run to the kitchen and lock the door. Nigel, she wanted to be with Nigel, so why were all these people in her house?

"Be right back." She beelined for the kitchen, peeking her head in the door.

"Can you bring the rest of the wine, please? Everyone's here." Her voice was light, her tone joyful, but if her husband looked at her, he would see she was wearing her face. Surely he would come rescue her. He didn't look. Winnie lingered half bent in the doorway, waiting for him to acknowledge her. "Nigel…" she whispered sharply. Then he did look up—his phone was in his hand like he'd been texting.

"Coming," he said.

"The wine," she reminded him. He nodded toward the bottles on the counter, the last case they had from Marrowstone Vineyards. Hopefully it would be enough—Winnie planned on drinking tonight. To hell with her rule about alcohol, she decided.

Just then, Subomi's mom texted to say she was outside to pick Samuel up. Winnie spotted her son talking to Malay and made her way over.

"Samuel, grab your things. Subomi's mom is here."

"Aww no, leaving us?" Malay teased. It was a rule not to have any of the kids at Friendsgiving, the reason being everyone wanted to get drunk. After a quick goodbye to Malay, Samuel dashed away to get his duffel. Winnie had just turned back to say something to her friend when she heard Dakota curse loudly from behind her.

"Fuck, kid! Be careful."

She turned to see her brother looming over her son, beer dripping down his arm and onto the floor. Sam looked genuinely frightened, all previous excitement drained from his face.

"Dakota..." Winnie was temporarily stunned.

"Don't fucking talk to my son like that."

Nigel stood just outside the kitchen, a bottle of wine in each hand. He looked...over it. He was calm, but Winnie could tell he was livid. She had a brief vision of her husband leaping over the couch and smashing the bottles on Dakota's head. She'd never seen her husband look *that* angry. She was oddly turned on.

"'Kota," Winnie said urgently, trying to draw his attention. Red-faced and already drunk, her brother turned toward Nigel.

"He ran into me, man. Didn't your momma ever tell you not to run in the house?" Dakota directed this question at Samuel. Winnie didn't have time to process what happened next: she saw Nigel set the wine bottles down on the hutch, and then he had Dakota by the shirt, shoving him against the wall. Nigel was going to take care of things, just like he had that night. *"It's done. No one will ever know,"* he'd said.

Her husband had the body of a gymnast—tight and hard—and he used surprise to pin Dakota for a good five seconds before the bigger man shoved Nigel backward with a great whoosh of his arms.

"Hey, hey, hey!" Uri called out, moving forward to step between them. "You're a guest in this house," Uri said. He bent his head solemnly to look Dakota in the eyes. Her brother jerked back, his face obstinate.

Winnie knew what was coming, and her insides shriveled up like little raisins. Dakota was looking at her—he wanted confirmation that he was more than a guest, he was her precious twin brother. But it didn't work like that anymore.

"You should leave," Winnie told him. His eyes held on to hers for a painful second before he looked away. Winnie knew 'Kota; he'd see this as a betrayal: blood was thicker than water. But Winnie had other blood to consider.

"Samuel, come here," she said. Samuel didn't hesitate. He didn't seem thirteen at this moment; he was a little boy again, and he was hers to protect. "Go, Subomi's mom is waiting. Everything will be fine." She kissed his forehead, and for once he didn't look embarrassed.

"Okay." He said it so only she could hear. Winnie licked her lips and gave him her best smile. Samuel looked unsure for a moment, and then he skirted off to the front door where Winnie had set his duffel.

There was an electric current in the room. Winnie could see the excitement in her friends' eyes. She blinked around the room, disbelieving. They were hoping, she realized, that her brother would disobey. This would give them something to talk about for weeks. They were poised all over the living room, on her chaise and couches, her glasses held in their hands. It hurt her stomach to think about them talking about her family, sending their group texts back and forth. She hated them in that moment, every single one of them. She wished she could tell them all to get out of her house.

Then Nigel sniggered from where he stood, shaking his head, and Winnie saw Dakota's whole body go tense. Any regret etched on his face was suddenly gone, and then her hotheaded brother was straightening his spine and spreading his feet wider apart. Her brother reminded her of a young lion, and her husband reminded her of an old one looking for a fight. She groaned deep inside herself, but not on the outside—on the outside Winnie kept her composure. No one was going to gossip; she was going to shut this down right now.

"Dakota—GO!"

"Yeah?" He looked right at her, and Winnie's heart cleaved in two. Things would never be the same with them.

"Fuck you, Nigel," Dakota said, shoving past him and out of the room.

Relief eased the beat of her racing heart, but the worst was not over; she had to get Dakota out of the house in one piece, and, oh, God—was she really going to have to continue with this stupid dinner?

"You okay, Win?" Vicky put a hand on her shoulder.

Dakota came back a minute later, a duffel slung over his shoulder. He had his phone out and was concentrating hard on the screen as he headed for the front door.

"Dakota!" she called after him. He didn't turn; he lifted one hand over his head to signal goodbye, and he was gone. Winnie heard the traffic outside, a buzz that suddenly got louder and then abruptly stopped when the door slammed closed.

"Maybe you should go after him," Malay said. "What if he does something stupid? You don't want to be blamed—"

Winnie didn't need to ask Malay what she meant; Malay's

cousin Alfie killed himself when they were all in college—ate the barrel of his father's gun. They had all known Alfie and were sad when he died, but Malay treated his death like a crutch for everything she did now.

"Shut up, just shut up," she hissed at her. She was spitting mad at all of them, but Malay had opened her damn mouth first. Now she was going to hear it.

"He's not Alfie, and Nigel had every right to be angry."

Their shock pleased her. Winnie had never so much as raised her voice at one of them. As the people pleaser of the group, she fought to stay in everyone's good graces; her favorite place to be *was* the favorite.

"You've all been under a lot of stress, you're right. We shouldn't be commenting." Don nudged his wife, who looked like she'd sucked a lime without the tequila.

"Let's have risotto!" Vicky pumped her fist into the air.

She was still holding her wineglass, Winnie noted—her true best friend. Where had that come from? Winnie rubbed her temples, chiding herself. Vicky wasn't the enemy, no one was. This was just a sticky situation. She felt so, so tired.

Despite Winnie sticking up for her husband at the dinner party, they were currently not speaking. The minute their last guest left and the door closed behind them, he'd turned and given her a look. Winnie had felt battered by that look, betrayed. For once, she'd stopped caring what people thought of her and had been rude to her friends. She could barely wrap her mind around how he could be displeased with her; she'd done exactly what he always asked her to do, which was to be on his side.

"What was that for?" But he was already en route to the kitchen, so she'd posed her question to his back.

"I'm going to bed, Winnie." He'd said it with so much finality she'd stopped dead in her tracks. She'd felt very small and stupid in that moment. She'd meant to say something to call him back, but she was in shock. And then he'd left her downstairs with the dishes and a million questions. *That,* she thought, *is not my husband.* The thought had scared her so much she'd marched upstairs after him if only to reassure herself. How much had he had to drink? She'd been too pre-occupied with keeping face to count his drinks. Dinner par-ties were the one night she never got on him about drinking, though she liked to keep tabs.

She felt smashed and crashed. Her brother was never going to talk to her again. He was still holding a grudge against their sister Candace, and they'd fought years ago—Winnie couldn't even remember about what. Not to mention the residual fall-out with the rest of the family after he spun his own version of the story to the rest of the siblings. What had she been think-ing anyway? Inviting all those people over when the emo-tional temperature in the house had a broken gauge. Hadn't her husband always accused her of making rash decisions? She always did the wrong thing, made the wrong choice.

Nigel was coming out of the bathroom when she walked in, and for a moment she didn't know what to do. She was nervous, she realized. Her toes curled and uncurled on the hardwood as Winnie stood a few feet inside their bedroom, watching as Nigel pulled off his T-shirt in the way that al-ways made her stomach do a little flip—by grabbing it from behind his neck and pulling it over his head. She watched for the peacock, as she called it, the cowlick that always shot up when given the chance. When he was shirtless and walk-ing toward her, Winnie forgot that she was supposed to be angry with him. For a moment she thought he was coming toward her to kiss her, like one of those romance novels she sometimes read, but at the last minute he breezed right past where she stood and out of the bedroom.

She followed on his heels, refusing to be so easily dismissed this time. He was back in the kitchen, opening the fridge and bending down to see inside. Winnie watched him pull out a Gatorade, snapping off the lid and taking a long drink. She had time to wonder when he'd shaved and if his Adam's apple had always been that pronounced before he replaced the lid and headed for the door, the bottle held loosely in his hand. He was still acting like she wasn't there, so she stepped into his path, blocking his way.

"We need to talk." She folded her arms across her chest and immediately felt childish. To make matters worse, Nigel acknowledged the action with a little raise of his eyebrows. He tucked his bottom lip under his teeth and stared at her through half narrowed eyes. If Winnie had wondered if he was drunk, she had her answer.

"I don't know what I did to deserve—"

"No, you never do know, do you?"

Her lips were still curled around her last word when he cut in, and they stayed that way as her eyes narrowed in disbelief.

"Know what, Nigel? How am I supposed to know if you don't tell me?"

His eyes rolled toward the ceiling like he was searching for something in the skylights.

"I did... I have... Winnie!" He ran his hands through his hair, yanking on it in frustration. Winnie frowned at all of this, pushing air loudly through her nose.

"I have no idea what you're talking about, but if this is about my brother—I stood up for you ton—"

Again he cut her off. "I didn't want your brother to move in, I didn't want to have this fucking dinner party, and if we talk about this right now I'm going to say things I regret. So do you really want to do this, Winnie, right now?"

She heard herself say "yes," but it was all smoke; she was afraid. Her husband had never spoken to her like this, and after all this time, after everything that they endured together, it could only mean one thing: he was over it. *It* meaning her and their marriage, the fascination he'd once held for her—gone.

That's when the shouting began, and true to his word, he said things he couldn't take back. Winnie pressed her lips together, the hurt rocking around in her chest like a wild horse. Didn't he know that once words were out, they stuck in people's minds like barbs? *She* only ever brought up that night when she absolutely needed to—why couldn't he do the same? For the most part it was around anniversaries that the grief woke up in her chest like a hibernating thing. She'd found that even if she didn't consciously remember that it was that time of year, an unexplained sadness would creep up on her. She didn't always know what was wrong; sometimes it took a few days of depression to figure it out. It was as if her entire body grieved on a sort of rhythm. Nigel shouting those ugly words at her had woken her grief, and now it would follow her around like a shadow.

8

JUNO

They were fighting tonight. Juno could hear them through the floor, their voices drifting to where she lay curled up in her bed. Her feet were cold; that's what she'd been thinking when the fighting started. With Sam gone, his parents fought like they were releasing all the fizz that had been bottled up and shaken. She supposed that was better than the alternative: a young boy hearing firsthand all the things his parents hated about each other. She knew from experience that what was good for the kids wasn't necessarily good for the marriage; if you were wizards you could balance everything, but for the rest of the nonmagical population, children put a strain on marriage while simultaneously keeping it together. It's what Juno called a good ol' damned if you do, damned if you don't situation.

Winnie's voice rose an octave; she was really working herself up. Juno lay still, eyes closed and trying to sleep, but their voices were invading her space. She felt the budding of panic in her chest, its petals unfolding. She was tired tonight, a little depressed, and she just wanted the day to be over. She could hear Nigel trying to reason with Winnie, who wasn't having it.

"You're dismissing my feelings again," she shouted. "I can't move on, you know that—"

"Winnie, you don't have a choice. We go over this year after year. I'm tired of it." Nigel's voice, which initially sounded calm, was curling around the words like he was struggling to pronounce each one. *He's fed up*, Juno thought—any minute he's going to blow.

"You're tired of it? Oh my God, Nigel. It was the worst night of my life and *you're* tired of it?"

She couldn't hear what Nigel said. Juno found herself leaning away from her pillow, trying to—

"It wasn't you! You can't know how this feels!"

Juno rolled on her back as Winnie dissolved into noisy tears.

"No. You're right. I don't know what it's like to steal someone's infant—"

The whole of Washington State could have shaken just then, and Juno wouldn't have noticed. She was frozen in shock as reality wobbled around her; then there was a very loud clap that she assumed was Winnie's hand meeting her husband's face, followed by a much louder eruption of words. They continued to shout for a while longer before Winnie stormed off to the bedroom, her footsteps pounding up the stairs dramatically.

Juno lay very still, Nigel's words playing over and over in her mind. *Steal someone's infant…?* What had Nigel meant? Surely not Sam. Juno had gleaned that Winnie had worked as a mental health counselor for some years before shifting to a management position in a similar field. Perhaps she'd reported someone to child protective services, and they'd had their baby taken away unfairly. But Nigel wouldn't have said those words with such bitterness if that were the case—if Winnie had just been doing her job.

She rolled onto her back, staring up at the ceiling. Could that be the secret Winnie had been harboring? The reason behind the depression she wrote about in her journal? That Sam wasn't hers and Nigel's—that she had *stolen* him? But Sam looked like his mother. Juno had always thought that—that he looked like his mother. They shared the same high forehead and wide-set eyes. Her son's hair was darker than Winnie's, though Juno suspected she was a bottle blonde—but so what? Kids didn't always precisely resemble their parents. But what bothered her was Nigel and Winnie's wariness around him, like they were tiptoeing over everything. Sam knew it, too, didn't he? *Wolves know when they're being raised by bears.*

Yes, that was it, Juno thought. Sam was the minefield they were tiptoeing around. But how had it happened?

9

WINNIE

When Winnie woke up the next morning, Nigel's side of the bed was undisturbed. It made her feel empty to see the space so untouched. Last night, when Nigel didn't come to bed, she'd found him sleeping in his den...*sleeping*. Winnie had never understood how men could fall asleep in times of emotional crisis. How could he sleep when he knew she was upstairs crying? She wanted to wake him up, yell at him for not being more upset; in the end she'd wandered back upstairs and climbed into bed, still in her dress from the dinner party. She wouldn't give him the satisfaction of knowing the little stabs he made were stinging.

She rolled out of the tangle of blankets, wobbling on her feet when she stood. She was a wreck, a hot mess—makeup was swirled across her face in streaks of color that reminded her of Dalí's distorted art. She heard Nigel's voice in the back of her mind telling her that it was very generous to compare herself to a Dalí—especially if it concerned her cry face. Or, as her mother would say—she had the face of a whore who'd been out whoring. Her pillow agreed, though she hated that she was using her mother's voice to slut-shame herself. Winnie most definitely did not want to be judged for the number of men she'd slept with.

She washed her Dalí face off during a quick shower, after which she threw on her sweats, parted her hair and pulled it into a low bun, and applied some mascara. She had to be Samuel's mom today, not Nigel's angry wife. To at least look a little angry, she wore large gold hoops in her ears. Nigel would understand what they meant. Then with a confidence she most definitely wasn't feeling, she marched down the stairs looking fresh out of a nineties music video. Pausing to grab an apple from the bowl in the kitchen, she flicked her eyes upward and found her husband dressed and drinking coffee at the dinette. She kept her cool, grabbing the keys from the hook as she stepped through the door. Her descent was halted.

"Sam's already home," Nigel called. He'd waited until she was down the last step. Winnie had to walk back up, which was cherry-on-top humiliating.

"Subomi's mom dropped him off. She said she texted you…"

Maybe. Probably. She hadn't checked her phone since last night. Where was it even? Winnie tried to move with indifference, but Nigel had that knowing look—*you're wearing your face, slim.*

She refused—refused—to speak to him. Marching straight upstairs, she went to Samuel's door and knocked. He called out a lazy "Come in," and Winnie did just that.

"Hey," she said. Samuel looked up from his book for a second before his eyes found the page again.

"How was it?"

"Fine," he said. "They think I'm weird."

"They do not. You're not weird." Winnie frowned at her son. She'd have to text Subomi's mother and get to the bottom of this.

"You are weird," Nigel said. Where had he come from? He was standing in the doorway, scratching the back of his head. Why was he saying this?

"I'd beat you up. Possibly shove your head in the urinal till—"

Samuel was cracking up, his face broken of its usually stony boredom, spread into a rare, crooked laughter. Winnie took a moment to appreciate it.

"Dude, weird is better than boring. Every time, man, every time."

Samuel shrugged but Winnie could tell he was pleased.

"I guess so," he said. "But I think they're weird. Just to get that straight."

"My man," Nigel said, walking over to fist-bump their son. He strolled back out of the room and she blinked after him. The smell of his cologne on the air was overpowering; she cleared her throat once, twice.

"Did you need something, Mom?" Samuel was no longer smiling but staring at her like her presence was an intrusion.

Her mother's heart wilted. "Nope. No—just checking on you...and I guess I wanted to talk to you about last night and Uncle Dakota..."

"Dad and I already had a talk. I get it."

"Oh," Winnie said. She bit back the rest of her questions, not wanting Samuel to know she was clueless. *Thanks, Nigel.*

"Well, if you need to talk about anything."

"Thanks."

She wanted to hug him—that's what they always did after they resolved a conflict together—but as Winnie leaned toward her son, he'd already gone back to his book. And nothing had been resolved. Not that included her anyway. Winnie had never had fewer friends in her own home.

And then, as she left the room, a thought seized her so aggressively she took a little step back, away from them. *What if Nigel told Samuel? What if he told him what I did?* Winnie felt light-headed. There was nothing to steady herself on, so she just swayed on the spot, one hand reaching for a wall that wasn't there. If Nigel had told Samuel, she'd lose her son forever.

Sometimes Winnie wondered if she'd taken the job at Illuminations Mental Health to prove something to Nigel. Once, when they were dating, he'd made a joke about her not being athletic; within a week she'd registered for indoor soccer and got a gym membership. It didn't end there, no—Winnie actually became what she wanted. She began to like soccer, enjoy playing it. *Can't say I'm not athletic anymore, can you?*

No, he really couldn't. And since he'd called her spoiled within the first year of their marriage, she'd gotten to work, hadn't she? He'd laughed at her when she spoke about the occasional dollar she passed to the homeless, had mocked her in one of his crueler moments. "You don't care about homeless people," he'd said. "You just have upper-middle-class shame you feel compelled to atone for!"

It was as if he'd issued some silent challenge to his wife. And so Winnie found herself working at Illuminations for two years. Two years of dedication to people less fortunate than she both in spirit and in bank. Two solid years. Before the incident.

He would have believed in her commitment to the cause,

too, had she not done what she'd done. "The incident" was the name Nigel gave to it, but it was a weak word for what happened that night. It wasn't an incident; it was a crime. One Winnie had committed.

10

JUNO

The autumn rain tapped incessantly against the windows in Winnie's book nook. Juno settled into a chair with the book she'd started the day she fell. She'd bent the spine, and she regretted that; she had a deep respect for books. That entire day was a bit hazy in her memory. She hadn't fallen since, but she knew that all it would take was falling the wrong way and her bones would snap like peanut brittle. She settled herself more firmly in her seat. No! There would be none of that. Juno was sick, sick as hell, and if she were careful, she could finish out her days without breaking a hip, or a leg, or whatever old people broke when they fell. As if on cue, Juno's hip began to ache.

She was trying not to think about what she'd heard the

night before as she lay in her own bed. *You misheard*, she'd told herself a hundred times since that morning. But she hadn't misheard, and now those words were repeating themselves in her head like a goddamn two-year-old whining in a toy store. She rubbed little circles at her temples and tried to read the words on the page. But she wasn't thinking about the story; it wasn't fiction in which she wanted to immerse herself. It was the truth.

Juno got up from the chair with some difficulty and walked over to the family computer. The screen was dark, but she knew that if she gave the mouse a little nudge it would spring to life, revealing the family vacation screen saver. She hadn't touched a computer in years—well, except when she'd nudged Sam's mouse much the same way the other day—but her life before had held all of those things: computers and jobs and credit cards. She didn't miss it. She had very little and having very little yielded fewer complications. It had taken Juno time to adjust to a life without—stuff—but once she had, she found that she preferred it.

She sat down in the chair facing the computer, flexing her fingers. It was no big deal; Juno knew how to work a damn computer. She wasn't one of those timed-out old people who poked at an iPhone screen with a shaking index finger. She just didn't want to be part of that world anymore. She almost got up right then and there, but Nigel's words played again in her head. Call it human curiosity.

There they are! Juno thought as the photo of the Crouches appeared on the beach. She tried not to look at them as she pulled up the internet browser, but she could see them out of the corner of her eye, staring at her with their sunburned faces. Her fingers found the keys easily. *Slipping right back into it*, she thought, sitting up a little straighter. Not bad for a sixty-seven-year-old, not bad at all. She typed *missing children Seattle*

Washington, and then, as an afterthought, added the year into the search box. Sam was thirteen years old. That would have made him an infant in 2008.

The Center for Missing and Exploited Children was the first site to appear, and Juno clicked on it. She was given the option to search for a missing child by name, but since Juno didn't know what Sam's real name was, she scrolled past that and saw there was a section where she could search by the city and state from which a child had gone missing. She typed in *Seattle Washington* and entered the year 2008 into the missing date option. Then Juno hit the return key and waited.

There weren't many. She scanned through the single page of results in less than five seconds. There were no infants reported missing in Washington in 2008, but that didn't mean anything. If the Crouches had kidnapped Sam, they could have taken him from anywhere. And maybe he wasn't an *infant* infant; Nigel could have used that word "infant" and meant it broadly. She widened the search to all fifty states, which yielded a considerable number of results.

She leaned back in the chair—*think, Juno*. She knew that of the nearly 800,000 children under age eighteen who went missing each year, more than 58,000 were nonfamily abductions and only about 115 were stranger kidnappings. That was almost two stranger-danger kidnappings to a state every year. That calmed Juno's nerves. Her previous thoughts sounded kooky, even to herself. A kidnapper's emotional motive was desperation, and Winnie and Nigel were hardly desperate—selfish, mostly, with a side of entitlement.

Just because she was already on the web page, she copied down a list of names on the notepad Winnie kept next to the computer—names of children who went missing in the US and were never recovered. *Recovered* was the word the website used. Juno thought that was a silly police word; no parent whose child had been kidnapped would use such gentle words as "never recovered" to describe the lack of closure to their personal tragedy. What she did know was that if a baby had gone missing in 2008 from a perfect little family, it would have been national news, she was sure of it—especially if it were a white baby. That was how the world worked. But there was something else not sitting right with Juno. She tapped the desk with her index finger, lips pursed and eyes narrowed. It was a little like staring at shadows in the dark: she could make out the shapes but the full picture of what was there was missing. "You're getting old, girlfriend," she said, exiting out of the internet windows. "But you still have time to expose the truth."

She groaned as she lifted herself from the chair and limped off to put her laundry in the dryer, but not before tucking the list of names into her pocket.

That night, Juno lay in bed listening to them fight again as she held the piece of paper in her fist. Their fight was the same old, same old. Nigel and Winnie making the rounds, revisiting the wrongs. She was bored of it; she didn't know how they weren't.

"I can't even believe you're guilting me about something I do for myself after you spent all of that money on the addition!"

"The addition that would be making us money if you let me rent it out!"

"And I made it very clear that I don't want a stranger in my home—then or now."

"Well, you got your way, Winnie, per usual. The three of us, secluded in this little world you've made for us. I suppose you want thanks, too. Sam is so very grateful that you've forced him to be a vegetarian. I am so very grateful that you choose my underwear brand, and schedule my weekends, and tell me how to use my time off."

"Rent your stupid apartment out," Winnie said. "But I'm not living here if you do."

PART TWO
THEN

11

JUNO

At first, she had only followed them around the lake, staying a few yards behind as they bickered—or on the very rare occasion, chatted amicably. More often, they walked with their faces turned away from each other, and when they did, Juno would remember the way Nigel had wrapped his fingers around her biceps that first day and squeezed gently. She'd believed in them in that moment, cared about their outcome. She was content to have something to do, to have something to study. The depression that choked her on most days ebbed back in the wake of new purpose. At a quarter to six, Juno would find a bench near the theater and wait for them to begin their loop around the lake. It became a game to spot their faces among the walkers, and then she would get to her feet, which suddenly seemed lighter, and stroll behind them for the rest of the way.

On the days when they couldn't bear to look at each other but could tolerate a walk together, Juno saw their real connection. She caught words, sentences—but mostly it was their body language that interested her. They were never more than three feet apart—even when angry. It was like they were connected by a rubber band with only so much stretch. She'd known couples like this, had sat them on her office couch for counseling. But none had ever interested her like these two. She told herself it was harmless, her fascination with them—like watching reality television. Wasn't that what everyone was into nowadays? But somewhere deep inside, Juno knew it was more. They walked late in the evenings when the foot traffic at Greenlake Park had thinned out for the day and they wouldn't have to share the path with a fleet of strollers. She'd never followed them after they left the park, because they were just that—her park family, something to be interested in other than her own tired problems. They had a child—a boy with wavy hair that hung in his eyes. During the week he'd join them, scootering ahead so fast they'd frantically call out for him to wait, but he wouldn't hear. It was Juno's opinion that he chose not to hear. That always made her laugh. Prepubescent boys had a way of wringing their parents' nerves dry. They called him Samuel—never Sam—but Juno thought he looked like a Sam with all that hair and those big eyes that stared so intently.

How many weeks had she trailed them around the 2.8-mile loop, sometimes trotting to keep up with them, cursing their youth? It went from interest to obsession for Juno in a matter of days. She couldn't sleep; she could no longer eat for fear of missing out on something. All Juno could think about was this family. For weeks she'd stopped near the utility shed and watched as they'd crossed the street and gone into a monstrous brick house on the east side of the park. Then, one day, just out of curiosity, she'd taken a peek into their mailbox, just to see their names. And there it was, right on a postcard from their car dealership reminding them to get an oil change: Winnie and Nigel Crouch. The names fit them well, Juno decided. Out of boredom, she'd Googled them on the library's computer, a fat gray machine that hummed louder than she did, and found that Winnie currently worked for a nonprofit called None the Richer as coordinator for their fundraising events, while Nigel worked as a web designer for an athletics company called Wella.

Juno liked how the information made her feel. Like she wasn't without all the things that made up a person: a family, a home, history. Just to hold theirs for a few moments left her heart racing. She wasn't doing it again. No, that's not what this was. She shook her head, narrowing her eyes at her own inner voice, that old liar. The last time, she knew she'd been wrong: she'd allowed herself to get too involved and it had cost her everything. But this time, she didn't have anything to lose; this time, Juno could throw herself into the project. And the project was the Crouches, who needed her help.

She hadn't decided to move in with them; an opportunity had presented itself and Juno had merely taken it like any person would. She'd needed a place to stay, and the Crouches had plenty of space—so much space in that monstrosity of a house. And yet they were adding rooms! She couldn't believe the greed of it. For weeks she watched from the park as the crews arrived early in the morning and worked through the day. The workers would carry their lunch across the street to the park and sit under the trees, sometimes napping in the shade until it was time to go back to work. Once, they'd come to the same tree where Juno herself was napping.

"Oh, shit," one of them had said. "She's homeless. Let's go sit over there," and they'd ambled away to a different tree. Juno, who had pretended to be asleep the whole time, had rolled over to watch them. There were three of them: two looked to be in their early thirties, and the third—who was on the outskirts of the friendship but had clearly latched on—was just a baby. *He can't be twenty-one*, Juno thought. He laughed at everything they said but a little too loud and a little too hard. She'd heard them call him Villy, as in "Villy, you dumbass" when he didn't know who Chris Farley was, and "Villy, you punk-ass bitch" when he admitted to listening to Justin Bieber. Juno felt bad for Villy. She'd rolled up her sleeping bag and left it in the crook of the tree, and then she followed them back to the Crouches' house.

She'd wanted to get a better look at what they were doing; it was just regular old nosiness, she told herself. To the workers she looked like nothing more than an old lady taking a walk down one of the more prominent streets facing the park. Old ladies wore sweatshirts and sweatpants in the winter, they waved at babies in restaurants and stopped to tell the parents, "Soak up every moment. It goes too fast." So when she started sitting on the wall watching them work, they'd thought nothing of it. She waved at them some days, and they waved back. She'd asked one of the workers once about the addition, and he'd said they were adding a multiroom structure to the side of the house.

"Wow," Juno had said dumbly. "Isn't that nice. Must be expensive." And he had looked right through her, as most young people did. For weeks she watched as they filled in the framing, then plastered the walls. They'd installed the wide window that would look out at the flowered backyard a few days ago. But then it was almost finished; any day now, the workers would pack up their things for the final time. Juno wanted to have a closer look before that happened, so around lunchtime she went to sit on the little wall across the street, the low brick one. She had a ham and cheese sandwich and an orange soda, and she swung her legs as she ate, kicking the backs of her heels against the wall and watching the last of the men leave for lunch. She noticed with satisfaction that none had stayed behind today as they sometimes did, probably on account of the good weather. She left her trash on the wall and gingerly crossed the street that ran parallel to the house. The addition was being put on the south side of the house, a compact limb jutting from the body. Juno gazed around. There was an old-fashioned lunch pail sitting in the corner, and someone had left a waterlogged John Grisham novel on the windowsill. She looked for more human touches but found none. Then her eyes found the double doors at the back of the room.

The doors were white, they opened inward toward the interior of the house, and where the doorknobs were supposed to be were two holes. Lying on the ground next to the door was the hardware for the doors waiting to be installed—probably after lunch. Juno reached out one sun-spotted, gnarled hand toward the doors and pushed.

The door swung inward, and Juno stepped inside. She was in a den area. To the left of the doors and slightly behind them was a recess with a brick fireplace. It looked to be old, probably part of the original house; a few empty cans of Coke sat on the mantle next to a staple gun. Juno turned away from the fireplace and walked through the den. A large television box sat in the corner unopened; she glanced at it briefly, musing at how careless the workers were to leave the door open. Anyone could just walk in and rob the Crouches blind. The den led to the family room, and then a sunroom facing the back garden.

The house was bright. Juno blinked around the room, taking in the color with wide eyes. How long had it been since she was inside of a home? She looked behind her then, past the den and through the addition. The birds chirped incessantly. No one was coming—not yet. The workers were all safely napping in the park. They wouldn't be back for another thirty minutes.

She could turn back now. Juno very clearly knew that what she was doing was wrong, and yet she took six more steps until she was standing in the middle of their family room. From where she was, she could see a hallway that led to the kitchen, and past that the front door. *No one notices when you're around anyway*, she thought—so she walked through it.

She wandered the Crouches' home, almost floating through rooms.

Juno hadn't meant to linger. She'd gone through the downstairs quickly, stopping briefly to look in the pantry when curiosity got the best of her. A house of fiber, a family of champion shitters. No plastic water bottles, no refined sugar, no fun whatsoever. Juno helped herself to an apple from a bowl on the counter. She ended up at the stairs. The staircase was a double wide—her mama had called them that if they were fancy, and this one was as fancy as they came. It was the same rich mahogany as the floors, polished to an elegant sheen. Juno laid a hand on the nearest bannister and began to climb the Crouches' double wide, and hot damn if she didn't feel like Scarlett O'Hara.

The stairs bent once like an elbow; there was a massive, gilded mirror hanging on the landing as tall as she was and as gold as it was gaudy. As soon as her reflection appeared, Juno averted her eyes. She knew what she'd see if she looked closely and—no, thank you very much. The stairs came to an end and opened into a wide hallway. On one end of the hallway was a bay window that looked out at the park. Two rocking chairs sat side by side with a small gold table between them, the quaint little setup laid over a Turkish rug. She wondered if they drank their coffee together on those chairs, or maybe had a nightcap. Her eyes went back to the four widely spaced doors, two on either side of the hallway. Between them ran a lush runner—leopard print, Juno noted. Winnie had a pair of leopard-print sneakers she sometimes wore on her walks, and some evenings she carried a leopard umbrella on a wristlet, though Juno had never once seen her open it. Turkish rugs, and neon busts, and leopard-print carpets—*my God*—Juno's own house had been a plate of beiges: brown, taupe, linen, cream, froth, camel.

She moved toward the first door. It was on the right and turned out to be a bedroom, probably the spare. She closed the door without going in and moved on to the next; this one belonged to Nigel and Winnie. The master faced the street, and it boasted a huge window overlooking the park. The bedroom, Juno noted, was less of a color bath than the rest of the house, mostly done up in grays. The bed was made, but the coverlet folded down to reveal deep purple satin sheets with a cream duvet over the top that looked like whipped frosting. In the corner of the room stood a four-foot fountain that bubbled and gurgled like a happy baby. Juno could finish out her days in a room like this; it was magnificent. Their bathroom was attached, and it was so white it made her feel like a lesser person. A bathroom had never made her feel inferior before. What would she have said to one of her patients if a bathroom so spotless and white had made them feel like the most worthless piece of shoe dirt? *You're allowing it. You're giving the bathroom permission to make you feel that way...*

Juno laughed. She didn't even mind that it was loud because everything seemed ludicrous: the bathroom so white a single pubic hair would mar it. Who wanted to live in a world so easily toppled? Even the fact that she was here in this damn house was funny. She laughed as she left their bedroom, closing the door behind her. Next were the two other—but then, voices. In the house.

Eyes wide, she fell to her hands and knees, crawling on the floor to remain out of sight. She heard the stomping of work boots on the floor downstairs. Someone called out, "Grab the rest of the shit, too..." and then more stomping. *Do or die*, Juno thought. She was going to have to make a run for it. And even if they did see her running out the front door, what were they going to say to the homeowners—that they were irresponsible and had left the door open, allowing a homeless woman to wander inside? No, she was fairly certain they'd keep their traps shut on the matter. As she charged down the stairs, she still had the apple clutched in her hand. She stuck it in a pocket as she reached the landing, rounding the corner and trotting down the remaining stairs. But whichever worker had been in the house, he'd obviously hightailed it back outside with the "shit" because the downstairs was blessedly empty.

Juno dashed for the front door. Aches and pains forgotten, she moved like twenty years had just fallen off her limbs. She'd moved like this once before, when she'd stolen a block of cheese from the corner store; the cashier had spotted her sliding it into the pocket of her hoodie. The front door faced the park, so if she walked out casually enough, maybe no one would notice her.

She was five steps away; she could see the stained-glass windows that flanked the door when the handle started rattling. Juno skidded to a stop, balancing on her heels, quite certain she was having a heart attack. There was movement on the other side of the stained glass. Was it normal for a heart to beat side to side, up and down, side to side, up and down? Juno had always been fast on her feet—she'd spent her sixties being homeless, which had certainly improved her survival skills—and in that moment, her instincts told her to move. As a key fitted into the lock, she reached for a different door handle—was it the coat closet or the junk closet? She couldn't remember; without pause she backed herself into what she thought was the junk closet—the one with the golf clubs and the snowboards leaning against the back wall. What else... what else had there been in here when she'd looked? She remembered a crate of tennis balls, old textbooks...nothing they would need, she hoped. She let a jagged breath out through her nose; she was trying very hard to hold still, but her body was shaking.

The front door opened; Juno held her breath. She held still, everything so still. There was suddenly a whoosh of noise as traffic and other outside sounds filtered into the Crouch house, into the closet where Juno was hiding. She thought she could feel a breeze on her ankles from under the door, but then it was gone as the door slammed closed. The sound of footsteps moving away from the closet and Juno. Light footsteps, she noted—Winnie. Had she come home to check the progress the men were making? Clearly she'd surprised them, too, as they'd been scrambling to collect whatever they'd left in the house.

She strained to hear. If Winnie was in the kitchen looking out at the work, then Juno could slip out of the closet and make the three steps to the front door. *And what if someone does see you, one of the workers, or a cop—can you outrun them?* Juno flexed one of her feet and felt pain roll up to her hip. Movement equaled pain, and while some days were better than others, it seemed that the exertion of reaching the closet would now prevent her from being able to run from it. She reached one hand behind her to the wall and leaned her weight there as she tried to catch her breath. Goddamn if this wasn't the most foolish, ass-hearted plan. She hadn't been thinking straight, a lapse in judgment. Juno felt like she couldn't breathe. *But you can*, she told herself. She said it in the same authoritative voice she used on her patients. She placed a hand over her heart and counted the beats, counted her breathing. Her vision swayed in and out of focus. Juno focused on the hand that wasn't on her heart, the one that was still braced against the back of the closet wall. *Feel it*, she told herself, *it's rough and warm. Count your breathing.*

When it was over and the worst had passed, she hugged her arms around herself, shaking now from exhaustion and cold. She was clear of mind and furious at herself, but, though she was thirsty and light-headed, she could do nothing but wait. Winnie had the front door open, and for a moment Juno thought she would leave, but then the sound of more voices joined her, children's voices.

"Sorry about all the construction." This was Winnie's voice, calling this to someone outside the door. Juno flinched as feet pounded into the house and up the stairs. Another voice—female—said something to Winnie from a distance, and Winnie laughed. Juno couldn't see it, but she could picture it: a parent idling on the curb in their car. Parking was impossible on the slanted streets of the city.

"Yeah, if you text me, I can send him out tomorrow, so you don't have to try to park." There was a response Juno couldn't hear, and then the door slammed shut. Winnie's heels began to clack away, and Juno tensed her body, ready to sprint if she got the chance. Two minutes later the doorbell rang again, and this time the voice was right outside the door.

"Roman, take off your filthy sneakers! Don't! No, leave that with me..." And then, after a swift goodbye, more clat-

104

tering of feet on the stairs above Juno's head. The voice came back, this time without the parental lilt; this was the voice of a woman who'd seen too little time for herself. "God, you're a saint for having them over. What time tomorrow...?"

Winnie laughed stiffly. "Ten. I'll feed them breakfast."

"Perfect," the voice said. "See you then."

It was a sleepover. As Juno realized this, she slid quietly to the floor. Her pelvis was throbbing—*her pelvis!* Oh, the places you'll throb! They never read *that* story to her as a child.

To her left were the golf clubs in their big leather bag. Juno could smell the leather. She was thirsty. Leaning her head sideways against the inside of the doorframe, she closed her eyes.

She didn't know what time it was when she woke up. It was dark then, and it was dark now. Juno pulled her shoulders away from the wall, tilting her head back in an attempt at a stretch. She could hear the noises of boys in the living room. They were playing video games, and every few seconds there would be a burst of gunfire followed by cheering and donkey-like guffaws. *You should just stand up, walk out like it's nothing,* she told herself. *You'd probably get away with it.*

But the truth was she couldn't stand up, not without help. She should have known; she'd felt the shift in her body, her mind loosening and her joints tightening. Her disease was predictable, and she always knew when a bad spell was coming. You knew. You just didn't want to acknowledge it. The pain was stiff and sharp. She slid her butt down lower to ease the ache that had spread from her pelvis to her hips and slid down onto her knees.

Juno's mind was clear partly because of the pain; it hadn't gotten overbearing yet. But, it would, oh it would. She was so thirsty; had she ever been as thirsty as this in her life? She didn't think so. She found herself fantasizing about the Crouches' medicine cabinet. She hadn't opened it, but she imagined there was at least a bottle of Tylenol. She needed a pill, something that would knock the grinding from her joints. She shifted again, sweat breaking out on her face. They would sleep eventually, and that's when she'd sneak out.

The closet was roughly five feet by seven feet and carpeted. It was cream-colored and newly installed—she could see the flecks of rug the contractors had left behind when they cut it to size. She picked up a curl of carpet and rolled it between her fingers. She shimmied even lower until she was lying on her side, her knees curled up to her chest. The golf bag was to her back now, and Juno could see underneath the closet door to the faint light of the entryway. She could see the boys' sneakers lined up as well as a pair of muddy cleats and flats that she presumed belonged to Winnie. She thought to check the pockets of the golf bag—maybe Nigel kept a bottle of Advil in there—but it hurt less to lie still; even the tiniest movement jarred the pain. She was still for so long that she fell asleep again.

The next time Juno woke she knew where she was right away. The smell of the carpet, fresh carpet—she still had the thread in her hand, the little curl. The light in the entryway was off, the closet filled with deep darkness. She moved her leg first, testing the stiffness. It was bad, but not as bad as it could be. She rolled onto her belly, huffing with the effort, and then slowly rose to her knees, keeping her head lowered in case she got light-headed. You learned tricks like that when you couldn't afford the medication. Tricks to survive, tricks to make things easier, but never tricks to make the pain go away—that, only the pills could do.

She could stand. She took a minute to regain her balance and reached for the doorknob. The door was a well-oiled thing and didn't make a sound as she opened it. Her heart would wake everyone up; Juno could hear it ringing like a bell in her ears. She stepped into the foyer, keeping her eyes on the door to the living room. If someone came through, she'd be able to see them first, but there would be nowhere to hide. *Relax*, she told herself, *the boys are sleeping, Winnie and Nigel are sleeping.* But she had no concept of time; she could have been in that closet for two days for all she knew. She'd passed out for large chunks of time before, often not in the most desirable of places.

She took steps toward the front door, the wood floors creaking under her feet as she went. And there it was. She hadn't noticed it, and why would she have? None of this was supposed to have happened. There above the light switch was a little keypad. Juno took a step toward it; maybe they didn't put it on tonight on account of the boys being in the house. But there above the number pad was a red light, and the words below it read: ARMED.

Her eyes moved to the door. If she bolted, she could probably get across the street to the park before anyone saw her—couldn't she? She had to try; Juno walked decidedly for the door. She had to grind her teeth to keep from crying out. The pain wasn't humming anymore, it was death-metal screaming. Juno had to relieve herself. She'd seen a bathroom, just around the way. She'd be quiet; boys slept *hard*. It was that or—she didn't want to think about it.

Creeping along the wall, she passed the kitchen, moving away from the family room. Under the recess of the stairs was a small half bath. She didn't turn the light on, and she only closed the door enough to shield her from being seen first.

The splash was loud. She tried to get everything done as quickly as possible, and then she was hoisting her pants up. Before she left, she opened the tap and bent her head to drink straight from the stream of water. She slipped noiselessly from the bathroom, once again passing the kitchen, but instead of turning toward the door she walked straight to the family room, her left shoulder brushing lightly along the wall.

Before she reached the family room, she spotted the blue glow of the TV. She listened for voices, even a snore, but there were no sounds—just the bouncing light of the TV on mute. She took a breath and looked around the wall. Two lumps lay under a mound of blankets on the floor and a third lay on the couch—that one was Sam. Juno could see the sandy hair in the TV's glow. She didn't move a muscle, but her eyes roved to the other side of the room. A table was set up, a light blue tablecloth spread over it. A sign that said *Happy Birthday Samuel* hung on the wall over the table in metallic blue letters. Juno could see the remains of a birthday cake—the side that Winnie had cut neatly into, and the side the boys had torn chunks out of when they went back for more. She was hungry; when had she eaten last? The sandwich outside on the wall; that had been yesterday, and she'd eaten that apple. She looked at the three mounds again, in a sugar and social exhaustion coma, and stepped lightly to the table.

Juno ate cake with her hands, great big chunks of it. It hit her stomach like a grenade. The frosting was blue and green like the Seahawks—no, Sam was a soccer kid—the Sounders.

There was a bowl of chips next to the cake (Juno didn't dare eat those; they would crunch too loudly) and a tray of sandwiches sliced into little triangles. She took a plate, piled as many on as she could, and carried them back to the closet to wait.

No one opened the closet the next morning; she was so sure that Nigel Crouch would come to retrieve his golf clubs or Sam would get the itch to play one of the board games stacked on the shelves above her head. But no one came. The boys noisily ate breakfast, and they were picked up promptly at ten o' clock by mothers who didn't push their luck. Juno lay hidden behind the ski suits and winter coats as each of the boys said goodbye, her head resting on one of those airplane pillows. If someone were to open the door to her little hideout and really look, they'd spot her easily, but no one was looking. Her pain wasn't any better, but her comfort was. She was ashamed to admit that lying on the freshly carpeted floor of the Crouches' closet was the most comfortable place she'd slept in over a year.

After all of Sam's little friends were gone, the family collected their shoes from the foyer.

"Will Grandma wait 'til the end of the night to give me my present or will she just let me open it right away?"

Juno didn't get to hear the answer; the Crouches were out the door and heading to what Juno presumed was a family celebration for Sam. Before the door slammed behind them and the key turned in the lock, she heard Nigel punching the code into the alarm box.

Sure enough, when Juno opened the closet door five minutes later, the little screen read ARMED. The red light glowed above the word like an all-seeing red eye, mocking her. She shouted every curse word she could think of, shaking her fist at it. Had she really thought she was going to be able to just walk out of here? And then her arm fell uselessly at her side and hung there. Where did she have to be? *Nowhere, Juno, you dumbbitch.* She'd graduated from calling herself an idiot to a dumbbitch.

Things were going downhill fast. She wondered if the house was armed with motion sensors. Well, she'd soon find out. She took two steps forward, two steps sideways…then she shimmied to the kitchen door and back. Nothing happened. Juno laughed. She went straight to the bathroom, but this time she climbed the stairs to Winnie and Nigel's, lowering herself over their toilet. And as she sat with her head resting on her fist, she looked around at lush towels and bottles that clearly hadn't been bought at the drugstore.

Why not? Juno thought, flushing. There had been so many "why nots" lately; maybe the fact that she hadn't been caught made her take such a big risk. First things first. She swung open the door to the medicine cabinet and her eyes scanned the bottles. When she found what she was looking for, she popped the lid and poured six of the pills into her palm. She replaced the bottle and popped two of the pills between her lips, pressing them to the roof of her mouth with her tongue.

Blessed relief. They hadn't even melted into her yet, but it was comforting just to know she'd taken them. She had the vague sense that she was floating as the sour powder of the pills coated the inside of her mouth. Juno worked harder, warming it up with her spit and her tongue. Who had taught her to do this? Bless them, she thought swallowing the glue. It was bitter, but it would get into her system faster this way. Whomever had taught her the trick was temporarily forgotten as she stepped out of her clothes and into the bath.

She could avoid the mirror all she wanted, but there were her feet—filthy, the nails jagged and yellow—resting on the spotless floor of the tub. She wriggled her toes and reached for the faucet. When was the last time she'd had a bath? Sometimes she got into the shelter early enough to use their shower, and sometimes she just cleaned herself over the sink in any random, unoccupied bathroom she could find. But a real bath? They'd had a tub in the Albuquerque house, the one on which the bank had foreclosed...when? Five years ago? It wasn't the time or the place to summon the desert into her current state of bliss. She dismissed the thought because she could, because that was one thing she was great at in her old lady days—forgetting.

The water rushed around her, and Juno sank into it. A

noise came somewhere from the back of her throat; she didn't know if it was from pain or pleasure, but she allowed herself to lie back until her ears were submerged and her hair wafted around her face. There were bottles lined up along the lip of the tub; she selected one at random and poured it into her hair. The smells were clean and fresh, reminding Juno of her childhood, when her grandparents had owned a laundromat. She scrubbed herself, using Winnie's nail brush to clean every speck of grime from her hands.

When Juno finally climbed out of the bath and the water drained away, there was a rim of grime where the water had leveled. She found a sponge and powdered Clorox and scrubbed at the filth her body had left behind. When it was spotless, she found a towel at the bottom of the hamper and dried the bathtub before shoving the towel down to the bottom again.

Now for the problem of clothes. Her own lay in a pile at her feet in different shades of filthy. Juno was still naked, and her less-filthy clothes were in her pack, shoved underneath a bush in the park. She carried her clothes downstairs, walking to the closet opposite the one she'd found herself hiding in, and opened the door. There was a garbage bag tied and sitting at the ready, a pink Post-it stuck on the front with the words DONATIONS scrawled in Sharpie. Juno quickly worked at the knot, and then the bag was open. She lifted things out quickly: a sweatshirt that had *Baywatch* printed on the front, a pair of women's yoga pants, and there were shoes, New Balance, nicer than anything she'd owned in years. She even fished out a pair of Thanksgiving-themed socks before shoving her own filthy clothes to the bottom of the bag and reknotting the red drawstring. The Post-it note repositioned, Juno closed the door firmly and began to dress.

The clock above the back door ticked its slow circle; it had been two hours since the Crouches had left. Juno wanted to be back in the closet long before they got home. Long after they could smell her moving through the rooms of their house. She'd considered looking for a safer place, but none provided the quick exit she would need. In her new clothes, Juno walked to the kitchen feeling both 100 percent better and 100 percent worse. Her shame was magnified by her hunger. In the pantry was a loaf of bread and peanut butter. Juno made herself two sandwiches, cleaning as she went. She ate one as she used the facilities for the last time and tucked the other into a paper towel in her pocket. Making one last trip to the pantry, she found some boxes of Lärabars and took one of each flavor, a can of peel-top SpaghettiOs, a can of green beans, and a jug of apple juice she hoped they wouldn't miss. Oh, what did she care? She was already squatting in their junk closet. She carried it all back to the space behind the coats and snowsuits, stacking everything in the corner.

Juno made one last run-through of the house, keeping her eyes on the street whenever she was in view of a window. They'd be back any minute, she just knew it. Call it a sixth sense. Animals had it, too—they knew when a predator was near. And that's all people were, really, wasn't it? Animals dressed up. She found a small puddle of water on the bathroom floor that she'd missed before, soaking it up with a wad of toilet paper. She dropped it in the toilet and flushed. Good as new. In the kitchen she dried the sink with a piece of paper towel and replaced the knife she'd used for the peanut butter in the drawer. No crumbs, no errant wrappers, no wiry gray hairs. Everything was as it should be.

12

JUNO

Ten minutes after Juno rested her head on her airplane pillow and closed her eyes, the front door opened and the Crouches returned. They walked into the house laughing, wrapping paper and gifts bags crackling in their arms. She was clean and comfortable, her belly was full, and most importantly, she was warm.

She slept.

It carried on like that for the weekend. She knew her best shot at leaving the house was on Monday when the Crouches went back to their weekday schedules. So she rested, listening to the voices of the family she had been watching for months while lying beneath the hems of their abandoned winter gear and Halloween costumes. It was comforting to lie on the new carpet, her back pressed against the wall, which was always warm. To herself, she'd started referring to the closet as Hems Corner. It was a safe space, comfortable and warm and familiar.

She turned from her side to her back to her other side, listening to Sam ask his mother if she could make bacon and eggs for breakfast, and then to Nigel rapping along with Eminem as he washed the dishes from the bacon and egg breakfast. She heard Winnie on the phone with someone from work as she opened the door for a delivery. "If we have to, we can replace her with Joanne from—yes I said replace—"

Her voice was indignant. There were two sides to Winnie, indignant and vulnerable.

Juno had eaten her second sandwich for dinner on Saturday night along with a few large swigs of apple juice straight from the jug. And then at night, while the Crouches slept off their Saturday, Juno snuck out during the early morning hours to use the bathroom. She wasn't as stiff as she thought she'd be and was in an exceptionally good mood. Safety and a good night's sleep and a family to nose around in. She'd become a true geriatric. Kregger would have howled.

On Sunday morning she ate a cherry pie Lärabar for breakfast and drank more apple juice. She figured it was early since the Crouches had yet to come downstairs. In the two days she'd slept in their closet, she'd come to decipher the way each of their footsteps sounded on the hardwood. She strained to hear even the muffled sound of footsteps, but the house seemed fully asleep—aside from Juno, the closet mouse, that was.

Suddenly, she felt like taking a risk. She rolled out from her hiding spot and got to her feet. The ceiling of her closet was surprisingly high. She stretched her arms above her head and did the yoga poses of her youth to try to ease out some of her stiffness. She'd been taking the Crouches' Advil—two pills every four hours—and it had staved off the worst of the pain through the day. She stretched out her neck, rolling it back as she breathed deeply and opened her eyes to the ceiling. But then she heard someone stirring upstairs, the sound of running water. She stretched once more—Tadasana, mountain pose—before crawling back to Hems Corner.

Juno was anxious. She rubbed a spot behind her ear, staring into the darkness. Even in the closet she could hear the sound of the rain outside. What would happen if they caught her? *You know what would happen*, she thought. *They'll haul you back to your favorite place in the whole world.* Juno didn't want to think about that. She didn't want to die in prison, either. And the truth of the matter was that she *was* dying. She could feel the rot; her kidneys like two old fists that were losing their grasp.

The spot behind her ear was stinging, but her fingers kept their back-and-forth rhythm. *Be present, be grateful.* She lifted her old mantras from her other life and tried them on for size. *Where would I normally be?* A series of images flashed through her mind, and she flinched from them. The more accurate question was probably where had she not slept? For a while Juno had had a blue tent. Wherever she pitched it, the police would eventually tell her to move in their deadpan way that made her feel less...and less...and less. The humiliation brought by those hard-faced men in uniforms, their faces stoic but their impatience loud. *Go, you can't be here. Leave, you have to move. You can't squat here.* She had nowhere to go and still she was commanded to leave.

It became easier to sleep in the day. Juno took naps on benches, in the grass, sometimes in a coffee shop where they thought she was just a shabby old lady dozing with her morning joe.

You'd be in the park, she told herself, turning toward the wall. The park itself was good, peaceful, but having to live there was not. She pulled the hood of her sweatshirt up over her head and, tucking her palms between her knees, began to shiver. She had a master's degree in psychology, she knew about Pavlov's dogs, and she knew that the sound of the rain made her cold and afraid because it had become an enemy—something that threatened her safety and comfort. And wasn't safety a basic human need? Of course it was. As was shelter. *And you are safe.* Her mouth formed the words, though she didn't dare say them aloud. *You're safe...you're safe...you're safe...*

When she woke there was music playing. Juno rolled onto her back, carefully tenting her knees. If she stayed still for too long her hands and feet would swell up like puffer fish. She breathed deeply, trying to make out the melody. She smiled as she caught a few of the lyrics. Dale had liked that song. Dale, her youngest, sweetest son. She mouthed his name, *Dale... Dale... Dale...*and felt better for doing it. Dale with his wiry brown curls; he had a bend in his nose, and long bony fingers that could play the piano more nimbly than hers. She missed him so deeply that the missing had become an organ. A throbbing, volatile organ. She curled into herself, into the pain. She deserved to feel it, and so when it came, she allowed it in, like a woman in labor.

Failure as a mother should hurt. It should feel flat and dull and never-ending. Juno would take all the pain in the world, carry every single bit of it, for one chance to see Dale again and tell him how sorry she was.

The song changed, and now she could hear the individual voices of the family singing along—Winnie off-key and Sam with his unbroken voice that would soon start cracking. Nigel, who was a good singer, sang around them, harmonizing with their squeaks and squawks in good humor.

She ate the canned beans for lunch, listening along with the Crouches' movie: *Sense and Sensibility* (Winnie had won at rock paper scissors). That evening, Nigel opened the door for the pizza they'd ordered, and Juno heard the rain really coming down.

"Is that thunder?" Nigel's voice was incredulous. She could picture him peering over the pizza guy's shoulder toward the flashing in the sky.

"Yeah, there's a lightning storm. Pretty cool."

Pizza girl, Juno corrected herself. When she'd first come to Seattle it had surprised her that thunder did not often accompany the watery days. In her old life, she would have told anyone that she liked the sound of the clouds colliding, but in this life, it scared the shit out of her.

An awful memory bloomed as she lay on the closet floor. The first time she'd not had the money to pay for her dirty little room at the Motel Palm she'd slept in her car, pushing the seats down and laying an old comforter across the trunk space. The lightning had woken her from an alcohol-induced sleep. And five seconds after she opened her eyes, Juno had thought a semi was rolling over her car. Thunder bellowed from nearby, and then the rain had come in fat, fast drops. Bullet rain being shot from some heavenly AK47.

Realizing that she wasn't in immediate danger had done little to soothe the fear and despair that had woken up with her. She wasn't going to die right now, but her ticket had been expedited with her disease. It was up in the air how— if hunger or cold or being hit by lightning could outrace the lupus, but she was fine with that. It was all talk; she was a small woman without options, without friends. Regardless, it had rained for three days while Juno lay huddled in her gasless Prius, stranded in a Walmart parking lot. She'd run in for food and to use the restroom, but had otherwise remained sedentary, frightened, and in shock.

What now? What now? That thought marched through her

head, demanding to be heard. She didn't know what happened now. She'd given answers to people during her career, and yet here she was as answerless and lost as any of them had been.

She smelled the pizza, wanted it. They were in the kitchen now, opening cans of soda. They were happy, and there had been a time when Juno's family had been happy, as well. Humans had a way of uprooting happiness. They found flaws in it, picked at it until the whole system unraveled. Juno had been bored with her life once upon a time. Instead of being professionally distant, she'd festooned her life with the stories of her patients. She'd become too involved; she knew that now. An idle mind leads to mischief, her mother had said. And she'd paid, oh had she paid. She'd lost everything.

Pizza was over; the Crouches were heading upstairs. Juno was glad to be rid of them; she'd be even more glad tomorrow when she could leave. She peed into the empty apple juice jug, took three of the Crouches' Advil, and drifted off to sleep.

13

JUNO

Monday came; Sam was the first to leave, slipping out the door before the sun had fully woken up. Juno could smell the nutty, sweet aroma of the waffle he carried out the door, and she registered hunger for the first time in days. The desire to eat would pass, though the need for it would not. She pulled a handful of oyster crackers from her pocket, placing one on her tongue with extreme concentration. She couldn't afford to eat something and then get sick in Hems Corner. Thirty minutes later Nigel and Winnie left together, stopping at the back door to check that the first of the workers had arrived. Juno listened to them have a brief conversation, jiggling her hips in her desperation to pee.

"I think they're coming in the house to use the bathroom,"

Winnie said. "I specifically told them they'd have to use a public toilet or get one of those construction toilets. We can't just have random men in here."

"A porta potty?" Nigel offered.

"They shouldn't be coming in here," she said firmly. "I don't like it."

"You don't know that they did. You're making assumptions."

At this she got huffy. Juno heard the clipping of her heels as she moved from the kitchen to the front hall where their coats hung in the closet opposite Juno.

"I hate it when you do that. Act like I'm blowing things out of proportion."

Her voice was needling. Juno needed to pee. She needed to pee, she needed to pee, she needed to pee... She put another cracker on her tongue and pressed it to the roof of her mouth.

Nigel was quiet as he shrugged into his coat. "I'm sorry," he said. "I'll talk to the foreman again. See where they are with the portable."

"Thank you," Winnie said stiffly. The cracker crumbled and dissolved against Juno's tongue.

She heard the sound of a kiss—a quick, perfunctory one— and then the front door opened. No alarm. She waited as long as she could stand it, though probably not long enough, and then crawled toward the closet door. She was reaching for the knob when the front door abruptly swung open again. Shoes pounding on the hardwood: Nigel's. What if he was looking for something in here? She backed slowly into her corner, lowering herself beneath the coats. For the first time in days, Juno was scared. She'd been lured into sleepy comfort and had forgotten the danger she was in. Danger of being discovered, of being cast out like a rat. How long had she lived outside, scouring around for change to buy dollar bags of chips, feeling so cold she was sure she was dying?

Footfalls echoed above her head; they were picking up speed and becoming more urgent. She held her breath, heart throbbing like she was having a heart attack or running a marathon. Juno pressed the hem of a Halloween costume to her face, a full-body foam hot dog. She held a portion of the bun over her eyes, trying to block out what she was 100 percent certain was going to happen. Nigel would come in looking for whatever he was looking for, his shoe would nudge some part of her body—a hip, or a thigh—and then he'd bend down to see what was shoved beneath the snowsuits and the hot dog Halloween costume.

She developed a crude plan to play dead: then, when he'd go to call for help, she'd hightail it out of there as fast as her old ass would carry her. Which probably wasn't very fast. Her finger reached for the spot behind her ear. The footsteps returned to the first floor, heading straight for Juno. The doorknob rattled, and that's when her bladder made one final squeeze before it lost its will. She felt the warmth spread beneath her, not unpleasantly, but she knew it would be soon. God, she was as old as she was pathetic. She'd never hated herself more than she did in that moment; not in prison, and not on the street. This was so much worse because she'd already come through those things and nothing was better; there was no reward if you behaved; there was no reward if you got clean. Society would continue to see you the same way they always had…and then, eventually, you would, too. The rattling had stopped, she realized, and the front door slammed once again. Nigel had most likely brushed against the knob on his way out.

She waited longer this time before coming out. It was just as awful as she anticipated; she could smell the sour tang of urine—urine filtered through failing kidneys. She crawled most of the way, not wanting to feel her wet clothes clinging to parts of her skin. When she reached the wood floor of the entryway, she did something bold, even for her—she stripped off her clothes until she was standing naked two feet from the front door. If someone were to open it, they'd get a great big surprise.

Juno opened the other closet, the one she knew less about, and hauled out the bag of donation clothes. She found a pajama top that had a series of *zzzz*'s on the front of it, along with a sizable red stain she presumed was wine, and she slipped that over her head. Down lower, toward the bottom of the bag and underneath the filthy clothes Juno had arrived in, she found a pair of men's jeans and an old T-shirt. She didn't put those on; she tucked them underneath her arm and put everything back the way she found it.

Carrying her wet clothes to the laundry room, she shoved them into the washer, tossed a fancy little square of liquid soap into the machine, and hit start. Too scared to risk a shower, she quickly washed herself using the hand soap and a hand towel. As she dripped onto the rug, she used the towel to dry the mess she'd made and then carried it to the washing machine, where she opened the lid and dumped it in with her clothes.

The next part was harder. Grabbing a cleaning bucket from the shelf in the little laundry room, she filled it with hot water from the sink, then poured a little liquid detergent into it until there was a good amount of foam. As she carried the bucket back to the closet, she slipped into the pantry to get a roll of paper towel.

The men were using the saw; she watched them working in the mist outside and actually felt sorry for them. Sorry that they were out there in the cold having to work. She cackled at the absurdity of the thought, then pressed a fist to her lips. She hadn't meant to laugh so raucously. As she skirted out of the kitchen with the paper towel, glancing back once more, one of the men looked up from where he stood, briefly making eye contact with Juno. She felt a rush of blood to her head as she ducked out of view. Had he seen her? He was probably just looking at his own reflection in the window, she told herself. It didn't matter, she knew now she had to just clean her mess and be gone from this house. She had her pack to see to—who knew how long it would be before someone else stumbled across it? Juno turned the light on in the closet and closed the door. She could leave it; she knew that. The Crouches would start smelling something foul in a few days. She could picture Winnie on her hands and knees, sniffing out the source of the stench. No, Juno had stayed in their home, and she was not a houseguest who left her dishes unwashed. She began the long process of soaking up the urine with wads of the paper towel.

It was when she was scrubbing the carpet with the T-shirt that she found the string of loose carpet—a run. Juno tried to break the piece off. Yanking on the string, she pulled up an edge of the carpet instead. She hissed a "dammit" under her breath. Today was the kind of day Kregger used to call a dumpshit. Instead of flattening the corner, Juno tugged on it. With some tugging, the carpet lifted away in a perfect rectangle. She turned it over to see a stiff board underneath, hidden by the carpet.

As Juno peered down at the wooden trapdoor, she could smell the laundry detergent, clean and floral. She could also smell something else, something closed and dank coming through the trapdoor. It wasn't made of the hardwood that ran through the rest of the house; it was a thick slab of nicked oak that looked like it had been there for as long as the house had.

There were two metal latches holding it in place, old and corroded. She had to work them open, jiggling the latches before they would release. Standing up, she used the strength in her legs to yank it open. She felt the grinding in her joints and ignored it: something else had her attention now. A gust of old air hit her in the face, and she screwed up her nose against it. The closet's lone light bulb hung above the trapdoor, and Juno could see dirt floor and rough pilings. She lay on her belly and peered into the hole. The dark swallowed up most of the space, allowing her to see only a portion of it, but it was clear that this was the house's crawl space. She didn't hesitate—sitting on the edge, she lowered her legs over the side.

Juno was on her hands and knees in dirt. Chunks of concrete rolled under her palms, making her flinch as she crawled. A grown man would have trouble fitting through parts of the crawl space, especially where the ground rose in lazy waves. The ceiling of the crawl space was made of wood and dusty with mold. It was like a cave, and it was almost cozy. Ten-year-old Juno would have been delighted at this discovery. The thought was so ludicrous she cackled aloud. It was the ugliest sound she'd ever heard, even uglier than the time an inmate had cut the tip of Rhionette Wicke's pinkie with a sharpened rock, and she'd screamed like a hyena. Aside from the musty smell, which was probably coming from a few dead rodents, this was a better, safer space than any she'd slept in.

Juno had run out of Advil and the ache was settling in, an ache made worse by the cold. She knew her kidneys were failing, and she also knew homeless women didn't get new kidneys. She was dying, and she didn't mind one bit. She had nothing left and that was that; she wasn't sad, she wasn't grieving anymore, she was waiting. And she would like to wait somewhere warmer and safer. Last year at this time, a bunch of punk teenagers had pushed her around, and she'd hit her head on the curb trying to get away from them. An ambulance had taken her to the hospital during which the ER doctor had spotted the butterfly wings on her face and told her gently that she likely had lupus. Juno had known her diagnosis for years, but she'd never told anyone, not even her sons. She denied it to the doctor, and he'd known she was lying, but that was her business. The last thing she wanted was some wet-behind-the-ears do-gooder trying to help her live a less homeless life. Juno wanted to die; she just wanted to do it on her terms, that was all. And perhaps this crawl space would be the perfect place.

She crawled back up to the closet and finished cleaning the carpet. The men left for lunch, and Juno hastened to empty the apple juice jug in the guest toilet. She was already in planning mode as she flushed the weekend away. She felt like a wisp today, lithe and not quite there. She was rested, though, by God was she rested. She threw the wet clothes into the dryer and headed for the pantry. She had about ten minutes before the first of the Crouches would start showing up.

The pantry door was already propped open and Juno slipped inside, her eyes moving across the shelves. She took one of Winnie's reusable grocery bags, a deep canvas tote with the words *Fat Mousie* on the front, and, shaking it open, she began to put things inside. She looked for multiples, boxes of individually bagged snacks, and took inventory as she went: one sleeve of Ritz crackers, one sleeve of garlic Triscuits, a can of corn, a can of creamed corn, a two-liter jug of water, two bags of fruit snacks, a pouch of Tasty Bites. She eyed a can of chili, but it lacked the pull tab that she would need in place of a can opener.

She knew she was running out of time. She stepped over to the fridge, her breathing loud to her own ears. Yogurt, eggs, butter things Juno missed. Her stomach grumbled. She searched the vegetable bin and found two wrinkled apples and a green pepper long forgotten, stuffing those into the bag, too, as she reached for the freezer door. The freezer was stocked to overflowing. Juno found a bag of frozen peas and tossed that in. She stopped by the silverware drawer and took a butter knife to unscrew the latches on the trapdoor more easily. That would have to do for now. Her heart was pelting in rabbit time against her ribs. Was she really doing this? She was. Fear and adrenaline were racing at a breakneck pace; she'd spent her first year in prison with the same jacked-up awareness. *And your first year on the street*, she reminded herself. But nerves eventually went away as you adapted to a new norm.

Back in the laundry room, she grabbed her still-damp clothes from the dryer, snatching a single toilet paper roll from the shelf. Her head jerked toward the direction of the back door—men's voices. Before they'd even picked up their tools, Juno was inching through the crawl space with the first of her supplies.

PART THREE

14

WINNIE

Winnie had pins and needles in her limbs; she'd been sitting for too long on the sofa, staring at the blank TV, her legs curled underneath her. When she stood up, her heart felt heavy, like it wanted to be left on the couch. *Heart down,* Winnie thought. Sometimes she felt ashamed of her own thoughts because she knew what Nigel would say about them: "So dramatic!"

Nigel was in his den; that's where he always was nowadays. Lying on his precious Lovesac couch, looking quite happy with himself and his situation. She hobbled over toward the bookshelves, not intending to read a book but to walk out the prickly feeling in her legs and feet. She made it all the way to the computer before the ticklish feeling set in. Winnie hated that feeling. One of her busts was crooked—the orange one. She stared at it until her pins and needles dissipated and then got up to straighten it. She saw the door that led to her husband's prized den. It was a barn door, and it created a large deal of hassle and noise to pull to the side. He'd done that on purpose so he'd always know she was coming. *Always thinking the worst*, said the Nigel voice in her head. He'd been sleeping down there for days, sleeping like a log while Winnie tossed and turned in their marriage bed. Tossed so much that she'd told herself to go downstairs to make herself a mug of Sleepytime tea, but that's not what Winnie wanted now. She was too anxious to eat or drink anything.

Unsure of what to do, she sat in front of the computer. Her elbow nudged the mouse as she leaned down to massage the last of the tingling from her foot, and a photo of the family on their last vacation materialized on the screen. Winnie studied the photo. Looking at it made her feel more depressed than she ever had in her life. They'd had such a lovely time, hadn't they? Things had felt right back then, their family structure firm. She'd been happier for sure; and Winnie subscribed to the "happy wife, happy life" theory. *You've lost yourself*, she thought. That trip had been a year ago; maybe what they needed was another holiday. Maybe she was the one who was dragging everyone else down. She would bring it up to Nigel…tomorrow. She could get up early, make him his favorite breakfast, use the latte machine they never had time for, and butter him up. Samuel, she thought, needed his parents on the same team. Suddenly Winnie felt a steely resolve settle in the bottom of her spine and work its way up. She straightened her back to accommodate her new determination. She could and would fix this; the smile was already on her mouth, the type of smile she'd make while reading a nice card.

She reached for her notepad; she could start making plans

instead of sitting around being useless. Retrieving a pen from the desk drawer, she pulled her notepad toward her. She wouldn't have discovered the words etched on the pad if her fingers hadn't grazed the deep grooves a pen had made in the notepad, a pen struggling to pull ink from its near-empty supply. She lifted the notepad to the dim blue light of the computer and tilted it to make out the words. She could see it had been a list and was about to dismiss it when she realized she could make out a name: Lisa Sharpe. Winnie didn't know anyone named Lisa Sharpe. In fact, she didn't know any Lisas at all. There was a longer name printed below that, but she could only make out the first name, Daisy, and part of the last name: Sawat.

She wondered if maybe Samuel had been using this computer. He had his own, but sometimes...

Out of curiosity, Winnie opened a browser on the computer and went to Facebook. Sam had an account—very restricted, everything approved by her. She found the little box where his friends were and typed the name *Lisa Sharpe* into the search engine. Nada, zilch. Lisa was a name common to Winnie's generation, not Samuel's.

She switched on the overhead light and studied the imprint of handwriting on the page. Had she examined it more carefully straightaway, she would have seen right away that it wasn't Samuel's.

And then, her fingers pressing compulsively into the little grooves the pen had dug into the paper, Winnie was suddenly sure her husband was cheating on her. *Nigel*, she thought. *Could he...?* Winnie spun around in her chair so that it was facing the family room. She was being silly and irrational. Why would she think Nigel was cheating on her just because a woman's name was written on her notepad? There could be a perfectly good explanation.

She Googled Lisa Sharpe instead. Chewing on her lip, she frowned at the screen, wishing the computer could hurry up and do its work because her stomach was a mess. She thought about going upstairs to find her Tums, but then her computer churned out the results, and Winnie no longer remembered her heartburn because her brain was exploding.

Lisa Sharpe. In the photo, she was wearing a red-striped dress, her blond hair up in a ponytail. She held a ragged-looking Barbie doll up to her face for the picture, head tilted toward the doll, smiling sweetly. She had been two years old, taken from her front yard in 2008. The toddler had been in her swing when her mother stepped inside to get her cell phone. When she returned, no less than sixty seconds later (or so she said), Lisa was gone.

Winnie read through the articles, her confusion mounting—but not nearly as high as her fear. Why would Nigel look up this child? This Lisa Sharpe? She could think of only one reason her husband would be interested in a case like this, and that was something she didn't want to think about.

Lisa was never found. Twelve years later, and her mother still held Facebook Live vigils for her every Sunday. Winnie stood abruptly, ripping the sheet of paper from the notepad and crumpling it in her fist. *No, no, no*, she wanted to say, but her tongue was glued to the roof of her mouth, dry and useless. How could he? Or more importantly; *why* was he? And why now?

15

JUNO

Juno spent the next forty-eight hours confined to the crawl space as the Crouches passed around the stomach flu. It wasn't the longest she'd been down there, but she was less prepared this time. With Nigel sleeping in the den downstairs, she hadn't been able to risk sneaking up to replenish her supplies. Her waste bucket was in bad need of emptying, and last she counted, she had just five water bottles leaning against the wall opposite her bed.

The weather dropped to thirty-nine degrees, and all she had left for food was a sleeve of saltines. She'd been careless; her focus—her obsession, she corrected herself—had been finding out the truth about Sam, and in the meantime, she'd forgotten to take care of herself. Again.

Her side was aching, despite the layers she'd put beneath

her sleeping bag. She rolled onto her back, groaning. She tried to change her position every twenty minutes; it helped with the pain. Years ago, Juno had a patient with lupus—Cynnie Gerwyn. And who could forget a name like that? But what Juno remembered most about Cynnie was the butterfly mark on her face and the way her thirty-year-old frame was bent and warbled like a wire hanger. She distinctly remembered feeling sorry for the woman. It would be years before Juno was diagnosed herself.

Cynnie had gone on to have a kidney transplant, and Juno had seen her twice weekly after that as she worked her way through a depression brought on by her disease. Back then, Cynnie had been just a client, a woman who paid Juno to listen to her talk, but she'd thought about her more and more since her own diagnosis, wondering what Cynnie had done with her life since the fresh kidney.

Juno moved her hands from where they were pressed between her knees to keep warm and held them close to her face; they were blue. Not from the cold—not yet, anyway. The swollen, blue hands were a sign of her sickness. She bent them at the knuckles and flinched when her joints popped painfully. Juno didn't have so much as an aspirin down in her cave, not with the entire Crouch family quarantined.

She returned her hands to their place between her knees and wished she were already dead. And she might be by the end of the week: her immune system worked like a bunch of fat old ladies with gout. There was nothing to do but think as she lay underneath the Crouches' house, below the humming bodies of the family who owned it. She wasn't ashamed of what she was doing. When it came to survival, in Juno's opinion, anything was acceptable. She'd watched them, wanted them, and found a home with them.

By the time the Crouches purged the virus and left the Turlin Street house to return to their outside worlds, Juno hadn't eaten anything in three days. She wasn't hungry; she wasn't anything, really—barely existing outside of the pain in her body. She had to talk herself into sitting up, and then slowly she crawled forward, the exertion of leaving her nest enough to leave her gasping for breath. The smell of her body made her gag, and she realized that at some point she'd wet herself, probably in the middle of her pain-hazed sleep. It took her close to an hour to get through the trapdoor where she rested briefly in Hems Corner before hauling herself to her feet.

The house smelled like bleach and flowers. Winnie had done a number with the de-germing. It was terrible, but not as terrible as her own smell, she decided. She very slowly made it to the bathroom to relieve her bladder, and then, stripping off her clothes, Juno walked naked to the washing machine, dumping her things in. She didn't have the energy to go down for the rest, but there was a new donation bag sitting by the door. She took the first thing she found on top, a shapeless T-shirt and butterfly leggings, and pulled them on. She walked to the kitchen, feeling rather gloomy.

A darkness had settled over her thoughts as she lay in her filth. The past always came to visit when she was too still. She headed for the sink where, with no joy, she opened the tap and drank until she was heaving. She didn't bother with eating yet; her stomach was deciding how it felt about so much water at one time. She had to wash, but washing was a want and eating was a need, so supplies had to come first. Juno paused at the door to the pantry, swaying slightly. She was an impulsive bitch, an irrational bitch, but she wasn't the type of bitch to make the same mistake twice. Grabbing without thinking, she took as much food as she could carry, armload by armload, until she was weak from the effort. Dumping it all down the trapdoor into the crawl space, she heard the satisfying thuds of cans and bags and even the log of tofu she'd taken from the fridge. Her clothes in the dryer, she headed upstairs to take a bath.

Juno sat in the warm water until it turned cold, and then she filled it up with hot again. When she felt moderately better, she drained the water and clambered out of the tub. She was drying herself very slowly and very carefully when she heard the front door open. Her mouth opened, and she heard the whoosh of air she sucked in. Juno felt cold all over, then her face grew hot.

Red meat or fish, sparkling water or still, gold or platinum—those used to be her everyday options. Today, it was hiding under the bed or hiding in the closet.

She ran for Winnie and Nigel's bed, a sizable four-poster. She'd planned for this, she was ready. Juno had a viable hiding spot in every room in the house in case something like this ever happened. And it was happening. She could hear fast steps on the stairs. As Juno dove to her stomach, she used her hands and knees to shimmy under the bed, an image of a salamander in her mind. She backed against the far wall and crouched into a ball, as small as she could make herself. She could see the digital clock blinking across the hall from Sam's nightstand: 1:20. Her body remained silent, thanks to the oxy she'd taken from Nigel's bottle. Her mind, however, was flicking around like a bad radio connection.

She knew it was Sam before his Vans came into view, knew by the sound of his footsteps. *Doom, doom, doom* like he carried the weight of his angst in his feet.

But instead of turning into his own room, he abruptly turned into his parents'. Juno saw his Vans up close and personal. Her heart was beating so fast it ached in her chest. How would he react to finding the sweet old lady that he'd chatted with in the park hiding underneath his parents' bed? God, if she had a heart attack under this bed, how long would it be before they found her congealing on their hardwood? He briefly stopped at the foot of the bed, then turned sharply and made his way to the dresser. Her breaths were shallow, but to her own ears it sounded like the beating of very large wings. A drawer opened. What was he looking for?

And then his phone rang, a little chirping noise she'd heard before.

"Yeah, I can't find it."

His voice so loud—so close. She closed her eyes, feeling light-headed.

"My dad has oxy, though..."

No, no, no, Juno thought. She needed that oxy. How many had she stashed away? Sam moved to the bathroom and she heard the medicine cabinet opening, the rattle of those precious, white pills—and then a minute later he was walking back out the door—faster, like he had somewhere to be. The *doom, doom, doom* went back down the stairs, and then she heard him in the kitchen, the clink of glass and the slam of the front door.

Juno was momentarily stunned, too stunned to move. Had she seen that coming? No. Sam was not supposed to be like his parents; she believed very strongly that nature could overpower nurture and vice versa. He was becoming like them, she decided, crawling from her hiding space and stretching her back with a groan.

She looked toward the bathroom. Padding lightly across the floor, she saw the way she'd left things. Close to the tub, just near the medicine cabinet, was a small patch of wet floor. She pursed her lips at this and then moved her eyes slowly to Sam's room. He was a teenage boy, and apparently he'd found the fast social connections a couple of oxy could get you; that didn't mean he knew anything was amiss in his own home. She doubted he'd paused long enough to study the bathroom.

She wondered if he knew anything was amiss with his family—specifically, his own birth. She thought again of his blog: *A wolf knows when it's being raised by bears.* But how much did he really know? She found herself wandering back into Winnie and Nigel's bedroom. Or, as of late, Winnie's bedroom.

She stood over Winnie's nightstand, thinking. Remembering the cryptic, depressing journals she'd read, she found herself reaching a gnarled hand toward the handle. She'd been innocently looking for nail clippers when she'd found those journals; she hadn't even been trying to snoop. But now she had other things on her mind, more sinister things.

And there it was, predictably, in the bottom drawer of her nightstand: a fireproof lockbox. Juno lifted it from the drawer and placed it on her lap. A little key was still attached to the metal hinge of the box, secured by a plastic loop. She had no problem sliding the flimsy key into its equally flimsy lock. If this was the Crouches' way of protecting their documents…

The lock clicked over, and she opened the lid.

Inside were three stacks of documents, two of them wrapped together with rubber bands. Juno picked those up first, unwrapping them with renewed speed. The shadows outside were shifting, the light in the bedroom turning from yellow to orange as the sun dipped into the park. She studied the shadows on the bedroom wall for a moment and then turned back to her task. She was nervous.

Passports: hers and Nigel's. Sam's was not among them. Rewrapping the passports, Juno put them back as she found them and reached for the next, larger stack of documents. It was exactly what she'd been hoping to find—in a plastic sleeve were Winnie's and Nigel's birth certificates, Social Security cards, marriage license, and life insurance policies. Juno took everything out of the sleeve and then put everything back, one by one, just to make sure. There was no birth certificate for Sam, no Social Security card. That was odd. It was possible that Winnie kept it somewhere else, but Juno couldn't imagine why. It was as if he simply didn't have any documents. She knew she was jumping to conclusions, but what she'd been hoping to see was a birth certificate that would settle the matter and quiet the nagging voice in her head. She remembered Sam's words that day in the park, the day he said he didn't feel like he was their kid—"I looked for my birth certificate once. My mom said it was ruined in storage when all the things got covered in mold and they hadn't gotten around to applying for another one."

Juno had seen plenty of women come through her office who were just like Winnie. They were predictable in their order: Winnie wrote Samuel's name in Sharpie on the labels of his clothes, she balanced his meals with the precision of a nutritionist, and his Halloween costumes had been handmade his entire life—there was an entire album of photos to prove it. This was not the type of mother who lost or forgot to apply for her child's birth certificate; quite the contrary. Juno lifted her hand to the smooth patch of flesh behind her ear.

If Sam didn't have medical records, he wouldn't be allowed to attend public school. Right? Right.

Maybe Winnie knew Sam's birth mother and had manipulated her into giving away her baby. To Juno, that would explain Nigel's outburst. She was grasping, and a headache had eased its way into the back of her head and was moving toward her forehead in a crawl.

On to the last item in the box—it was rolled and wrapped with rubber bands like a fat joint. It took Juno a good three minutes to get them off, and it only occurred to her after that she wouldn't be able to replicate the complicated wrapping system. "Is there method to this madness, Winnie?" she asked the room.

It was too late now...two envelopes unfolded in her hands, the paper crackling from age. It was like one of those Russian nesting dolls, she thought; things inside of things. That told her a little bit more about Winnie. She set the rubber bands aside and stared. Instead of licking the strip, Winnie had tucked the flap inside and then rolled the envelope up, binding it over and over. Juno had the feeling that she'd open it and there'd be nothing in the interior. *Wouldn't that be hilarious*, she thought. But it wouldn't be. Juno was already on edge, digging around where she shouldn't be. And what did she care, anyway? Why was she digging around—these people were not her problem. Juno had come here to retire, to die. She told herself it was curiosity, crumbs left behind from her former trade, as she tented the opening of the envelope. It was empty aside from another rolled piece of paper, this one thin enough that at first Juno thought it was a hand-rolled cigarette. She had to use her fingernails to unroll it, being careful not to rip the paper. She spread it out on her knee and saw that there were two printouts, the writing so faded and grainy she could barely make out what they said without glasses. They looked to Juno like police reports. She'd seen a few in her line of work. The words were a series of blurred black lines. Sometimes she used Nigel's reading glasses, which he kept in the side table next to his bed. Juno stood, padding lightly over to Nigel's nightstand, and slid the drawer open. They were there next to a bottle half-full of cough syrup. She slipped the glasses on and reached for the syrup, screwing off the lid even as she eyed the abandoned papers where they lay on Winnie's coverlet. She eyed them long and hard as she took a generous swig, the tomato red of the syrup coating the inside of her mouth like cool cherry blood. Licking her lips, she put the bottle back in the drawer and moved to Winnie's side of the bed. The words on the papers were easier to see now. Juno held one of them in front of her face. Her tongue made a strange clicking sound as she read, the words becoming increasingly more disturbing. Juno realized she was clicking her tongue at Winnie. Finally, folding the papers neatly, she tucked them into her pocket. She stared once more into the envelope.

There, at the bottom corner was something... *Something,* Juno thought—but probably nothing. She turned the envelope, shook it a little, and into her hand floated the strangest thing.

A tiny piece of paper towel...no—cloth. It was old and scrunched up. It looked to Juno like there was embossing on it, like on a hankie her grandfather had kept in his breast pocket. She lifted it closer to her face, rolling it a little between her fingers. The yellow color, she realized, was blood, very faded old blood.

Juno dropped the scrap in disgust. Why would Winnie keep this tiny rag? And whose blood was it? She lowered herself very slowly to her knees to retrieve the square, bending all the way down to the rug to pluck it up. For a moment Juno wasn't sure if she'd be able to get back up; her back seized at the same time her knees locked like two defunct wheels, Nigel's syrup not yet coating her pain. She pushed through it, stumbling to her feet. Breathing like a winded rhino, she returned the scrap to the envelope. It could be anything, she supposed, depending on how weird Winnie truly was. Juno had once had a patient who collected his fingernail clippings in a mason jar. There was one more envelope, and this one felt heavier. Bracing herself, Juno wrinkled her nose as she tented it, hoping to see something else, but when she looked inside the second, there were not one, but six bloody pieces of cloth.

She'd never wanted to be rid of anything quite as badly. What exactly had Winnie's mother been smoking when she was baking the twins? Hands moving quickly, she started to roll the envelopes back into the wad. Her knuckles locked painfully, but for once, she was too preoccupied to notice. Shaking her left hand to loosen some of the stiffness, she lifted her right hand—the one holding the envelopes—up to her face. Juno's old eyes worked hard, probably so hard she'd have a headache later. But there it was: two envelopes and six bloody scraps. After she put the box back, she walked stiffly to the bathroom where she held her hands under scorching water.

Juno knew from a lifetime of training that she had to get inside the head of the person, burrow deep until she knew not only how they worked, but *why* they worked. Once she had that vital piece of information, the circuit board to that person's brain opened up, allowing Juno to press the right buttons. Two envelopes: six bloody little scraps. Were they trophies? No, Winnie considered herself the trophy; she would never keep something dirty and soiled as a souvenir. They were keepsakes, like a lock of hair or a love letter. And judging by the way they were wrapped up, painful ones. And then the thought came, dragging out of Juno, snagging along the way. What if no one knew Sam's mother had even been pregnant? What if Winnie was the only one who knew? Juno had been looking for a stolen baby, but perhaps the real truth lay in finding the mother. This thought settled over her like a mist, and she felt cold to her very bones.

16

WINNIE

At ten o' clock the following morning Winnie was sitting at her desk at work, checking emails and making a grocery list. Her kid was eating them out of house and home. She missed the days when he was little and they shared meals at his little Paw Patrol table; with the way their schedules were now, they hardly ate dinner together anymore. She was only required to be in the office three days a week, and she used that time to catch up on paperwork. The other two days she spent in the field, mostly in psychiatric wards to place patients in home care. She preferred this job to the one she'd had at Illuminations. She didn't have to work with the patients herself, for one thing, not after the initial placement; after that, they belonged to their case workers. It was more of an overseer's position and that suited her well, she thought. She got much too involved with her patients. That's why Nigel had wanted her to find something different after Illuminations. Winnie reached for her coffee and found it cold. She was working to get a patient placement in one of the more coveted adult homes, but her mind kept drifting to the name of the little girl, Lisa Sharpe. Why had Nigel searched for missing children on the internet and then written their names down? It felt like the deepest betrayal, the cruelest thing he could do after...and yet hadn't she done the same thing? Scouring the news for stories of missing children? If she were to be honest with herself, she would admit that it was the parents she was most interested in. She wanted to see their hurt, to experience their pain alongside them like she had some part in it. She got off on the hurting. She got up from her desk, abruptly leaving her office to look for fresh coffee. That's what she needed; she hadn't had enough today and her mind was fritzing. She laughed a little as she made her way down the hall and back toward the kitchen. It was the type of laugh a woman made when she was uncomfortable with something, and Winnie was uncomfortable with her thoughts. She'd never say any of it out loud, no way. She was pouring coffee into one of the company mugs when her next thought derailed her so thoroughly she forgot to add her usual cream and sugar. She stared down at her mug of black coffee once she was back in her office and thought, *I can't do this. I can't pretend nothing is wrong when it is.* She needed to talk to Nigel, face-to-face. Tell him that she knew that he'd been looking at...things on the internet. She grabbed her jacket from the back of her chair, relieved at her own decisiveness. But she always had been the confrontational one; she just had to work her way up to it. Nigel, on the other hand, wanted nothing to do with the battle; he wanted to win like everyone else, but he had other ways of doing it. Winnie didn't want that type of fight in her marriage. What she really wanted was to turn back time, go back to the night she'd made the worst mistake of her life, take it all back like it never happened. If she could take that one moment back...her marriage, her son...everything would be healthy as it should be.

It was raining when she stood under the awning of the building just a few yards from where her car was parked. Winnie stood huddled there, her eyes looking at the bruised color of the sky and not really seeing it. Where would she go if she got in and drove right now? She didn't know, so instead of walking to her car she flipped the hood up on her jacket and began walking along the sidewalk, dodging a couple of guys who had their eyes on their phones. The rain was more of a mist, and it swept into her face with an affection only Seattle rain offered.

If they fought it would get ugly, because that's how people with secrets stepped into the ring. If she told Nigel she knew he'd searched for Lisa Sharpe online he would get accusatory, make her feel awful for snooping and then thinking the worst of him. And maybe he'd be right, or maybe he'd be gaslighting her; she was fairly certain she did her fair share of gaslighting herself. But Nigel wasn't like Winnie; he wasn't trying to punish himself for his role in her mistake. No, if he was searching for information it was to benefit himself. You couldn't live with someone for years on end without knowing their patterns; good or bad you learned them.

Winnie licked the water off her lips. She wasn't aware of where she was walking, or how fast; she was only vaguely aware of the people she passed and how they stared at her. *It must be my makeup*, she thought. The rain that was kissing her face was probably making her mascara run. A voice in the back of her mind was telling her that she was deciding how people were seeing her instead of facing the truth about how she actually looked; the voice sounded suspiciously like the therapist she'd seen for three years, the man's voice more distinct in her mind than her dead father's. He'd ended up losing his license, after which Winnie quit therapy indefinitely to become a full-time control freak mom.

It was when Nigel brought up renting out the apartment downstairs to help with bills that she'd started looking for a job. The thought of some stranger in her house, watching her, terrified Winnie. She just couldn't do it, even though she'd agreed to put in the separate entrance. She stopped on the corner of a street she wasn't familiar with and looked around for the first time. *Calm down*, she told herself, but she was calm. Almost too calm. Why was that? Because he *couldn't* leave her, and that was her ultimate fear. She laughed, a raucous burst that made several people who were waiting for the light to change step away from her, the woman in the Burberry coat with the smudged mascara. But it was funny, wasn't it? She was afraid of the thing that couldn't happen. The smile wilted from her lips. It wasn't that he couldn't leave, it was that he wanted to and couldn't. Perhaps it was too much to ask after what she'd done, but she just wanted her husband to love her...to want to be with her.

She'd somehow walked home, wound herself through streets she rarely drove down until she'd reached the opposite end of Greenlake Park and was now standing in front of her own house—a mess of wet clothes and running face paint. Her car was still in the parking lot at work. She'd walked four miles and hardly noticed. The last thing Winnie wanted to do was schlep all the way back to the office just as people were coming back from lunch. If people from work saw her show up, drenched, to pick up her car, they'd assume the worst. They were always looking for something scandalous to chew on; it made the days go by faster. And the worst they could imagine would not be as bad as what Winnie had actually done. She'd have to take an Uber to work tomorrow, concoct some story to go with it. She decided that she'd tell Nigel she'd left work to find her car battery dead. That would be enough. She was back to her old ways: sweeping pieces of her crazy under the rug.

She stilled for a moment, standing at the edge of the park; her house was across the street and for a moment she saw it as the park-goers saw it. "One of the neater homes," she'd once heard an older man say to his older lady friend as they walked past it. "Mmm-hmm," she'd agreed as she scooped her arm through his. Winnie agreed with the old dude; she saw the red brick and traditional angles as charming, but some of her girlfriends made snide comments, saying it could have been the setting for a Wes Craven movie. It was barely noon, yet the sky already had a six o' clock shadow. Her house was framed by agitated clouds that seemed especially dark right above her roof like they were specifically congregating there. That was ridiculous. It was like she was having a mental breakdown or something; this whole day was just—and then her eyes moved downwind toward the bedroom windows and the thought slid from her head. What she saw made her stomach clench and her thighs squeeze together. Someone was standing in her bedroom window looking out at the park—looking out at *her*. Her mouth dropped open at the same time a man walking his dogs crossed in front of her, blocking her vision for two seconds at most. After he passed, the window—her bedroom window—was empty. She darted across the street, yards from the nearest crosswalk, and a Mazda honked at her. Winnie held up an apologetic hand as she ran across the three lanes of traffic, her eyes firmly glued to the window of the bedroom she shared with her husband. She was pulling her keys out of her bag as she ran up the pathway to the house, now searching the other windows for signs of the intruder. She could see Mr. Nevins's Tahoe parked along the curb. He was home; she could call out to him if she needed help. The rear of his house faced the rear of her house, separated by a narrow alley. Winnie ran past his truck and the yellow bumper sticker she hated with a passion, to the back alley. Mr. Nevins was nowhere to be seen, the windows of his Cape Cod dark. The gate to her own house was undisturbed; she opened it quietly, pulling her phone from her purse as she kept her eyes on the back door. If someone were to run out it would probably be from here. But then Winnie straightened up, remembering one important detail: the house alarm. She blinked at the back door, fingering her keys. She'd peek in, see if the alarm was still on. She ran across the grass in the backyard, the flowers overly bright in the strange light that was filtering through the clouds. As soon as she was within five feet of the door, she could see the red light on the keypad in the kitchen. It was armed. Winnie felt a chill run down her back and pool indecisively in her toes. She wanted to call the police, but Nigel would have a fit. He'd be embarrassed, and more than that, he'd think Winnie was "losing it". He'd give her that look again, like she was a dangerous thing that could snap at any moment. She chewed on her lower lip, trembling slightly. She couldn't call the police, and she couldn't call Nigel. She'd have to go explore this herself.

Winnie opened the door like a woman preparing to be mugged. Had she imagined it? She'd been thinking about those dark clouds moments before and then...looking around, she tapped the alarm code into the keypad, jumping when the fridge started to hum its tune. The alarm beeped once to tell her it was off, and she took a cautious step deeper into the kitchen listening for any sound. The house was old; it had its noises and she heard those as she strained to hear the intruder. When nothing unusual sounded, she crept toward the hallway, seeing it as empty as the kitchen. She walked toward the stairs, convinced she'd made it all up. She'd been in a horrible frame of mind this morning; she wouldn't be surprised at all if she'd seen something frightening in a shadow. Her heartbeat calmer, Winnie went upstairs.

In her bedroom, she spun in a slow circle, her eyes darting carefully and impatiently over the familiar objects. Nothing was…wrong, but something was off. She couldn't place her finger on it. It felt like someone had been here, even if they weren't there now. Skirting the window, she made sure not to turn her back to the doors. This was ridiculous, she felt ridiculous, but fear was a compelling argument. She'd look more ridiculous if she ended up dead. *You don't really think there was someone in the house*, she thought. The alarm was on. So what did that leave…?

Shoving the curtains aside, she stood in the same place she'd seen the figure. Something had looked at her from this window; she was certain she'd seen it. "No," she laughed, turning away. The only thing haunting her was her past decisions. She was more afraid of that than ghosts.

17

JUNO

The grass was wet and spongy under Juno's tennis shoes; she turned her face toward the light drizzle and breathed all that good Washington air into her lungs. The outside was now a special treat to her; if only life could balance out its problems. She saw Joe down the way a little, working his cardboard sign, a bottle of orange juice at his feet.

"Orange juice, Joe?"

Joe looked around until he found the source of the voice. His face lit up when he saw her. "Some motherfucker gave it to me, Juno. You know I want the fizzy shit." He laughed so hard he slapped his knee. Juno hardly ever saw him without a bottle of soda; Crush, preferably, but any soda would do. She caught a look at his sign and raised her eyebrows. Joe wasn't the "Please help me out" type. In very bold, block writing he'd jotted three lines of a Johnny Cash song Kregger used to listen to. Juno read them with amusement. He was niche homeless: his signs drew the attention not of the bleeding hearts, but of the edgy music lovers with a soft spot for good lyrics. Joe did pretty well on most days. Joe, who referred to the entire world as "those motherfuckers," was an eternal optimist. He even called the mutt that followed him around Mother. Juno didn't see the dog now; it was just Joe trying to get her attention. Juno smiled and walked on, but he called after her. "Hey! Hey, Juno! Where have you been, girl?"

"I'm no more a girl than you are, Joe!"

"That's right! You're a motherfucker!" She heard him laughing before she turned the corner, eager to be away. Joe was an insatiable gossip, and she wanted no part of that today. She took the long way to the library, stopping at the corner mart for a hot cup of soup. The guy who worked there on weekdays had always been nice to her. He did a double take, then bopped his head at her as she headed over to the soup counter. She had been gone for a while. It was nice that he noticed. Choosing the minestrone and ladling it into the to-go container, she headed to the register to wait her turn. The soup was two dollars fifty, and she set the money on the counter and asked for a single stamp, fishing the extra change out of her pocket. She had just enough left to use the printer at the library, which was five cents a page. With the stamp tucked away, she drank her soup straight from the paper bowl as she walked. The guy at the register had slid her a pack of Mentos before she could walk away—no charge. She ate half the pack as she sat at the computer terminal in the library, slipping them discreetly between her lips. When she had what she needed and the printer hummed out its last warm sheet, she headed out. Samuel would be home in an hour.

He'd take care of the alarm, and Juno would slip in through the kitchen while he did his homework. The problem was Mr. Nevins, who occasionally peeked out of his windows into the alley that Juno had to walk down to reach the back gate. If she took her eyes off the windows, she might not see him, but he would see her, and then he'd call the police. She didn't cross the street from the park and approach the house from the front; instead, she crossed the street early and took the long way around. Her heart was racing like a Derby horse, and she hadn't even gotten in the gate yet. What if Sam was making a sandwich in the kitchen and saw his old homeless friend walking through his back gate? Mr. Nevins's truck wasn't on the curb. Walking down the alley, making every effort to look like a harmless old woman, Juno kept her eyes on the gate. Samuel had left it open; she wouldn't have to reach over the top to knock the latch free. She slowed when she neared it and looked around furtively, but there was no movement from Mr. Nevins's windows. Someone else could see her, she supposed, but chances were they'd think she was the cleaning lady or something. People came and went in the city without the same nosiness you found in the suburbs. Juno had known everyone's comings and goings when she was a suburban mom. She slipped through the gate and immediately recognized her mistake. A male voice called out to her as soon as she was on the house side.

"Hey! What are you doing?" She turned to see Joe trailing her down the alley, a filthy Mariners hat perched at a cocky angle on his head. He was walking a little loose limbed, his head wobbling around like his brains were too heavy for his neck. Juno knew that wasn't the case, which meant he'd probably had a recent hit. Joe liked some crack to go with his soda. She slipped back out, pretending she hadn't heard him, and continued on her way toward the street. Her heart was doing a jackrabbit run in her chest. Why had she called out to him earlier? She looked around for the dog, expecting to see it, but Joe was on his own and by the look on his face, he had an appetite for some trouble.

"Juno! Juno, you motherfucker!" She sped up, turning right down the street toward Greenlake Park. If she crossed the street fast, she could lose him. But when she turned around to see how close he was, she couldn't see him at all. Juno backtracked, peeking around the corner. Joe was standing in front of the Crouches' open gate, swaying as he stared in. It was a frightening sight. If Sam came into the kitchen and saw—

"Hey! I'm here, Joe. What do you want?" He didn't seem to hear her this time; his attention was focused on the house. *Dear God*, Juno thought. *What's happening in those drug-addled brains of his?* Now Juno wished Mr. Nevins were looking out of his window.

"Joe!" she called. "Hey, shithead! Let's go get a doughnut, you motherfucker, before they're out." Joe still didn't move, his attention for once laser focused. Juno had met Joe at the doughnut shop, which was no more than a one-room fry house that smelled like heaven. The owner was a former addict and sold anyone without a roof over their head doughnuts for twenty-five cents apiece; first come, first served. He was a lot younger than her, so it wasn't like they were friends, but when you were homeless, you became part of a community you hadn't exactly asked for. She took a few steps closer to where Joe stood, careful to keep out of his reach. Crack made him unpredictable. "Joe," she said again. "I'll buy you a—"

His head swiveled toward Juno so suddenly she jumped back. "What was in there?"

"What?" Suddenly he looked a lot more coherent than she'd initially thought. *Maybe he's not high.* Joe took a step toward the gate, extending his hand to push it all the way open.

"Come on, idiot," she said through her teeth. "What if they're home? Come on…" The sound of a car punctuated Juno's sentence, and suddenly Joe started moving. Hesitantly. She dug her fingers into the underside of his arm and hauled him away. He allowed himself to be pulled out of the alley and a few steps down the sidewalk. Juno stopped in front of the little wall she'd once sat on to watch the construction on the Crouches' house and glanced around nervously.

"What are you doing following me?"

Joe had a look on his pale face Juno didn't like. As she looked at him, she noticed the skin was burned pink around his cheeks and nose. What she'd mistaken for him being high was actually him being perfectly sober.

"You lifting something from that house, Juno…?"

"Yeah, sure, Joe. I was trying to get to the TV," she joked. "Thought I could carry it down to the pawn shop to—"

"You were a shrink in your last fancy life, weren't you. Yeah, I remember."

Juno emptied her eyes and smiled dully at him. "Sure, yeah." She tried to keep her voice calm, but Joe's questions were making her heart run fast. He had that knowing smile on his thin, crusted lips. He took a moment to turn his head back to the Crouches' house and study it, picking at the dead skin near his mouth.

"Yeah, I think you've got something going on, you old motherfucker." He leaned all the way down so that she smelled the rot in his mouth and saw the pockmarks on his nose. "I think you've got something…" And then he walked off toward the park in the same loll-headed walk. She stared after him, tiny pinpricks of fear tickling at her stomach. *He's just a junkie. He'd forget they even had this conversation by tonight*, she told herself. But he hadn't asked her again where she'd been; it was like he…knew. And if she wanted to get inside the house before Winnie and Nigel came home, she was running out of time.

"Hurry up, you old motherfucker," she whispered to herself, echoing Joe, as she made her way once more toward the alley. She glanced up at Sam's window and saw the light on. What would Sam do if he caught her sneaking through his house?

18

WINNIE

Winnie hadn't looked through the mail in three days. That wasn't the only thing she hadn't done: dishes were stacked around the sink, and there was a load of moldy wet clothes in the washer she'd been too lazy to transfer over to the dryer. Lazy wasn't the right word, no, she was *spent*. Meanwhile, she lay awake all night waiting for the dark figure to materialize next to the window so she could shake Nigel awake and prove she wasn't crazy. There'd been no apparitions after that day, and Winnie had spent a good portion of her nights convincing herself that what she'd seen had been a figure of her imagination. This was an old house, after all. She was standing with her foot propped on the pedal of the garbage can, dumping various store catalogs and flyers inside, when she came across the envelope.

It was the hand-scrawled address that drew her attention. There was no return, just Winnie's name and address and a stamp.

She ripped it open, and a flurry of paper drifted out, landing across the kitchen floor. Swearing, Winnie knelt to pick up the pieces. They were cut in different-sized rectangles. She held one up to her face and saw that they were printouts of online news stories. The first one read: *Baby abducted in supermarket!*

The story was of Rosie Jhou, taken from her stroller in the late nineties from a chain grocery store. Winnie remembered the story. As far as she knew, Rosie Jhou had never been found. That would make her over twenty today. But why would someone send Winnie this? She reached for another clipping, this one asking, *Where is Karlie Karhoff?* in bold across the top. Eight-month-old Karlie Karhoff had last been seen in the nursery of her family's home in Montana. Her distraught parents said they'd put her to bed the night before, like usual. "She had a cold and was sleepy," her mother, Hillary Karhoff, told authorities. But to their horror, they found her crib empty the next morning, baby Karlie gone.

Winnie reached for another, this time her stomach in her throat; it was about a missing Detroit girl named Hellie Armstrong. Hellie hadn't made it to her second birthday party; she was taken from her yard a week shy of it while wearing her yellow Princess Belle dress. Her mother said it was going to be a Disney Princess party. By the time Winnie was finished picking up the pieces of paper, she held over a dozen clippings in her hands, which were shaking so hard she dropped them all over again. She stuffed everything back into the envelope, every child who had never been found, and quickly dropped it into the trash. The lid closed and Winnie placed a hand over her racing heart.

Rosie Jhou's little face was in her mind as she took deep, gulping breaths. But she paused, the toe of her shoe pressing hard on the pedal of the trash can so that the lid sprang back. She stared down into the peels and rubbish, at her name and address handwritten on the envelope, and a chill swept across her body. That was a woman's handwriting, she was sure of it. She shoved the envelope farther down, pushing the rest of the trash over it. Someone knew.

She spent the rest of the week and the weekend in a kind of shocked stupor. Everything made her jump, and the sound of Samuel's loud TV shows set her on edge, their laugh tracks making her want to scream. Why did kids have to watch things that were so obnoxiously loud? On Friday night she put her hair into a ponytail, got into her sweats, and hid in the bathroom, citing cramps. Nigel and Samuel retreated to the den to play video games, leaving her to her own devices, which included obsessively Googling the stories of the kids in those articles. None of them had been found. None. She paced the bathroom floor in her socks, one arm wrapped around her waist, the other over her mouth. It was Josalyn she was thinking of, the petite blonde with the thin, ratty hair. The girl had one of those faces; she'd looked insolent and angry even when she hadn't meant to. She'd looked no more than fourteen, though she'd been a woman of eighteen when she came to the program at Illuminations. Winnie remembered the bitten down fingernails, and the sleepy way her eyes looked when she'd first sat in Winnie's car on the way to a doctor's appointment. She had two STIs and half of her teeth were rotting in her mouth; other than that, Josalyn had been healthy of body. Her mind, on the other hand, was a stewpot of issues and she was often suicidal—the evidence of that on her wrists, scars slashed the wrong way, the way a fourteen-year-old girl might attempt. Sitting at a little table in Starbucks, Josalyn told Winnie that she'd almost overdosed on sleeping pills the year before in California. Winnie distinctly remembered the flat way she'd told her about her suicide attempts—very matter-of-factly. Her therapist said she was suffering from PTSD and handed her a diagnosis for Bipolar-1. She'd just been a kid to Winnie, some kid who needed help. Winnie had come home each night thinking—no, obsessing over Josalyn's fate. Her coworkers told her that it was normal to have those feelings when you started out. But she'd gotten under Winnie's skin, for whatever reason. Did it matter? She wanted to help her. She'd done the opposite.

19

WINNIE

When Winnie's phone lit up on Tuesday morning with a text from Amber, she was crossing Pike Street with her arms full of dried flower arrangements. She'd volunteered to pick up the flowers for the winter banquet at Samuel's school.

The flowers, which you could buy from the market in huge, inexpensive bouquets, were sold dried through the winter. Winnie found that depressing. They crunched slightly in her arms as she waited for the light to change. She was freezing, her nose still raw from the cold she'd had last week. She wondered who on the school board thought bouquets of dead flowers were Christmassy, and why hadn't someone invented a heated coat?

She had to hike uphill back to the parking garage where she'd left her car, so she didn't read the text until the flowers were loaded neatly into the trunk, and even then, she was distracted as she glanced at her phone while she walked around to the driver's side door. She had to read the text again, sure it was a mistake, clearing her throat incessantly as she did when she was anxious. Surely Amber, who routinely drank two glasses of wine with lunch, had it wrong. But Winnie also knew that Amber, who'd grown up in Brooklyn and had once shoved a man down a flight of stairs for touching her rear, was not the type of person to raise false alarms.

So Winnie typed a reply: Send the photo.

She waited with her back leaning against the car door, feeling her stomach lurch repeatedly as the seconds ticked by. It was cold four floors up in the parking garage, the wind skating right off the Sound and passing through the open, yawning windows—but Winnie didn't want to get in the car yet. She shivered, staring at the side of a black Suburban. Someone had written *Idiot* in the dirt on the passenger door. It would be different if this were coming from someone else, but Amber was her cousin. If she came bearing bad news, chances were, it was valid bad news. Something you had to see but didn't want to see.

She opened her eyes to read the text again, just to make sure:

I debated sending this but I feel it's the right thing to do. I was at lunch yesterday at Palomino. I spotted Nigel and thought he was with you so I headed over to say hi. When I reached the table I saw that it wasn't you. He was with some woman. They were sitting on the same side of the booth, very close. Something wasn't right. They were turned toward each other. They didn't see me but I took a photo as I walked by. I'm sorry.

That was Amber; no butter on her toast, she delivered everything dry. Winnie's hands were shaking—no, her whole body was shaking—as she waited. The photo came, the notification lighting up the phone. She stared at it hard—so hard her eyes hurt. It was there; it was right there in front of her. The photo blurred as soon as it came into view, the faces of the two people disappearing as her eyes filled with tears. But she'd seen them, she knew the faces well: her husband and Dulce Tucker.

The photo was blurry; Amber had taken it on the move and there was a blur of a red fingernail in the corner of the shot, but there was no mistaking Nigel, whose body was turned sideways toward the woman next to him, his arm thrown casually across the back of the booth behind her. She was wearing a bright red sweater that accentuated the swell of her breasts. The thing that bothered Winnie the most was the hand that rested on her husband's chest, a hand so comfortable being there that it surely had been there many times before. And where else, Winnie thought. Where else had this woman's hands been? Both of them were smiling. *Isn't that something*, Winnie thought. *It's possible to smile while breaking someone's heart.*

Thank you, she sent back to Amber, and then she had a panic attack on the cold ground of the parking garage, her car filled with pretty, dead flowers.

Winnie dropped the flowers off then drove straight to Nigel's office. She'd yet to cry, she'd yet to feel anything other than a greasy dread that was working its way through her mind at that very moment. She was no longer in charge; some other woman had access to her husband's heart. Did he love Dulce? That was the question of the hour, nagging under skin like a splinter. Had her husband fallen in love with someone right under her nose? She'd been distracted, she definitely had been…between work, Samuel, and her volunteer hours.

She was a busy person, like everyone else. The truly rotten part about this was that she hadn't even suspected. *What did you think, you idiot? That he really wouldn't leave you eventually after what you did...?*

Nigel worked in a stout brick building in Belltown just off the railroad tracks. There were always a couple of homeless men wandering around outside at this time of day; Nigel called them the Belltown Hoppers. She saw one of them now shuffling up the sidewalk, holding a can of soda and walking slightly off-kilter. It made her uncomfortable that Nigel nicknamed them, but still, she found herself referring to them by the very name that disturbed her. It was 12:30, Winnie noted on her Apple Watch. Nigel took his lunch around this time; Winnie had often met him for a quick bite at one of the bistros in the area.

He hated it when Winnie called their lunches a quick bite. "This is a real quick bite—" And then he'd nip Winnie playfully on the neck. Now, apparently, he was nipping other women on the neck, taking bites out of things that weren't his.

She took a seat on a bench half a block away and, facing the entrance to Nigel's building, crossed and uncrossed her legs. If he left for lunch, she'd be able to see him from there. If he left for lunch with Dulce, she'd also be able to see him from there, and she was unsure as to whether or not she wanted to. The man with the can of soda was now feeding a dog scraps of a sandwich a little ways down the street. She renamed him Mr. Soda, thinking that less derogatory than Nigel's moniker for him. Winnie watched their exchange without really seeing it; Mr. Soda and his dog were just background. She was reviewing the last few months in her mind, looking for some clue to mull over. Exactly how stupidly blind had she been? And how sneaky had he been to pull this off?

Winnie desperately didn't want to be the idiot wife who

was cheated on by the bored husband, but ten minutes later, she found out that's exactly what she was. Nigel was wearing the sweater Winnie bought him for his birthday as he held the door open for Dulce. Winnie sat forward on the bench as the five-foot-four brunette stepped past her husband onto the sidewalk, smiling up at him with a surprising sweetness. They fell into step together, talking with their hands in happy gestures. It looked like the end scene to some happy movie, only with Mr. Soda in the background. They were headed to the quick bite places. *If he takes her to 360, I'm going to lose it,* she thought, standing up to follow them. She stayed on the far side of the street, a few paces back, trotting to keep up with them. All she had with her was a small crossbody bag, and as she walked she held on to the strap across her chest with both hands, her eyes never leaving them. She half expected someone else to join them, calling for them to slow down, but no such thing happened. This was a lunch date, and not of the business variety. *You don't know that yet,* she thought. But when they walked into the very restaurant Winnie feared they were headed to, she knew.

360 was *their* place, locally sourced and a favorite for date night. He hadn't told her that he came here during the day with other people. She waited five minutes before crossing the street and walking into the restaurant.

She didn't really know what her plan was other than to confirm what she already knew. She didn't feel crazy or unhinged as women were supposed to feel when they found out their husbands were cheating on them. Winnie felt suspiciously calm. The storm was coming, she knew, but for now there was the eerie stillness inside her.

They were seated in a cramped booth opposite each other; Winnie could only make out the tops of their heads when she walked in the door. When the hostess greeted her, she

pointed to a table near the window where she could see them
without them seeing her. As soon as Winnie was seated at her
own table, Dulce got up to go to the bathroom, grinning at
Nigel like they shared a secret joke. Winnie watched her walk
away; Nigel also watched her walk away. He even leaned to
the side a little when she was walking out of his line of sight
so he could keep his eyes trained on her ass. She was wearing a pinstripe skirt—white with fine gray lines, so tight you
could tell that she spent five nights a week in the gym.

She winced. So this was what Nigel liked? Twentysome-
thing women with hard, round asses and shaggy, pullable
hair. It was unsurprisingly predictable, and yet still painful.

Winnie's own blond hair was smooth and flat, her ass much
the same despite how often she lunged and squatted. She had
always wanted larger breasts, but Nigel insisted that he liked
her as she was. Clearly not. Clearly her short little gymnast husband was looking for something wild to ride. Winnie poured water into a glass from a carafe on the table. She
drained the glass and poured another, wiping her mouth with
the back of her hand. A swatch of lipstick came away with
the droplets of water. She must have smeared it all over her
face, but Winnie didn't care. Dulce returned to the table and
there was more grinning. They conferred over the menu as
the server waited, pen poised.

Someone came to take Winnie's order, and by the time
she was alone again, she saw that Nigel and Dulce each had
a mimosa in front of them. Winnie felt sick. So far nothing
had happened other than her pathetic, dumbass husband taking a much younger woman to lunch and staring at her ass.
Winnie had ordered coffee, but she'd only held the mug to
her lips, never taking a sip. She wanted to drink something
stronger, but she didn't know what to order. Their food arrived and Winnie's heart began to slow. They were…eating.

Like two colleagues. She felt ridiculous, stupid. Amber had probably seen them at lunch just as Winnie was now and had jumped to conclusions. Amber had been cheated on recently; it all made perfect sense to Winnie. God, she was embarrassed. She was about to pull out a ten to leave on the table for her coffee when it happened.

It was, in Winnie's opinion, as intimate as a kiss. Dulce extended her fork toward Nigel, French toast held on the tip; from where she was sitting she could see the syrup swinging from the bread. He must have opened his mouth for the bite because she returned her fork to her plate, grinning. Winnie could see his ears move as he chewed, hear the laughter as he wiped syrup from his face.

She'd seen enough. Setting her coffee down on the table, she lifted her phone from her bag. She had several missed calls from Amber, and one from her friend Courtney. She scrolled past these until she found her husband's name.

Hi, where are you?

She saw his head dip to look at his phone. For a minute Winnie thought he was going to ignore it but then the little bubbles appeared to say he was typing. With Nigel's attention on his phone, Dulce's expression was unguarded as she watched him text his wife.

Winnie felt something hard and primal unfold in her belly. Her immediate anger was directed at the woman and not the man. She recognized this as being off-brand with her feminism, but she didn't care. What was feminism to a woman who was being betrayed? This bitch had cozied up to a married father, and all she could do was grin like the Cheshire cat. She wanted to hook each of her index fingers into the sides of Dulce's mouth, and pull that grin wide enough to rip her face open. She'd never, in her life, had such a violent thought, and it made her whole body shake with satisfaction and disgust. Winnie stared down at the screen of her phone, her hurt burning like a fever. She read Nigel's answer, panting slightly.

At lunch

He wasn't lying. But omissions were the same as lies in Winnie's opinion.

With who?

She finally took a sip of her coffee, but when the server came by, she ordered a glass of white wine. If she was going to drink something cold, it needed to make her feel better. White wine was the medicine of the basic bitch, wasn't it? Winnie had never felt more basic in her life as she watched her husband pay the bill with cash. Dulce didn't even offer, she noted.

When Nigel finally answered her text, they were standing up to leave and Winnie had drained her glass.

Some people from work...

What was that? Winnie thought—an omission or a straight-out lie? Things got murky in that department.

She watched as he shrugged on his jacket, a lingering smile on his lips from something Dulce said. He glanced down at his phone once more before pocketing it. It was then that, in tandem, Nigel and Dulce turned toward the door, flipping up the collars of their coats. Nigel was walking straight toward Winnie, who was looking at him squarely, willing him to see her. It was an awful few seconds as realization kicked in; she was getting ready to scream and rail and cry at him, but what if that was what he wanted: a reason to finally leave her? A second later, his eyes found Winnie, and she leaned forward eagerly to see what he would do. Maybe it was the white wine medicine that made her so brazenly thirsty for conflict. Nigel stopped abruptly, like someone had yanked him back by an invisible string. Dulce didn't look back until she was at the door and Nigel wasn't opening it for her. The smile dropped from her face as she looked from him to Winnie.

"I'll catch up to you," he said, waving her off. He didn't have to tell her twice; she was out the door and hurrying past the window, her head bent like a shamed dog. Nigel slumped into the seat opposite Winnie. She searched his face to see what he was feeling, but his expression was neutral. He'd always been better than her at hiding his emotions.

"So you follow me now?"

"So you have lunch with work whores now?"

Nigel's head jerked back in offense and Winnie felt rage.

"She's a colleague," he began. "Don't be ridiculous—"

"She fed you food from her fork. Do you do that with Brady when you have lunch together?"

He was momentarily speechless. Nigel looked stupid when he was speechless; Winnie had never noticed that before. He looked like what her father used to call a dumber-than-shit idiot. His eyes were cantering around, blinking like the room was too bright.

"Have you slept with her?"

He'd been preparing for this for the last minute, thus the neutral expression, she thought. His systems were in overdrive trying to wiggle out of this.

"What? No!" But Winnie already knew it was true. She

could see it in his eyes. He was ashamed. He was bowing his head a little like Dulce had when she walked away.

"Nigel," she said firmly. "Tell me the truth. I deserve the truth at least, don't you think?"

He stood up, almost sending the table toppling. "You don't get to come in here and accuse me of things." Winnie was so lost in her shock that she found nothing to say. He was red-faced, though his lips were shockingly white, like he'd bitten into a powdered doughnut. It was Nigel's tell; when he was lying, when he was guilty. His outburst immediately embarrassed her.

Recoiling in her seat, she felt hurt rise in her throat, making her want to moan out loud. He slammed out of the door as she sat, still as a statue. People were looking; of course they were—Winnie would have looked, too. And then she knew—he'd done it to throw her off—to buy time for a better lie. Using her weakness against her was an all-time low for their marriage. She drained her water glass, left a generous tip, and took an Uber home.

Five hours later, Nigel walked in the door after work. Winnie had spent those five hours finding out everything she could about Dulce Tucker. She could hear him depositing his work bag in the junk closet, then his heavy tread up the stairs as he went to change out of his work clothes.

He came down a few minutes later wearing sweats and a T-shirt. Seating himself at the table, he folded his hands rather piously on the tabletop. "Can we talk?"

"I would say we *need* to," she said calmly. She'd been nursing a tea for the last few hours, just pouring hot water over the same tea bag again and again. It didn't matter; Winnie wasn't tasting anything.

"Winnie," he began. "There's just been a lot of stress lately—on both of us—I wasn't myself."

Winnie waited a few beats for him to say more, to apply some salve to the wounds he had inflicted with his actions. More, anyway, than just "I wasn't myself." She leaned closer— just an inch or so to urge him to finish his sentence.

"Oh…oh," she said. "Is that the end, are you—?"

"Goddammit!" Nigel slammed his fist on the surface of the table. Winnie's salt and pepper shakers wobbled. "Nothing is good enough for you."

She blinked at him for a few minutes in disbelief. Nigel was acting like she was chiding him for not picking up the right brand of yogurt.

"I didn't say that. Was that an…admission?"

Nigel's compact frame was tense, despite how relaxed he tried to appear. Her attraction to this man was primal because, even as gaslighted as she was, she wanted him in a way that made her feel shameful.

"Why are you like this, Winnie? So suspicious. I've never given you reason. It makes me feel like I've done something when I haven't."

"But haven't you?" Winnie couldn't help it, her face was incredulous. Was it really happening this way? She'd caught her husband having a cozy lunch date with Dulce fucking Tucker, and now he was angry with *her*? It felt too weird to be real. Winnie had met Dulce during the last Christmas party at Nigel's work when she was a new hire. She'd come over from a temp agency when their secretary was out on maternity leave, and then later, when said secretary decided to be a stay-at-home mom, they took Dulce on permanently. Nigel used to make jokes about her name, and Winnie joined in, figuring it was better than wondering if he was attracted to her. Turns out he was.

"Winnie—" he tried again. "We've both made terrible mistakes—"

"Have you slept with her or not?"

He dropped his head. "No."

She didn't believe him, but he'd never change his story. When Nigel lied, he stayed committed to that lie. She knew that better than anyone.

"But you were planning to?" She could see him mulling over this one—stewing would be a better word. Under the table her hands grabbed at each other, holding tight.

"Yes." He seemed almost relieved to say it.

"Why?"

"I don't know…boredom." He said it with a challenge. "You're always inside your head. I can't get in there."

"Ohh, that's not it." She pressed her lips together so hard she imagined they looked like Nigel's.

"Isn't it?" Something else had settled across Nigel's face. Winnie recognized it; Nigel got like that when he was playing a game and winning. She thought about the way he moved his bottle of liquor around to throw her off. Everything was a game to him.

"I don't want to talk about this anymore, Nigel." The truth was that she didn't feel capable of talking about it anymore. A line had been crossed, the trust they'd worked so hard to rebuild, kicked out from under them like a wobbly stool. She didn't know how to put into words what she was feeling because there were no words for it.

Everything in her life was coming off the rails: her marriage, her relationship with her son, and her mental health. She was either being stalked, or she was imagining being stalked, and quite frankly Winnie didn't know what was worse. There was no one to turn to, not a soul who would understand. She couldn't leave him because of what she'd done, and he couldn't leave her because of what he'd helped her do. They were tied together in this life. Winnie locked herself in the bathroom, wishing she had a bottle of wine.

Nigel retired to his den, where Winnie assumed he'd be spending the night. After he'd gone, Winnie made some tea and sat at her computer, trying to get her mind on something else besides the storm that was her life.

She was checking her email, aggressively sipping at chamomile tea, when she clicked on a message sent by the King County Library system. Winnie had seen enough of these back in the day to know what it was before she clicked on it. After Samuel was born, she'd read voraciously for years, making regular trips to the library with him strapped to her chest. Occasionally she'd read a book she really liked and then, instead of returning it, she'd read it again; that always amounted to fines. But she hadn't cared, they'd been worth it. And sure enough, when the body of the email downloaded to her screen, Winnie's suspicion was confirmed: a library fine.

But that couldn't be right. Winnie hadn't been to the library in years, like at least four or five. Not to mention she didn't have a clue where her library card was. It had to be an error in the system, or a ghost email haunting her from her inbox past. Looking more closely, she saw that it was a fine for a book that had been checked out on October 5 of this year. Winnie leaned closer to the screen to read the name of the book she'd supposedly checked out; it was in fine print like a little librarian elf typed it—*Child Abduction: A Theory of Criminal Behavior.*

For a moment it felt like someone had plugged her into an electrical socket. Fear charged through her limbs, settling in her bowels like greasy food. She doubled over, hitting her forehead on the lip of the desk, but hardly feeling it. Bent with her head between her knees and her hands clutching her calves, she pushed air through her lips to keep from wailing. Everything inside Winnie was screaming, but she had to keep control. She lifted her head again, glanced briefly at the screen before exiting out of it, and turned the computer off. She wanted to ask Nigel if this was some sort of cruel joke, but she knew in her gut he'd never do something like that, not when his hands were as covered in guilt as hers. There was also the fact that neither Nigel nor her son liked to read library books; it was new or nothing. Either way, she had to find out.

She texted Samuel. Did you check out a library book lately?

Last time I went to the library was on a fourth-grade field trip.

Why couldn't he just answer her? It was yes or no—that simple. Everything had to be a snarky little game with him. If she'd said that to her own mother when she was Samuel's age...

And then all of her anger evaporated. She was lucky he'd even answered; lately, he wanted nothing to do with her. That was the essential difference between her mother's parenting and her own: her mother didn't care what her kids thought of her. Winnie tried not to think about how much she cared as she got up from the desk to check the junk drawer for her library card. She rifled past a hairbrush with a broken handle, a jump rope, and a box of press-on nails before she found it. It was under the stack of instruction manuals and receipts, pushed to the far corner of the drawer. She held it in her palm, staring at it hard. The library must have made a mistake; she'd sort it out.

But when she called the library, they said she had indeed

checked out *Child Abduction: A Theory of Criminal Behavior* on October 5.

"It wasn't me," she said firmly. "I haven't been to the library in years. I don't even know where my library card is!" She glanced guiltily at the junk drawer.

"Well then somebody else has your card," said the guy on the other end of the line. "And they owe five dollars and seventy-two cents in fees. Will you be paying it? I can take your debit card right over the phone."

When Winnie ended the call, she cried. She hadn't cried in a long time and it felt good to let the drama loose, as her mother used to say. She'd been too busy to be scared lately, but here it was: a library book, reminding her that at any moment her entire life could be torn apart.

If she told Nigel about this, he'd just blow it off, and then it would end up in another big, fat fight. She was tired of those, obviously, since she even refused to fight about his infidelity. She was desperate for peace and for her son to like her again, and for her secrets to stay secret.

She went to look at the library card again, really examine it under the light. There was chocolate melted on one corner and most of the writing was scratched away.

She walked straight to the pantry and pulled out Nigel's secret bottle of Jack Daniel's—this time hidden in the bread box. Without bothering to get a glass, she unscrewed the cap and drank directly from the lip. A trickle of whiskey ran down her chin as she coughed and sputtered. Her eyes burned like she'd poured the whiskey straight over her pupils, and she squeezed them closed as her stomach lurched in protest. *Better,* Winnie thought. *When I'm retching my guts up, I don't think about the scary shit.*

No wonder her husband liked this stuff. She held the bottle up to the light, swirling it around. Her father had been a whiskey drinker, and when Nigel ordered it stiff on their first date, just as her father would have, she'd fallen for him right then and there. And then of course she'd banned him from drinking it (after the death of her father, due to said whiskey), but that was only to put the fear of God in him. Winnie knew he drank, but because he wasn't supposed to, he watched how much, and where, and who with.

She wandered around the rooms downstairs, holding the bottle of whiskey by its neck and occasionally taking tentative sips. By the time she walked through the kitchen for the second time, the bottle was considerably lighter, and Winnie could feel every single ounce of alcohol chortling through her system. It was awful and wonderful at the same time. She made a right out of the kitchen and found herself swaying near the computer, and all of a sudden she remembered everything she was trying to forget, only now she was drunk. It was worse drunk than sober. Winnie was a sad drunk, a dark drunk; she thought of bad things when there was alcohol in her. It had been like that since before her dad died, the nature of his death only solidifying her distaste for the foul stuff.

She leaned her hip against the wall and a few seconds later, her head. Winnie was dizzy and she wanted to hurl. That's what her dad used to say—hurl. She started to cry, and then she did hurl.

20

WINNIE

As it turned out, the alcohol wasn't the only thing swirling around Winnie's stomach. The following day unearthed the virus. It hit them in tandem, so it was hard to know who to blame. At first Winnie thought she was being punished with a hangover the size of Kilimanjaro, but when she heard Nigel stumble through the door at noon, heading straight for the downstairs bathroom, she knew Samuel would probably soon follow. Winnie, who had never left for work, was upstairs in a similar position, her face noticeably green as she leaned over the toilet, expelling her bad choices along with the virus. They met in the kitchen accidentally, both in search of water. It was an awkward standoff, one in which Winnie felt like the victor when Nigel looked away first and skulked toward the fridge. It was as she watched the back of his head that it occurred to her that he had brought home this sickness, brought it right from Dulce fucking Tucker. Winnie and Nigel had both shared the same almost empty bottle of Jack Daniel's, slurping after hours to hide their sin. It was the insult that sent her over the edge, the audacity of Nigel to humiliate her by entertaining another woman. How he hid his bottle all over the pantry, too drunk to put it in the same place as before. Was life with her so unbearable? It wasn't like she'd let herself go, or that she ignored her husband. He'd just chosen to do this to her and now she was sick as a consequence, sick as a dog. She couldn't wait her turn for the water, her stomach was rolling. Winnie ran for the stairs angry as all hell.

She came out of the bathroom a good deal later and stumbled over to her side of the bed, feeling moderately better. She'd glanced at herself in the mirror on the way out of the bathroom and had seen a gray waxy face bearing two dark holes instead of eyes. Her hair was matted down and stringy, stuck to her face. She swept it back into a low ponytail as she walked slowly toward the bed. Her phone lit up on the nightstand and she grabbed for it as she pulled down the covers, hesitating briefly when she saw that it was Dakota who was texting her. Dakota, who'd been staying with their mother, was getting worse instead of better. Despite all of her brother's grandiose efforts to win back his wife, Manda wasn't having it this time. He'd left message after message, begging each of his sisters to reason with Manda. Winnie set the phone facedown on the nightstand and crawled into the bed, already beginning to shake from fever. It was as she gazed longingly toward the bathroom, wishing she'd drunk straight from the faucet, that she spotted the sweating glass of water next to the bed. At the sight of it, Winnie started to cry. Nigel had brought it to her;

Nigel had not abandoned her despite how cold he was being. She lifted the glass to her lips and drank it all.

Nigel, who'd been sleeping in his precious den, hadn't apologized as much as he'd shown concern. He brought her toast once, carrying it into the room on a tray with a glass of water and tea. Winnie had only been able to stomach a few bites of the toast, but felt soothed. There was no room for grudge-holding when it came to their marriage. Nigel had stuck it out with her and she would stick it out with him. They may not have signed on for the type of marriage that turned up, but here they were, somehow living it.

The virus worked its way out of the house three days later. Sam took the least of it, though he spent a full twelve hours in front of his own toilet and the other twelve in his room, playing on the computer. Winnie still wasn't feeling herself when she accepted Shelly's invitation to join them at their cabin for Christmas break. But before the plague hit, she vaguely remembered deciding that they needed a vacation. She also vaguely remembered other things she didn't want to think about at the moment. Being anywhere with Shelly immediately eliminated the possibility of relaxation, and that's exactly what she needed—to be distracted, to keep her mind off things. Mixed with the holiday mania and a house full of loud kids, it was exactly the type of distraction she needed. She accepted with forced gratitude, then texted Nigel to tell him the plan.

Can't, he texted back. I have that work conference.

Winnie vaguely remembered something about a work conference, but he'd been complaining about going.

Get out of it

Can't

Can't or won't?

Both...?

She was furious at him for that question mark because she could *see* his expression as he typed it—stick it to the wife, it said.

Where is the conference?

His answer came back impressively fast, so fast that he couldn't have made it up on the fly...or could he? If he'd planned it...

Puyallup

Wow. Okay. Priorities.

Winnie was so angry she tossed her phone in her purse and didn't look at it again until lunchtime. Didn't he understand that they needed this? It was like he wasn't making any effort at all to be a family lately. When she finally dug her phone from underneath all of her crap, she was sitting in Lola's with two of her coworkers, sipping coffee and working on a pastry.

Just seeing his name made her feel angry all over again, but after reading his text she excused herself to the bathroom to read it again.

I'm really trying here, Winnie. I can drive you up. Spend

Saturday and Sunday with you before I have to head back. That's the best I can do for now.

She nodded at the empty stall. Okay…she could work with that. She'd pack her pot, of course, she'd need it up at the cabin with Shelly.

21

JUNO

In the sixties, Juno's mother had owned a beauty salon called The Slick. Back then, women drove from all over the county to visit Hoida Pearl at her salon for a Vidal Sassoon cut, incredibly radical for the time. The salon was in a strip mall with a five and dime, a laundromat, and a butcher. Salon, chores, dinner, the women in the community joked—all in one! Juno spent many weekends and afternoons at the salon, washing and folding the towels for her mother, listening to the ladies talk. She learned that if they noticed her presence they'd share looks, pointing her out with their eyes. "Young ears in the room!" one of them would sing, and then her mother would sashay over to the register, her heels clipping on the tiled floor. Juno would hear the whoosh of the money drawer as it opened, followed by the clink of change as Hoida scooped some out. It was then that Juno understood that she was being dismissed and bribed all in one.

"An ice cream for you, *mija*, and cigarettes for me." The change was cold in her palm.

To argue would have been pointless, and Juno wanted the ice cream. From then on she'd learned that by staying out of sight—say, by the towel closet—they'd be more apt to spill their guts, dirty laundry tumbling out of their mouths a mile a minute. She'd known things about everyone in their town— the local Baptist pastor and her pediatrician, Dr. Mynds, included.

At this moment, she was grateful for the skills she'd honed in the salon.

Juno vibrated with something like anticipation as she lay in her nest. Above her, in the house proper, Nigel pulled open the door to the closet and tossed his work bag inside. She listened as his footsteps clambered up the stairs, calling out for Winnie and Sam. They were going away for a week to ski with Shelly's family; obviously, Shelly was speaking to Winnie again after the Dakota episode. Though from what Juno had gleaned, Dakota was anything but okay with what had gone down in the Crouch residence that night. He'd left two messages on the house phone, threatening Nigel in gruesome detail, and accusing him of ruining Dakota's life, in the slurred tones of a man who'd lost his family and was rapidly drinking himself to death.

Drunks seldom looked inward, and when they did, they usually ended up drinking more. Dakota was obviously looking for someone to blame and Nigel was the winner winner chicken dinner. Juno knew a ticking time bomb when she saw one. But Nigel had deleted both of the messages without Winnie ever catching wind of them.

They'd collected their snowsuits and skis from Hems Corner yesterday, loading everything into and onto Nigel's Subaru. Now she heard all three of them come down the stairs, their voices loud and excited. Juno would have the house to herself, and she had plans.

She'd spent days lying in the crawl space thinking of nothing but her growing suspicions. While her body throbbed around her, she withdrew into thoughts, accumulating theories into an overflowing bin in her brain. It wasn't good when she got like this; she couldn't sleep, couldn't focus on anything else. She ate aspirin (it was aspirin these days), chewing it to a paste and swallowing with a slight gag. She'd taken some of Winnie's marijuana, too, from a little Altoids tin she kept in her toiletries bag under the sink. Juno had laughed out loud when she saw the six little joints rolled to perfection. She'd taken one without even thinking about it. Her pain these days superseded her caution. With the aspirin still coating her throat, she slipped into a haze of dull pain and unwelcome remembering.

Kregger was telling her that enough was enough. He was angry and he rarely got angry. Juno was fighting back, defending herself. This was her job, she insisted; everyone took their job home to some degree. Kregger looked at her in bewilderment. You cannot be serious, Juno, you cannot...

The vibrations from the door slamming roused her slightly. The alarm was beep-beep-beeping as it prepared to arm. She breathed deeply, the smell of the marijuana mercifully covering the other smells in the crawl space. She lit the joint again, dragging on it heavily, the paper sizzling. It hit her where it mattered—all around her pain, body and brain. Leaning back, she edged the joint out on a Coke can to her right, then propped it inside the pull tab.

As the pain abated, Kregger came back, his voice so clear

183

it was like he was down here with her. She laughed at that: Kregger living in someone's crawl space like a rat! Her laughter was short-lived, though; the rawness in her throat from the pot sent her into a fit of coughing that brought up blood.

It's your career or me and the boys.

She spat into the dirt, out of breath, and leaned back. Her career or her family—that was the ultimatum her husband had given her. Entirely unfair, since Kregger got to have both. She'd said it, too, and he'd given her that look that said, you are crazy, and I don't know who I married. *You're obsessed, Juno, can't you see what this is doing to us? You're sicker than your clients, you know that? You're the one who needs help!*

She hadn't understood at the time, hadn't been able to spot in herself what she could so easily spot in others.

She'd known he'd wanted to leave her for years, in the same way she knew Nigel wanted to leave Winnie. When they began, they were in love, but problematic partners had a way of dissolving love faster than it could regrow. One step forward, two steps back. And then one day there wasn't enough love left to cover the sins. He'd taken their boys and left. Juno didn't feel as if she deserved that part. Sure, she'd fucked up her marriage, fucked up her career. She'd gone to prison for it, too, paid her dues. But they hadn't visited her once, and there had been no one there to greet her on the day she left those prison walls, a little bag of her things clutched to her chest. She'd stumbled into the bright sunlight, her new reality hers alone to face. She'd tried to find them for a while, living in a halfway house. She'd called every single one of their friends, people who'd eaten her food, babysat her children. None of them would talk to her. Kregger was gone and so were her sons.

A few months after getting out of prison, Juno had once taken a bus to her old neighborhood and knocked on a neighbor's door. The surprise on the woman's face when she saw Juno standing there, wearing too-big blue jeans and a Reebok sweatshirt from Goodwill, had been so painful, Juno had recoiled, ashamed. Her hair was now a wiry burst of gray that she'd tried to wind into a bun with no luck. From her temples and crown, Juno's hair burst forward in unruly coils. Did she look as alien to this woman as this woman looked to her?

"Juno, I'm not going to tell you anything." Her old friend wouldn't meet her eyes. Juno wasn't surprised by this; she'd once had a client who'd come to her because she had a panic attack every time she saw a homeless person. "They make me feel guilty and vulnerable," the client had said.

"Please, Bette, he took my boys…"

Bette's face had clouded over, and for a split second Juno entertained the thought that her old coffee date, her girls' night partner, was going to help her. Juno, after all, had been the one to start calling Elizabeth Brown "Bette" when they first met. It had caught on, and then suddenly everyone else was calling her Bette, too. And here was her Bette, with the high, round moon cheeks, looking at Juno like she was spoiled cheese. The thought was indulgent; Juno knew what she'd do in the same situation. Someone you're ashamed to know shows up on your doorstep demanding information they really didn't deserve.

Bette's eyes filled with ice. Juno was familiar with that look, but not from Bette; Bette had always been a little lamb. Now she suddenly seemed like something else. Had Kregger called to tell Bette that Juno was getting out and to keep an eye out for her? Of course he had; Juno knew Kregger just as well as he knew her. She took a little step back, which seemed to embolden the new Bette.

"Those aren't your boys, they're Kregger's. You had your

chance with them, Juno, and you blew it. Leave them be, they've started over." And then Bette shut the door in Juno's face.

Juno had a key to Bette's house once; a just-in-case key that she held on to in case they ever got locked out, or Juno needed to go inside to water a plant while they were on vacation. The pain Juno felt in that moment was unbearable; they *were* her boys. She'd raised them. They'd left Alaska after Kregger's ex-wife, Marnie, overdosed in her apartment in Albuquerque. A neighbor had found the toddlers, both wearing sagging diapers and wandering the corridors of the building. The worst part was, they hadn't even been crying; that's what broke Juno's heart the most. She and Kregger had taken the first flight back to New Mexico with no thoughts of returning to Alaska. They had sons now, and Juno had taken the boys willingly—of course she would raise them, of course she would love them as her own.

The boys had had nothing to do with her mistake; she just hadn't been thinking about them. That's how it always was when it came to mistakes; no one was doing any thinking. During Dale's freshman year of high school, Juno had an affair with his swim coach. She could say all of the regular things about how "it just happened" and how "she wasn't that type of person," but…if you did it, sorry, you were that type of person.

His name was Chad Allan, and the first time he'd walked into Juno's office for therapy it was with his wife, Julianna. They all startled when they recognized each other, and then, somewhat awkwardly, sat down. Juno went by her maiden name professionally, and the Allans had been a referral, so none of them had realized they knew each other until the day of the appointment. They had sons in the same grade; Chad and Julianna's son Michael was not an athlete and drifted toward the arts, separating the boys into two circles.

Juno was shivering. She needed to get up, move to where it was warmer. Hems Corner, she thought. No, the blue room; she could sleep in the blue room right off Nigel's den. When was the last time she'd slept in a bed? She groaned as fresh pain erupted in her stomach. She'd stay here for a little while longer, until she was strong enough, even if the memories were bad.

Chad Allan wasn't the reason her marriage and her motherhood ended, no. He was just at the ugly end. The whole thing had felt like a roller-coaster ride to Juno, one that she realized she didn't want to be on until it was too late. The adrenaline of secrecy paired with an angry woman. And Juno *was* angry—at Kregger. Mostly. Hadn't she put her life and career on hold to raise his sons? She'd done everything right, everything to benefit him—and yet by the time she met Chad, it seemed that Kregger barely looked at her. He looked at everything but her, in fact: the television, the paper, his laptop.

Chad's son had seen them together, walking out of a Motel Six hand in hand as he drove to his part-time job at the art store. Chad's wife, Julianna, filed a civil suit against Juno for sleeping with Chad, her client; and, compounded with the criminal charges brought against her, she didn't stand a chance and neither did her marriage. Good ol' Chad had played victim to save his marriage, the poor, wounded target of a predatory therapist who took her own issues out on her clients. While Chad reconciled with his wife on a trip to Tahiti, Kregger moved into an apartment with the boys. With the house in foreclosure, Juno slept on a friend's couch and waited for her sentencing. Kregger would never forgive her; she knew that. She forgot herself, as people often do. She forgot herself for three months of mediocre sex with a man whose favorite catchphrase was "No soup for you!"

She reached for her water, her throat starting to tickle and her mouth filling with the dust of the crawl space; Juno felt like it was choking her. She was tired enough to sleep again, but her thoughts were keeping her wired. Chad Allan had come for a visit.

All these years later and Juno could still feel his lips on her neck, the little circles his tongue would trace across her pulse and down the steep incline that dipped into her collarbone. He was funny; that's what she liked most about him. He made her laugh and he made her come: win-win. They hadn't loved each other, and they hadn't needed to because it was all for fun. She was in a fever then, crossing the line, wanting more, more, more.

And she was in a fever now, too—literally this time. Throwing off her nest of blankets, she let the air hit her damp skin. She was really sick, she realized. With whatever they'd had up above. The air was sharp, dragging its nails across her skin. Juno had been sick like this twice before: once, in prison, where the women passed around their illnesses like they did their cigarettes in the yard. That had landed her in the med wing for a week with pneumonia. And then once on the street, shortly after she'd moved to Washington, and *that* had made her stint in the prison hospital look like a spa retreat. She'd picked it up at the shelter, no doubt, and a day later, Juno was shivering so hard she could barely catch her breath. She hadn't known where to go, only that she needed to lie in place until whatever it was passed through her body. She'd been thirsty, too, but there was no way her legs would hold her up long enough to find water. She'd walked toward a bench near the water; there was a little park on the hill.

She was dreaming now. Chad was standing in a hotel room in his ridiculous Simpsons boxers, a warm bottle of beer in his hand. He was standing in front of the television, doing a little dance that made Juno laugh. Bart Simpson waved his

middle finger at Juno from the left ass cheek of Chad's boxers. Behind him, on the blue-lit screen of the TV, Juno saw
another of her former clients, Pattie Stoves. Pattie had been
seeing Juno about the guilt she had over having an affair with
the minister of her church, Pastor Paul.

"No, no, no—" Juno said as Pattie, on the TV screen, rode
the minister, her lips opening in pleasure. Chad, who thought
Juno was talking to him, looked momentarily over his shoulder, winking at her. He was a stocky guy, muscular, and for
a moment she watched him twerk as Pattie moaned from behind his torso. Juno was about to tell Chad to put on some
music when she realized a song was already playing: "Summer of '69" by Bryan Adams. Now Juno felt sick, even in her
dream. Her stomach rolled dangerously as Chad shimmied
toward her, his Simpsons underpants tented with his erection.

"Wheeeeeeeee..." Chad cried, bending his knees and
throwing his fists into the air. Juno's eyes switched to the
TV where Pattie Stoves was sitting on her minister's hairy
knee obediently. She was naked and seemed wholly unboth-
ered by it as he reclined behind her.

"Get out of here...get the fuck out of here, you're scaring
the kids."

Juno looked in confusion at the naked woman in the television. She could see the minister's chest behind Pattie, smooth
and muscular, dotted with sweat. He was massaging Pattie's
breast even as she screamed at Juno.

Pattie was really mad now; she stood up, her breasts bouncing sharply in her anger. And then she leaned through the TV,
her torso emerging from the screen like it had been nothing
but a box the whole time. She reached for Juno and grabbed
her by the lapels of her coat.

"You're a waste of life," Pattie snarled into her face. Juno
looked around for help. Where was Chad...? When Juno

looked up again, she was suddenly in Greenlake Park, lying on a bench opposite the playground, Pattie's scream echoing: "You're scaring them!" But Pattie herself was gone; so were Chad and Pastor Paul, and a man was glaring down at her, his hands fisted on the shoulders of her jacket. He was young, and behind him was a little girl in a yellow coat, looking scared.

The man was leaning over her, bearing down. Juno lay on a park bench opposite yellow and blue playground equipment. She read his expression, noted the tight pull of his mouth, and realized he meant to do her harm. Juno tried to shrink back, but he kept leaning down into her face, saying terrible things. Her eyes darted around, looking for help, but none came. Overhead, clouds of charcoal rolled like the sky was about to split. To her right was a playground surrounded by pines so tall they disappeared out of her vision, poking at the gray thunderclouds. Could she use the covered slide as shelter? She'd done it once before, her bottom half curled into the mouth of the yellow tube, the rest of her lying on the metal pedestal that fed children into the slide. It was covered by a plastic roof that resembled the turret of a castle. There was just enough coverage from the trees that passing cops couldn't see her. And then this man—this stranger—shouted her awake. He looked disgustedly at her as he shouted his next words: "Go!"

He released her abruptly, casting a look over his shoulder at the little girl. Juno fell backward, hitting her head on the bench, and then landing on her back on the concrete. She felt the pain burst in her head as she had then; sharp and blinding so that her vision blurred.

"Go!" he shouted again.

"Leave me alone," Juno screamed, thrashing on the concrete. Couldn't he see that she was struggling…that she didn't want to be here any more than he wanted her to be here.

As the first drops of rain fell over the playground, he called her horrible names. But she wasn't those things; she was a woman with nothing and no one, but surely she wasn't just the sum of her mistakes. Must he take her bench, too?

"Cunt," he'd said as he strode quickly away, snatching up his daughter like she was a cardboard prop. The little girl, no older than eight, met Juno's eyes even as she hung over her father's shoulder, bouncing with his steps.

Don't see me like he does, she begged silently with her eyes. The child looked unsure, her little eyebrows drawing together. It happened so quickly Juno had to replay the moment several times in her mind to fully appreciate it. The girl lifted her hand and waved. It could have been that she was steadying herself as her father navigated the playground, lugging her back to the car, but Juno didn't think so. She saw the girl's little palm lift in a bumpy salute before she looked over her shoulder to where her father was carrying her. That little hand hung in Juno's mind as she lay back on the bench gasping for breath. The porcelain palm of that child, accepting her with an innocent concern.

"I'm sorry," Juno said. "I'm not what you think." She wasn't just telling the child with the deep brown eyes: she was telling everyone who was willing to listen: *I'm not what you think. I'm scared, too. I'm sad, too. I want my family, but they don't want me.*

She woke with a start. The child was gone, the angry father was gone, Chad and his Simpsons undies were gone… the crawl space grinned at Juno. Her fever had broken.

She sipped timidly from the can of apple juice and thought of Pattie Stoves. Coy, shy Pattie—who wore Chanel N° 5 because her mother told her men couldn't resist it, and who knew how to line her eyes in just the right way to speak to a pastor. Pattie Stoves, who had been cheating on her husband with the minister of her church. She'd spoken more of their rendezvous than she did of her children. By their third session, Juno had gotten the distinct impression that Pattie didn't want help from a therapist at all; what she really wanted was a girlfriend with whom to share her secrets. It was a bragging thing, her coming into Juno's office and telling her every detail in that hush-hush little voice. Around their third session Juno came right out and asked the million-dollar question Pattie had been skirting around for the last two sessions.

"Are you here, Pattie, because you feel guilty on account of having sex with your minister, or do you feel guilty about cheating on your husband?"

Pattie Stoves had mulled over that one for a few minutes, her gold sandals and gold-painted toenails bopping along with her thoughts.

"The first one," she said sadly. But Juno didn't see any sadness in her eyes. Pattie was enjoying her affair. She described her minister in great detail, drawing a picture of a very fit golden boy who'd been pressured into marriage right out of college, and had nothing but Jesus in common with his wife. Pattie herself was nothing to write home about, but she had the sort of body that could pass for much younger, and Juno noticed that she dressed to emphasize it. After a year of biweekly counseling with Pattie Stoves, Juno felt like she'd been reading a particularly saucy romance novel, one in the taboo genre. One Sunday, when Pattie was visiting family out of state, and Kregger took the boys on a fishing trip, she'd put on a dress and gone to the church—Juno had learned its name from one of her sessions with Pattie. She arrived late and sat in the back pew, holding a Bible she'd stolen from a Motel Six a few years ago. Pattie's minister was exactly as Juno pictured him. She wondered if Pattie was the only parishioner he was having an affair with.

When she'd looked around the church, every female eye

was unblinking as they watched him deliver a sermon on… Juno couldn't even remember what. After that, her obsession had taken a slight turn, veering away from Pattie and her high-schooler tits and toward Pastor Paul Blanchard himself. Pattie told her that Pastor Paul liked to go to Tip Top Donuts on Wednesday mornings to do his devotions and spend time in prayer. Tip Top was at least thirty miles away from the church, closer to Juno's side of town.

Juno figured he'd probably told Pattie that to get some time to himself; affairs tended to be time-consuming. She stopped at the Tip Top on her way to the office one Wednesday morning, forgoing the drive-through to step inside. And there he was, Mr. Pastor Man himself, having coffee with a petite brunette. From then on Juno made it a point to always go inside on Wednesday mornings and was pleased to see that Pastor Paul was always drinking coffee with the same lady friend. It wasn't his wife, either—she'd seen the pastor with his wife at the Sunday service.

She supposed that if anyone were to see them, Pastor Paul would say he was counseling the woman; after all, they met in a public place. And as far as Juno had seen there had never been so much as a pinkie touch between them, and no one even spared them a glance. She'd started thinking that maybe there was nothing going on between them, and then one day she'd waited in her car, waited long enough to see them leave. Instead of getting into his own car, Pastor Paul waited five minutes in front of Tip Top, leaning against the side of the building, his head bent over his phone. Then, with barely a glance around, he crossed the parking lot, hopping over a short hedge, and approached a dark blue minivan. The door opened as Juno imagined the brunette's legs were ready to, and the good pastor would do his work in the back seat of the Honda. Juno waited thirty minutes before driving away.

She had a session with Pattie in an hour and was fascinated to know if her own view of the woman had changed with this new development.

But it hadn't stopped there. The next time had been by accident; Juno was going to the post office when she'd spotted Cayleigh Little through the window, heading for the Food Mart. Cayleigh, who went by Clee, was in her late twenties, one of Juno's weekly patients. Juno avoided run-ins with her patients if she could; it was awkward for everyone involved. But she abandoned her place in line to get a better look.

Peering through the glass and into the street, she followed the woman's progress across the parking lot. Clee Little was single, she lived by herself in the city, and she had no family in the area. She claimed to be a sex addict, often detailing her antics with pride in her voice. For a moment Juno wasn't even sure it was her, but then, she spotted the hot pink key fob she often saw in their sessions. It was dangling from Clee's free hand. Her other hand was attached to a child's, and she had a baby strapped to her chest in a carrier. The whole scene upset Juno, made her leave the post office and walk faster to catch up. Clee was dressed differently, in blue jeans and a T-shirt. Had Juno ever seen her in anything but one of her high-powered work outfits? She was on the sidewalk now, following the mother and her two children through the sliding doors. They headed for the freezer section, Clee with the baby, no older than seven months, attached to her chest. Juno watched, fascinated, as she piled frozen dinners into her cart, calling out for the toddler to slow down as he darted ahead of her. *She could be babysitting*, Juno thought, eyeing the carrier on her chest.

"Mama!" the little boy called, running toward Clee. She'd not seen Juno standing nearby and was cooing to the toddler. Why would she lie and pretend to be single? Claim that she didn't have children when she so clearly had two of them? For some people, the lie was the escape. Or perhaps she really was a sex addict and didn't want Juno to know that she had a family. Clee never found out that Juno followed her around Food Mart. Neither did any of the others. For a while Juno was able to be as invisible as she felt and if anyone ever saw her—which they occasionally did (once at a restaurant)— she'd act like it was purely coincidental. She hadn't needed to follow Chad; no. He'd pursued her from the start. Juno had his number and every other man who started their game with the same line: "I'm not like this, you're the exception."

Fourth degree criminal sexual conduct carried a minimum two-year prison sentence. The law frowned deeply on the abuse of power; for a therapist to have sex with a client was certainly that. And if that's all she'd been charged with, perhaps there would have been something to fight for, but by the time Juno served a four-year sentence (two for the sexual misconduct and two for intentional affliction of emotional distress and sexual harassment by a professional) everyone from her life had moved on. She didn't recognize them any more than they recognized her, those old friends. Her hands had touched things their hands would never touch; her eyes had witnessed things that would make them wet their practical high-waisted panties. Even as Juno scurried away from her former neighborhood, she'd realized that she didn't want to be there anymore anyway. It felt soiled now; a white shirt you could never get the blood stains out of. Could a person change too much to go back? She used to say no, but now she lived the yes.

It was thirty-two degrees outside, according to the news, which Juno watched from Nigel's den, wrapped in a thick fleece throw that smelled of Nigel. Juno knew the smell; she knew all their smells. Nigel smelled reedy, like grass and spices. Winnie didn't have a smell of her own anymore; she coated herself with expensive perfumes and she smelled like a department store. And Sam, well, he smelled salty, like a kid. He left behind the faint scent of baloney.

She stared mindlessly at the TV, her hair still damp from the shower she'd taken. The shower had tired her out. On TV a reporter was standing in grass, wearing a thick puffer jacket. She looked uncomfortable in it, despite the resplendent Christmas tree behind her. Everyone was sick to death of winter, and it was only December. *How long until Groundhog Day?* she thought.

She turned off the TV and stared resolutely at the blank screen. It had become more difficult for her to get up from the crawl space in the last few weeks, the pain in her joints flaring beyond the help of the aspirin from the Crouches' medicine cabinet. She wished there was still a stash of oxy in there, but that was gone now, thanks to Sam.

Most days she chose instead to lay curled in the nest she'd made with the foam mattress she'd snuck from the camping supplies. She'd taken blankets and a sleeping bag, too, from the linen closet upstairs, and once Winnie donated a garbage bag of old throws, as she called them, which Juno ferried down the hole before Nigel could cart it away. No one ever noticed her thefts, though Juno supposed they weren't really thefts, since everything was technically still in the house, and it was stuff they were getting rid of anyway. Winnie and Nigel were too busy with their own shenanigans to notice hers.

She'd amassed a small wardrobe of discarded sweatshirts and sweatpants from the giveaway bags, things she washed weekly in the Crouches' laundry room. When the weather got very cold, and the ground in the crawl space turned icy, Juno would crawl up at night and sleep in her old digs underneath the snowsuits and Halloween costumes in Hems

Corner. That was a treat. On those days, she stayed upstairs for most of the day, collecting supplies and standing near a window for a few minutes to soak up some of the sun (if it showed itself). She washed her clothes and blankets, took a bath, ate a warm meal, and watched the news. By that time Juno was nearly asleep on her feet. When she lowered herself back to her crawl space after a day at the Crouches, she was tiiiired. *Or maybe it's your kidneys that are tired,* she told herself. But as dandy as her growing nest and wardrobe were becoming, nothing compared to the bliss of sleeping in the apartment during this glorious week without the Crouches.

She could hear the faint rumble of the dryer from where she sat, trying to read but too distracted.

She took the clothes out, warm and smelling of the dryer sheets, and folded each one into the grocery bag she was borrowing from Winnie. She knew the vacation was temporary, and soon she'd head back to the crawl space. But if Juno were honest, she was able to spend multiple days in the crawl space in moderate comfort: changing out her clothes, sleeping without worrying about people messing with her or cops chasing her off. Cops young enough to be her son, boys who had little to no respect for people her age, never mind homeless people her age. No, she preferred it down here under the Crouch house, suffering in peace. She had a fleet of apple juice and water jugs now: three for waste, two for water, one for trash. She kept those in what she considered her toilet area—the farthest corner of the crawl space. Juno considered her crawl over to be exercise, which she got very little of these days. She figured it wouldn't matter for long; her kidneys burned like coals in her body, hot and sweating under the pressure of too many work hours and poor work conditions.

"Sorry, ladies..." She used one hand to reach back to massage a kidney and the other to slam the dryer closed. Juno's things were packed and ready to go. She carried the bundle to the closet and lowered everything into the crawl space, the smells of dirt and ammonia sweeping around her in a gust of dead air. She was used to it, though Juno had no doubt she was now sharing her lungs with mold spores.

Standing up, she looked down with satisfaction at the things she'd managed to get done this morning: laundry, a shower, TV time, and she'd even got a little exercise in. The last thing she needed to do was eat.

The walk to the fridge was a long one; Juno never knew if there would be food to take. Glory hallelujah, someone had gone to the market, and if Juno could bet money on it, she'd say that the someone was Nigel. Leftovers were vegetarian meat loaf and real mashed potatoes. By the time they got back the food would go straight to the trash anyway. Juno ate it cold, straight from the tub. Then she washed and dried the Tupperware, putting it into the drawer with its fellows.

Outside it was raining; the grass was a spunky neon. The blue-gray clouds drooped like bellies over Seattle. Despite the clouds, there were spears of light breaking through, hitting the lawn and sidewalks and street beyond with the type of light you'd see in a Thomas Kinkade painting. Two memories surfaced uncomfortably in her mind. She looked away despite the beauty of the scene in front of her; in fact, *because* of the beauty of it. Juno the therapist had loved grass, a rarity in New Mexico. It had become a fascination in Washington to Juno the newly homeless. There was always grass, deep-watered, green and soft. When she slept in the park, she'd kept Kregger's Swiss Army knife by her side, though the thought of trying to stab someone with the tiny blade held in her swollen, arthritic hands was laughable. It made her feel better to have it there, nevertheless. She hadn't known where else to go, and there were always people chasing you away. The park had been the only welcoming place for Juno, so she stayed through summer and into fall. But Washington changed come fall, the never-ending drizzle coating the ground she slept on and leaving the grass wet. She remembered the damp seeping through her clothes night after night as she tried to get warm. She was never dry for those months and she'd become deathly ill, her fever spiking so high she'd been delirious. Some good Samaritan—a jogger who'd seen her in the same spot the day before—had called the ambulance. After that, she'd had the blue tent for a while.

Juno knew about Skinner and his rats, had studied his methods in school, so her aversion to wet grass was just a fact. It was how humans worked, picking up pieces of their experiences and choosing to fall either to the pain or triumph. If anything, Juno was just sad it had to be that way, that she associated terrible things with something she once loved. She suddenly felt hot all over as she had that day, before she slipped into that fevered sleep. The last thing she'd seen before her eyes had sealed shut was a blade of grass, so lush and bright she'd focused on it with all her might, her teeth clacking together. There were a hundred drops of the finest rain clinging to that one blade of grass. It was sharp around the edges, like the blades of her old carving knife. Juno had looked closer and seen that there were tiny writhing hairs, reaching their little arms toward her grotesquely. *You're not really seeing what you're seeing*, she'd thought. *You're sick, not stupid.* And then she'd blinked a few times, her vision clearing. She'd had to remind herself to see things from the right perspective. It was just too much thought about grass, and when Juno woke up in the hospital, she found she hated it, simple as that. There was no grass in the crawl space, though, just dirt, dirt, dirt.

Enough is enough, she told herself. *Get your chores done and crawl back into your hovel.*

Or maybe that can wait, Juno thought as she spotted the family computer sitting dormant on the desk. It was the grass that made her want to do it, remembering how she'd blinked a few times, gained perspective and had seen the right thing: an inch-long blade of grass with two little drops of water balancing on its tip; something simple that her feverish brain had made ugly. *You're doing the same thing with Winnie that you did with that grass. You're making her the enemy.*

Yes, that was what she was doing. But still. She couldn't leave without checking Winnie's search history. Maybe that would give her some answers.

Juno scanned over the last few days of internet search history. Just a lot of normal shit like vegan recipes and celebrity gossip…and there it was. On Thursday night, Winnie had searched for a Josalyn Russel at 11:30 p.m.—hours after she usually went to bed. What she'd seen in the envelope must have left such a sour impression on Winnie's mind that she'd lain awake for two hours before finally going to her computer. That's what Juno imagined, anyway.

So there it was: Winnie had received Juno's envelope in the mail, and then, when Nigel was in bed, had searched for this woman on the internet. She clicked on the link, the last website Winnie visited, and it took her to the article that Winnie had been reading.

Juno rubbed a square of her shirt between her thumb and index finger as her eyes scanned the article. She was braced for something, but she wasn't sure what. She had always prided herself on excellent gut intuition. What she felt about people was usually right, and from the moment she'd moved in, she'd had a feeling. She read through the article twice, making sure she didn't miss anything.

The article was about Tent City. Juno's eyes stretched to their full capacity. She'd spent some—but not a lot—of time in Nickelsville, Seattle's portable, self-managed tent community. Intended as a temporary answer to the lack of bed space in shelters, they got by. Their purple tents were donated by the First Methodist Church of Seattle, and a rotating security guard kept loose order. She'd been there a few weeks when a rogue band of meth-heads staged a coup and took control. In the words of her mother and Ray Charles: hit the road, Jack. She did, but her options were either finding a bench, or joining those who set up camp in wooded areas along I-5. Juno chose the latter. But why would Winnie be interested in a homeless camp?

Juno devoured the article, looking for something that could possibly be of interest to Winnie. Thousands of teenage runaways go missing every year, the article said, their families never hearing from them again.

And then Juno found it: a quote from Winnie Crouch, an employee at Illuminations for Mental Health at the time.

"There are women in these camps, very young women like you and me who are living hand to mouth, with no sanitation or access to medical help. In fact, one of the young women I work with was pregnant and living in a tent when she disappeared."

22

WINNIE

S he lay in bed, listening to the sound of the crickets in Greenlake Park, drifting toward sleep. The trip to the cabin had been as horrible as she had anticipated—worse even. She couldn't wait to get home. But now here she was, back in her own bed, feeling just as horrible as she had then.

Someone was working against Winnie. At first she thought she was being paranoid, which was her MO anyway—poor, paranoid Winnie. But there was no way to explain the notepad, or the library book, or the envelope that had come in the mail with those clippings inside it. Deep down, she knew she'd told Nigel only half the story, established a firm villain all those years ago—Josalyn Russel.

Josalyn Russel hadn't left her home and family because she

was a drug addict; she'd become one as a result of what they'd done to her. Josalyn had run away from home three months shy of her eighteenth birthday. She stayed under the radar for those three months, and then, when she turned eighteen, came forward to access social services. She was bipolar and in need of medication. When Winnie was assigned her case, Josalyn had been a wisp of a girl, no more than a hundred pounds. She kept earbuds in her ears at all times, her message clear: she was not offering conversation. Winnie didn't push her, she never pushed them. She was there to be an advocate for Josalyn in a world that didn't understand her. On her arms were delicate tattle-tale scars of years of self-harm. She was a runaway: defiant, nonverbal, and had severe trust issues. She liked junk food—Funyuns and drinks that were blue. Winnie paved an avenue for trust with snacks.

Josalyn began talking a little. First, it was about home— her parents divorced, and her mother remarried a younger man. Then one day, she told Winnie her stepfather had molested her. "His friends, too," she'd told her, looking at the floor. "He passed me around, and when I cried, he acted like it had been my idea."

Josalyn wanted to stay under the radar; Winnie saw genuine fear in her eyes when she spoke about her stepfather. Her family had money—a lot of it, she claimed—and they used it to get what they wanted. Winnie now understood the rainbow curtain of hair she wore around her face; she retreated behind it when she needed space. So Winnie bought her more hair dye—pink and green and blue—and they developed a mentorship. Winnie was fond of the girl, protective. She'd seen what the world did to women like Josalyn and was afraid for her.

And then Josalyn became pregnant. She said she didn't know who the father was, and by then, she was spending the night in a tent and paying for her drugs with sex.

She hardly ever came to group, and she only met with Winnie when she needed something. Winnie tried to appeal to Josalyn on behalf of the baby, offering her programs, help, detox, but she'd wanted to keep her baby.

"It's mine. I'm keeping it," she'd said.

"Josalyn, you live in a tent. A tent isn't a home for a baby. Social Services will get involved. They'll take the baby from you."

"No," Josalyn said flatly. Her eyes were dull like she was checking out. Winnie softened her voice.

"Your family, Josalyn. We can contact someone in your family—they can help."

That's when Josalyn's demeanor changed, terror rising in her eyes instead of tears.

"No," she said firmly. "Never ever. It's better to live in a tent than with them."

When Winnie tried harder to make her see that she wouldn't be able to keep her baby, Josalyn had run. Winnie tried to find her, going as far as Tacoma, asking shelters about a pregnant, homeless woman with multicolored hair. No one had seen Josalyn, and Winnie's guilt took on a new corridor in her life.

Winnie rubbed her eyes. She needed to sleep; she couldn't think clearly anymore. She tossed and turned in her bed. How could anyone know about that night? What she'd done. She had been alone with Josalyn in that tent.

The call had come in the middle of the night and she'd slept through it, since she silenced her phone after 8:00 p.m. She'd woken up to use the bathroom and there was the missed call, lighting up her screen. Winnie had carried the phone into the bathroom and hit play on the voice mail as she peed. Josalyn's voice came through, shaky, her words as discombobulated as the noises behind her.

"I had the baby. It's not good, I'm not good. You said you'd help. I'm living in a tent near the overpass in Ravenna. Please..." And then the line had gone dead. Winnie called the number back right away, still sitting on the toilet, but it just rang and rang.

What she remembered vividly were the conditions she'd found them in: the piles of trash, the smell of sick and shit so overpowering Winnie had taken two giant steps back, into the fresh air, and promptly thrown up. When she'd composed herself, washing her mouth with the bottled water she'd put into her bag, she stepped back into Josalyn's tent. In her attempt to keep the baby warm, Josalyn had made a nest for him out of blankets, wedging him between her own body and that of her dog, who stared at Winnie balefully, unmoving.

Josalyn's face was pale, almost greenish along her eyes and jaw. She lay very still next to the bundle, a threadbare towel draped over her body. The smell of death was so present that Winnie's eyes had immediately gone to the baby and stayed there.

The child was her priority; the child had not asked to be put in this dire situation. She had to get him to safety first. She could reach him if she crawled around Josalyn; and so without thinking, Winnie dropped to her knees and crawled over the human and animal waste, the heel of her hand landing in dried vomit. The dog whined from where he lay, one drooping eye watching Winnie.

She closed her eyes, focusing on everything she was feeling on the inside: her desperate need to reach the child, the urgency, the adrenaline that was pounding past her hesitancy. What she was seeing and touching and smelling wasn't important; the baby was important. When her hand reached to touch the pale cheek of the baby, he stirred, and Winnie felt a mass of joy, thick and sustaining. Alive!

He was tiny, his weight no more than five pounds. Gently unwrapping him from the blankets Josalyn had used, Winnie lifted him from the cocoon and saw that he was wearing an Elmo onesie that was a size too large—relatively clean aside from his bulging diaper. Winnie eased him feetfirst into her jacket until he was pressed against her chest, splayed out like a little turtle. It would have to do until she could get him somewhere warm. Winnie zipped it up around him, leaving enough room for air to get inside. For the first time in her life, she was grateful that she didn't have huge breasts, which would have been suffocating to this small creature. Still on her hands and knees, she bent her head to peer inside her jacket where the baby lay, curled as if in a hammock; he was breathing, but not deeply. She crawled back out into the twilight, away from the smell and the filth, gulping in the sharp winter air.

It was bitterly cold; she had to get him to her car, and quickly, but it was parked up the steep embankment and nearly a mile away. Her only option was to scale the frost-slicked grass on her hands and knees. Winnie crawled; she was terrified of slipping. Keeping one hand firmly on the bundle against her chest, she picked her way to the top, never once looking down at Josalyn's tent, which hung in the mist below her, never once thinking about her. When she reached the top, she straddled the metal railing and swung her legs over the side, landing squarely on the asphalt. And then Winnie took off, racing for her crisp white BMW, which still smelled of new car. She was parked along a skiff of grass between a cluster of houses. She could see them up ahead as her breath chuffed out in bursts of white. She wasn't thinking about anything but the baby when she climbed into the front seat and jerkily pulled the SUV out of the grass.

If she'd just called an ambulance right away.

She'd meant to—as soon as she got the baby safely to the car. But that's where everything had gone wrong, so wrong...

23

JUNO

Juno broke the cable box. That was her big plan. She un-plugged the whole thing and then, lifting it above her head, threw it at the carpeted floor in Nigel's den. Once lightly...twice...she heard something rattle loose the third time. Then she put everything back the way she found it and waited. Nigel holed up in his den, watching an endless stream of CNN and ESPN for his mindless entertainment. To fuck with his cable box was to fuck with his precarious mental stability. But that's what Juno wanted—everyone unstable, so she could get some answers.

Nigel spent two days arguing with the cable company over the phone. Juno, who risked a night in Hem's Corner to hear everything, for once appreciated his loud anger. No, he would not be paying for a replacement…no, it was their faulty box, not his inability to handle it… Yes, he needed someone to come out, hadn't he been saying that all along? The soonest was when! No, that wasn't acceptable, there was a game he wanted to watch this weekend and he would not be put out by their incompetence…if that's all they had…Thursday. "And can you give me a window, so I know when to be home?"

"That's an eight-hour window!" She could almost hear the defeat in his voice. "Fine. Yes… I'll leave the alarm off for the day and the back door unlocked. If your guy can give me notice when he gets here and leaves so I can come and lock up. Is it in the notes? Put it in the notes."

On Thursday morning, Juno was waiting in the closet by what she guessed was 5:00 a.m. She'd had a carton of chocolate milk to drink and a few oyster crackers before she came up, and the sugar was making her feel squirmy. Squirmy was better than limp, she thought. She was wearing a gray Seahawks hoodie with the hood pulled up and a pair of Nigel's giveaway jeans, belted with twine Juno had found in Winnie's craft drawer. Nigel always left earlier than Winnie, usually heading out the door by six, and she wanted to be ready. On her feet were the same sneakers she'd worn the day she moved in—since they'd brought her here in the first place, she wore them for luck.

Nigel's steady, methodical footsteps echoed above Juno's head. She crouched beneath the coats and costumes, breathing through her nose and smelling the faint aroma of urine. A cough stirred at the back of her throat, and she tried to swallow it down before it became a thing. That was one of her biggest fears—discovery by coughing. Her thighs burned, muscles she hadn't used in weeks being forced to hold her weight, however slight she was. His boots were on the stairs now; soon he'd put off the alarm and open the closet to grab his bag. Juno heard him clear his throat, then the faint beeping of buttons as he tapped in the code, disarming the alarm. The code was Sam's original due date: 0602. She'd once overheard Winnie reminding Dakota of it. The door opened and closed, and Nigel was gone. He hadn't taken his gym bag today, and she stared at it hard before crawling over. She checked the zippers first, then the inside. There was a five stuck in the inside pocket; she smoothed it out on her knee and kept looking. She pushed past a change of clothes and a small bottle of cologne. At the bottom of the bag was an Altoids tin that didn't rattle with mints when she nudged past it. Juno brought it out and flipped open the lid. She didn't have time for this; Sam would be waking up any moment.

Her mouth went dry as she stared down at a credit card, a wad of twenties that looked like it amounted to about five hundred dollars, and a single, foil-wrapped condom. She unwrapped a twenty from the wad and shoved it into her pocket with the five. What she did next didn't surprise her as much as it amused her. Juno crawled back to the hot dog costume, the one she liked to hold against her face. She'd had a big surprise one day when the tip of a safety pin had jabbed her in the cheek. She'd reattached it to the hot dog, the sharp pin tucked away. Now she retrieved the pin with only minutes to spare; Sam was in the bathroom. With the aspirin coating her pain, Juno was actually pretty fast. She liked the way it felt to stick the sharp end of the safety pin past the foil and into the rubbery onionskin beneath it. She pushed the pin all the way through. Then she put everything back the way she found it; that was the trick. Juno was out the front door before Sam had even flushed the toilet. She had an eight-hour window.

At three-thirty, she carried a bag of cereal she bought at the Dollar Tree to a bench by the water. Pulling open the plastic, she sprinkled a handful across the dirt and in two seconds she was surrounded by the blue-barred chests of a dozen pigeons. They pecked away, stoic, their amber eyes casting Juno sidelong glances. She didn't prefer these little rats with wings, but they were always the first to come.

"There are usually three turtles over here."

Juno jumped, almost dropping the bag. The sun was out—a rare moment—and it was shining directly into her eyes, temporarily blinding her. But she knew that voice, she knew it well.

Samuel was standing close to the water, right where the dirt dipped into the lake at a sharp angle. He was wearing a green hoodie and a ratty pair of jeans, and a backpack much like Nigel's was slung over his shoulder. He wasn't looking at her; his eyes were focused on the lily pads a few feet beyond the mud. Juno knew that's where the turtles usually rested, craving sun like the rest of the folks in Washington.

"Yes. They were out earlier."

"I'm offended that they didn't wait for me."

She glanced over at him and saw that he was joking, so she offered a smile back. Juno sprinkled the last of the Fiber One on the ground for the birds and dusted her hands.

"What are you giving them?"

"Old cereal gone stale."

He took a step forward, examining the ground as the birds jackrabbited around his shoes; Vans, Juno knew. Her sons used to wear them. Sam toed one of the little pieces until a crow stole it away, hopping out of reach.

"It looks like hamster pellets. No wonder you didn't eat it."

Juno laughed. "Yeah, it was pretty bad. Fiber stuff."

"Breakfast should be fun. If you have a bad breakfast, you have a bad day."

"You sound like a commercial!" Juno exclaimed. "What cereal are you trying to sell me?"

"Froot Loops, definitely." He grinned, enjoying the joke. And then, "Hey, you're wearing a Landman shirt! I used to have one just like that."

"I got it at Goodwill." She shrugged. "I thought it was a green bean."

Sam found this hilarious. He laughed hard enough to make Juno smile, too.

"It was probably mine," he joked. "My mom gives all my stuff away."

"Well, if it was," Juno said, "it would be tiny on you now." She thought wanly of the giveaway bags.

Sam shrugged, his smile lingering.

"He's from a video game. Landman can morph from a man into anything that grows out of the earth. So basically, he has to defeat his enemies, the Gorgs and Spawns, by trapping them in, like, volcanos and rivers."

Juno listened raptly, nodding when he made references he clearly expected her to know. She imagined his parents' eyes glazed like doughnuts as they half listened to everything he said, nodding and *mmm*ing dutifully until it was time to talk about them. Kids needed to talk; they needed to empty themselves of their experiences so they could process them properly. And, more importantly, they needed to have someone who wanted to listen and who could gently guide. That's what Juno did. She listened.

Sam, finished discussing his video games, slid his arms through the straps of his backpack until it was hanging on his front. He wore a plastic bracelet on his wrist, the stretchy kind that had a little motto on it. A little dog on one of those retractable leashes skittered into the clearing, sniffing at Sam's sneakers before darting off at the sound of "Klipper!" Sam

212

bent down to pet Klipper, but it was too late, his little hind legs were working hard to get back to his owner.

"Anyway, my uncle broke my system and I couldn't play anymore."

Juno's ears pricked to attention. Could be talking about Dakota? It hadn't happened during Datoka's last stay; Juno knew that for sure.

"How did your uncle break your game?" she asked.

"He's an alcoholic." *So matter-of-fact about it, too,* Juno thought. She studied him with the eyes of her old profession.

Sam was a small kid, scrappy-looking, with bandy, muscular arms and a boxer's set to his chin. She'd never heard him complain to his parents about the kids at school bothering him, but that didn't mean anything. Some kids shared that stuff and others bottled it up. *Who are you, kid...the bully...or the bystander?* Juno watched as he cocked his head and then, almost as suddenly, his eyes returned to the water. He watched a couple of teenagers in a kayak with interest for a few seconds before turning back to her. He regarded her like he was seeing her for the first time, and Juno began to sweat beneath the Landman sweatshirt. She searched his face, though for what, she didn't fully know; a little bit of Winnie or Nigel, maybe. But in this moment, she couldn't see a trace. With a quick dart of his hand, his phone materialized from his pocket, and he checked the screen.

"Want a puppy dog? That's what my dad calls a hot dog." He kicked the toe of his trainer into the dirt, but then squinted at her. "I always bring money on Thursdays so I can get two before I go home, but we had a class party with pizza today so I'm still pretty full. I have to eat this stuff out here where my mom can't see." He grinned.

"Health nut?" Juno knew that Winnie was more akin to control nut than health nut, but Sam nodded. The kid wasn't allowed sugar, processed carbohydrates, soda, meat, or pizza unless it was a special occasion. As much as Winnie tried to control what he ate, Samuel worked equally hard to assert rights over his own choices by disobeying her. It would be an ongoing battle until someone yielded, and by the looks of the scrappy little boy in front of her, Winnie was in for a long, hard fight.

Before she could give him an answer, he was running toward the kiosk. Juno had ordered from it many times before; it was just a little metal-roofed shack that sold cold beverages and turned hot dogs slowly for hours on a greasy machine.

"You're fast," she said, when he came back a few minutes later carrying two paper boats, one in each hand. His backpack, sticking out like a turtle shell in front of him, had a stray blob of mustard on it. Juno took the meal without looking at Sam. When she raised her eyes to his face, he was already eating and staring at the lake where the teenagers had been floating earlier. The birds, which had forsaken their foraging for Juno's cereal, were starting to peck at Sam's feet for new crumbs. He consumed his food so quickly, never taking his eyes from the water, she was unsure how he could have tasted it.

She finally remembered her manners. "Thank you, Samuel."

He turned the full beam of his smile on her. And then just as suddenly it fell away. "Please, call me Sam," he said. "I hate my full name."

Juno would admit that she was out of touch with young people, but she was fairly certain most of them didn't sound like young British aristocrats when they spoke.

"Okay. Sam," Juno said slowly. "I like that better, as well."

He grinned at her. Then, "So you're still homeless?"

"Yeah," Juno said. "I am."

She watched as he kicked his legs against the brick wall, and then, all of a sudden, he spun around and sat down next to her. Juno found this almost childlike in its innocence. Most people moved away from the homeless, not toward.

"How come?"

"Life happened. It doesn't always happen the way you want."

He seemed to mull over this for a while before nodding. "Why'd you come to Seattle?"

"How do you know I'm not from Seattle?"

"I guess I don't. But most of the people I know aren't from here."

"Well, you're right," Juno said. *And that's interesting*, she added to herself.

"I'm from New Mexico," she said. "I used to be tan all the time, now..." She looked up to the sky where the clouds had obscured the sun again. Sam laughed.

"What was your job, before?"

"You make a lot of assumptions, Sam."

"That's what my dad says." Sam was unabashed, almost like he'd taken this as a compliment. "He says that making assumptions makes an ass out of everyone involved."

"That right?" Juno couldn't take her eyes off him. She'd heard Nigel say those very words in that very tone to the boy, but here she was, seeing how he interpreted them.

"I was a therapist once, a very long time ago." Juno paused to gauge Sam's reaction. She had his attention, his murky eyes fixed on her face. This kid ticked in a different way; she just couldn't tell how yet. She waited for him to ask the question she could tell was perched on his tongue.

"Why did you stop?"

"You never stop being a therapist."

He thought for a minute, sucking his cheeks in like a fish,

and then reworded his question. "What was your last day at work like?"

Juno felt jarred; he'd thrown her off again. In the end, she couldn't lie to him; there was something about him that told her he'd see right through it anyway. She'd always noticed that about him during their lakeside conversations. And really, what difference did it make? Sam knew exactly what Juno was, and yet he didn't seem to care.

"It was sad. I didn't want it to be my last day, but sometimes there's no way around these things."

Sam considered this, his forehead furrowed. "You felt out of control."

"Yes, Sam, I did," Juno said slowly. "Unfortunately, we aren't the only ones in control of our story arcs. Outsiders have an influence, too."

"But we let the outsiders have an influence."

"Yes and no. When you're an adult you can control who you allow into your life, but you can't control how they'll behave once they're there."

"Kids don't get that choice."

Sam didn't say this bitterly; rather, he was matter-of-fact, which hurt Juno's heart. He was so tender in this moment, so vulnerable. It was hard to learn your place in the world when so many people told you different things. She'd confused the hell out of her own kids, God forgive her. In youth, people were plenty stupid—mostly because they thought they were so smart.

"Hey, regarding our conversation earlier... I have a little something for you," she said, reaching into the paper bag at her feet. She grunted a little as she bent over, but Sam didn't seem to notice; his eyes were glued to the bag, curiosity on his face. Fighting her uncertainty, Juno pulled out the box of Froot Loops and presented it to him. It was a stupid gift, she was almost embarrassed—except Sam's face lit up as soon as he saw it.

"Wow. Now that's ironic! We were just talking about Froot Loops."

Juno laughed at this. It wasn't ironic, nor was it a coincidence. But she wasn't about to confess that she knew Sam loved Froot Loops. How could she explain why she knew that about him?

"Hey, I've gotta go." He looked over his shoulder in the direction of the house. Winnie would be getting home; she could tell that Sam was calculating how long it would take him to get around the lake and if he could beat his mother there. He had a dusting of cinnamon freckles across his nose that made Juno's heart ache in a way it hadn't in a long time. Marcus, her oldest, had freckles. It had been so many years since she'd seen him, and she had no idea if those freckles still appeared in the spring like the cherry blossoms had. Sam reached for the Froot Loops. Juno watched in amusement as he dropped to a knee and opened his backpack.

"Thanks for the snack, Juno!"

Juno thrilled. He was such a good boy.

She wanted to make the right decision. Sam did not belong to Winnie and Nigel; they'd taken him from a woman named Josalyn Russel. Her story was tragic: a runaway, young and afraid, got pregnant. She must have been terrified. But that meant Sam had a biological family somewhere: aunts and uncles and cousins, maybe even grandparents. Juno would never have the chance to be a grandmother to her grandchildren, and that cut at her heart. What these people had done was unthinkable.

In that moment, she made her decision: she would find these people, the Russels. She needed to see what type of people they were.

Running into Sam had thrown off the timing of her plan, so she spent the night on the west side of the park, too afraid to sleep, but tired all the way down to her joints. It was warm-ish outside, and from her bench she could see the Turlin Street house and that gave her some comfort. She considered taking something for her pain—the pills in her bag—but Juno pre-ferred being alert in the park at night. As if emerging from some horror movie, an old drunk stumbled by. Juno knew him from the area; Vic, they called him. Angry guy, from what she recalled. She'd always steered clear. Some of them knew you were there and didn't care to acknowledge it, but other guys—like Vic—they wanted to get right up in your face, make you uncomfortable. People were the same every-where you went: the suburbs, prison, the gutters of Seattle: everyone was afraid of their own existence. Afraid they were getting it wrong…afraid of what would come after as a con-sequence. And in Juno's opinion, that made people act like irrational assholes.

A dozen yards away, Vic tossed something into the lake. Juno thought she heard him yell "Fuck you, Howie!" *What does it take to get some peace and quiet around here?* she thought. There was one more anguished hail of "Howieee!" He set-tled down after that, probably to squirt something into his veins. Juno relaxed a little, fingering the pill in her pocket. She could think in peace. She had a view of Winnie and Nigel's bedroom—*and Sam's*, she thought, her eyes drifting to the window that belonged to the boy's room.

For Juno, there was the matter of getting back into the house the next morning without triggering the alarm. Her plan was to go through the kitchen door with the key she'd borrowed from the ring of spares. She'd have to time it just right, so that she'd be walking in the back of the house while Sam was leaving through the front. She had a three-minute window to get inside without triggering the alarm. Everything had to be timed just so.

Just so what? she thought. *You get back to your little hovel in the ground where you live like a mole.* It was almost spring, she could return to the park, walk away from the Crouch house. It had done its job; sheltered her through winter. Juno was certain she would have died if not for the crawl space. And she wasn't well—far from it.

But she'd chosen the wrong family to follow, a family with deep, dark secrets. *No,* she chided herself. There was no wrong in doing right. Juno, who'd never believed that there was a reason for everything, had never blamed God for the things that had happened to her—knew that people made their own fate. She was a walking testament to that. But Sam didn't belong in this mess. On top of that, Juno knew that the Crouches' marriage was falling apart. Where would Sam go if they got divorced? What would his life be like? He was entitled to a different life, one with his real family. The clock was ticking, and Juno wanted to make sure Sam was okay. Sam was her priority. Sam was caught up in all of this because they'd stolen him. She'd read the police report, seen the little swatches of blood. A baby had been taken. Like hers had been taken from her. And she'd had no rights, no legal standing to see them. Kregger had erased her from their lives.

Juno's body rocked with a different type of pain. She moaned softly, a purring sound in the back of her throat. *Her boys, her boys, her boys.* Dale and Marcus. One was the athlete, one was the student. She'd raised them. When Kregger was working long hours in the casino, she'd raised them. Two little boys and nothing but their stepmother. Good thing she'd been equipped. Juno had loved the boys enough to put her doctorate on hold, to be a mother instead of a student. She'd never once resented Kregger for expecting her to raise his young sons; she'd wanted to raise them. And he'd taken them from her. Like Winnie had taken Sam.

Vic let out a cry of pain from the brush. Distracted, she didn't notice the truck that circled past the house twice, nor did she pay attention to the way it idled on the corner of Aurora and Turlin, the driver tossing a cigarette butt onto Winnie's immaculate grass.

24

WINNIE

Winnie paused in the doorway of her bedroom, eyes flicking across the room; everything was as it should be. In here, at least, she thought. Maybe it was the stress of life that was getting to her. Yes, that had to be it. After all, hadn't these thoughts been toying with her mind for years, hounding her relentlessly? Her subconscious was probably clogged up with fear, and it was clearly manifesting in her life. She was still embarrassed about the shadowy thing she'd convinced herself she'd seen in their bedroom window. Maybe she needed more time in therapy. That season of her life was over, that part of herself buried so deeply Winnie had created a new person, a better one, to replace the last. She breathed deeply, coercing her mind into emptying itself of the negative. Everything was going to be all right...everything was going to be all right...

When Winnie went downstairs the next morning in her robe, Samuel was already in the kitchen, sitting at the table with his phone and a bowl of cereal. He was a sight, his hair flattened on one side and poking up on the other. He looked like the little boy she missed, the one who ran to her, eager for hugs and kisses. But she knew all too well that there was a simmering adolescent where her little boy used to be. And he didn't want his mother's affection.

As she breezed past him on her way to the sink, feigning indifference, she saw the rainbow Os floating in milk and bit her tongue. He knew he wasn't allowed to have sugar. But she kept her trap shut about it, to avoid an argument. It was Saturday, and she wanted to make the most of the weekend.

Winnie opened the fridge. "Want to take a walk around the lake after lunch?" Her hand tightened on the handle as she waited for his possible rejection.

Samuel looked up from his phone, unaware that his mother was holding her breath. He shrugged and followed with a weak, "Sure."

Winnie was relieved. Small victories. That was what her therapist had wanted her to focus on, small victories—not the giant, looming issues that chewed incessantly at her mind. She hid her smile and nonchalantly made her French-press coffee.

But all too soon, he left the kitchen. She cleaned up his empty bowl and the splashes of milk on the counter, wiping aimlessly until the kitchen was spotless. She felt disarmed by Samuel per usual; given favor one minute and having it taken the next. Being a mother was by far the hardest job Winnie had ever taken on, and she had roughly five years left before Samuel went to college.

Nigel often made fun of her for referring to parenting as a contract, but it was. The most unbreakable contract, excruciatingly unrewarding…and yet…it was the thing that most drove her in life, the thing that she simultaneously hated and loved at the same time. *No—that's wrong*, thought Winnie. She didn't hate being a mother, she hated parenting—being the enforcer, the teacher, and most often, the bad guy. Today was her day to be the good guy, to remind her son of the un-breakable bond they shared. She intended to make the most of these last years of his youth; it felt like Samuel was slipping fast from her grasp. He was solemn and slow to laugh, and he regarded both her and Nigel with suspicion. Winnie couldn't make sense of it. Lately she'd been thinking that perhaps they'd spoiled him. That was a thing with only children; she knew this because Nigel was one. There was an entitlement etched quietly into their minds, a sense that things needed to go their way. They had no one to contend with but doting parents—no siblings to scream in their face, no hair-pulling, kicking, or having to share. The world was their oyster. And on that rare occasion when things didn't go their way—well, that was when they sulked. These were all the things she told herself were going on with her son. The alternative…well, that she didn't want to think about.

What does Samuel know?

Winnie placed the washed and dried cereal bowl back into the cabinet harder than she intended. The mugs rattled as she slammed the door closed. It was then she stopped dead in her tracks, spotting the empty Froot Loops container propping open the lid of the recycling bin. Where had he got the Froot Loops from? Winnie had been so distracted by her thoughts that she hadn't asked herself this until now. There was no way Nigel would buy them for him after the last fight they had about it, and Winnie certainly hadn't. Unless Samuel bought them for himself. Was that possible? Winnie rode him so much about what he ate, maybe he was purchasing food on his own dime. Sometimes he was home alone after school before one of them got to him, though it had never been for longer than thirty minutes. Would that be enough time for him to walk to the Safeway and back? She put the box on top of the bin, took a photo of it, and sent it to Nigel. His message came back right away.

Where did he get those?

Winnie was relieved by his response.

I don't know??? She texted back. Nigel sent back an emoji scratching its head. Winnie set her phone down. She stared toward the stairs, wondering if she should say anything at all; it was just cereal. Maybe he got it from one of his friends—that seemed more likely—Subomi or Angelo. But Winnie knew both of their mothers, and they were of the Kashi, antigluten variety. *It's just cereal*, she told herself firmly before heading upstairs. But why did it have to be *that* cereal?

Their walk around the lake after lunch was unsurprisingly awful. Winnie tried to lure Samuel into conversation but was met with the cold indifference that he seemed to specialize in lately.

In her heyday she'd been the most popular person in any room, and that confidence, still ingrained in her personality, took a blow every time her son rejected her. When Samuel walked ahead to distance himself from her, she gave up, pulling her phone from her pocket. Manda had tried to call and then had resorted to texting. She kept half an eye on Samuel as she read the texts, her mood plummeting. Nigel had been right in his prediction: Manda was refusing to let Dakota back, her newfound spine made of steel.

As she was getting ready to text back, her phone rang, Manda's name popping up on the screen.

"Hey, I was just texting you back," Winnie said. She watched Samuel bend down to pet a fat bulldog up ahead.

"He's making threats." Dakota's normally timid wife sounded angry. "He's saying that someone is putting these thoughts in my head because he's never known me to be an unforgiving person. Can you believe the actual level of gaslighting he's using?"

She could tell that her sister-in-law was pacing; she'd seen her do it often when she was on the phone, her feet getting tangled in the skirts of the long dresses she wore. Manda claimed that the dresses were a souvenir from her Pentecostal upbringing.

"Wait, wait," said Winnie. "Threatening you *how*?"

"How do you think, Winnie? God, I know how you guys worship your brother, but he's not been right for a while. No one wants to acknowledge that."

Winnie took a deep breath as Manda called out to her boys. "Lincoln, ask your brother, all right? Go...right now. Go!"

"I'll acknowledge it." Winnie was tired of making excuses for Dakota; she had her own problems to worry about now. "What do you think he needs?"

Manda was quiet for a long time, and when she spoke again, her voice sounded much calmer.

"He hears people. I think he's schizophrenic or something, Winnie."

Samuel had moved passed the bulldog and was drinking from a water fountain, the toe of his orange Vans pressing down on the pedal. Winnie flinched. He did that to annoy her. He darted away out of sight, probably to avoid the look she was about to give him.

"What do you mean, he hears people...?"

"I don't know. Ask him yourself. I can't believe he didn't say anything to you. He said he saw a ghost in your house.

225

I'm not letting him near the kids, I'm not. Paired with the drinking and drugs, he's a ticking time bomb."

Samuel was making his way up the path toward the street now; she didn't want him crossing without her.

"Manda, he was drunk half the time he was at our place. He wandered around in his boxers crying. I don't know what he thinks he saw, but you're right not to let him around the kids. I'll call him, see where his head's at. I promise."

"I don't need you to call him, Winnie," Manda said dryly. "I'm done. He may have mental health problems, but he's also an entitled, drunk narcissist and it was all of *you* who made him this way."

"That's not fair. You know he lost his father when he was—"

"That's exactly the problem. Goddamn, Winnie, I thought you were different. He thinks he can do whatever he wants to me and the kids, and then just cry about his issues and I'll forgive him, just like your family always does. And you refused to see the much bigger problems he has because it wasn't convenient for you."

"Manda, you called me…"

"Yeah, to warn you that Dakota has it out for your husband. Goodbye, Winnie."

She opened her mouth to protest, but Manda had already hung up.

Samuel was no longer in her line of sight. She pocketed the phone, pressing back her tears, and sped up. What was that saying? It didn't rain until it poured.

Samuel was already in his room when she walked through the front door. She slid into a chair in the kitchen and sat with her face in her hands, trying to make sense of what was going on. First the envelope with the clippings, which, aside from the actual night of the incident, was the single worst day of

Winnie's life. Then there was the library card ordeal—she still didn't know what to think of that. And now the Froot Loops. Samuel was acting like a complete stranger.

25

JUNO

The obituary was short:

Josalyn Russel, daughter to Terry Russel and step-
daughter to Mark Gordon, died unexpectedly on February 8, 2008. Her funeral service will be held at the
First Baptist Church in Lima, Ohio.

Icy, Juno thought. That was *not* the obituary of a well-loved
girl. Juno had seen parents over the years who were distraught
over the behavior of their children. They brought their children to her like an ingredient for a recipe they didn't know
what to do with. One parent usually looked anxious and put
out, the other hopeful. It was like good cop/bad cop in the

family department: What is this? How do we make it work in our family? And there were too many times when the therapy wasn't working that Juno saw parents harden their hearts against their own children—a lost cause, the problem child, the child who just couldn't be reached. Emotional detachment was a survival skill. The person subconsciously muted their emotions in order to protect themselves. Josalyn, Juno thought, had been a problem child. She could see it in the wording: *Died unexpectedly.*

Drugs, she thought. That's what always got them young. "Died unexpectedly of an overdose" would have been too honest for an obit.

The Russels' number was listed. She wrote it on her hand, the pen making sharp, black lines on her skin. Then, sitting at the dinette in the kitchen, staring at the checkerboard floor, Juno dialed and waited. A stately woman's voice said "Hello," and Juno detected both class and vinegar in that voice. Here was a woman who had lost a child, who'd been forced to alter her reality to accept that she'd outlived the child she'd grown in her own body.

"Hello, Mrs. Russel. My name is Juno Holland. I'm sorry to bother you, but I'm calling to talk to you about Josalyn."

There was a long silence, so long Juno thought that Terry Russel had hung up, and then she heard a release of breath that she supposed was a sigh. Juno pushed on. "I'm a retired clinical psychologist, Mrs. Russel, and I was wondering how—"

"She's dead. She was twenty years old when she died. What else would you like to know? I don't know why you people are calling again."

Momentarily stunned, Juno blinked at the wall in front of her. Juno could hear Terry Russel breathing heavily into the phone, like she was restraining herself from crying. For some reason, though, she didn't hang up. Juno took the opportunity

229

to say, "People? I'm not sure what you mean. I had no idea
Josalyn had passed and for that I am very sorry, Mrs. Russel."

There was a shocked silence on the other end of the line.
Juno's mind was spinning. *You people*...had Winnie called
Josalyn's mother, as well? It made sense for Winnie to call if
she wanted to confirm Josalyn's death.

"Listen," she said, dropping her voice an octave; it was her
sympathetic but in-control voice. Whenever she used that
voice, her clients would look up at her like she was going to
deliver God's good word. "I lost my own sons, so I know
how you feel. I was very fond of your daughter. I had hopes
that Josalyn would..." She let her voice drop off, and Terry
Russel picked up where she left off.

"We all had that hope. Unfortunately, Josalyn was too sick
to even seek change."

Juno, who still had her eyes closed, frowned. She *had* sought
change, though, hadn't she? In the form of Illuminations for
Mental Health, where she'd been assigned a counselor named
Winnie Crouch.

"What was your name again?"

"My name is Juno Holland, Mrs. Russel. I met your daughter in Seattle, Washington...before she passed," Juno lied.

"Yes?" Terry said, a little impatiently.

"I worked with her briefly at Illuminations. I'm sure you
know of it?" Juno didn't wait for Terry to respond and she
didn't need her to. "She was a very good writer. That's how
I came to know of you. She would write stories and poems
about you for group session."

Juno didn't have the slightest clue as to whether Josalyn
even knew the alphabet, or if Terry would call bullshit. She
held her breath and was rewarded with Terry's voice a moment
later. "She won a short story competition once...at school..."
She sounded wistful. As a therapist, Juno hated to leave that

wistfulness untouched, but she wasn't on the phone to give Terry Russel therapy.

She pushed on.

"I'm sorry to bring up such a painful subject, Mrs. Russel, but something has been nagging at me for some time. Did Josalyn ever mention anything to you about being pregnant?"

There was a long pause on the Russel end, during which time Juno acknowledged a beast of a headache groping along the back of her skull.

"Yes…" Terry said uncertainly. "But she was on drugs. She said a lot of things. She claimed to be pregnant once when she was fourteen, too. We took her to the doctor and he said her hymen was still intact…"

Juno made a slight harrumph in the back of her throat. That was a topic she didn't care to get into today. It wouldn't make a lick of difference to Mrs. Terry Russel, who had already decided that her dead daughter was a lying drug addict.

"She mentioned it to her counselor at the time… Winnie Crouch." Juno imagined the name traveling across the space between them. She found the spot behind her ear and pressed her cool fingertips to it.

"No, Winnie wasn't her counselor, I know that name. Winnie was her friend. She said so. Winnie was helping her. She distinctly said that name the second to last time I spoke to her. I said well, who names their kid Winnie anyway, and how equipped is she to help you? And then she laughed at me."

Juno didn't just get chills, her body started to tremble. So, Winnie had secured Josalyn's trust enough for the girl to consider her a friend; so much so that she affirmed it to her mother. Her mouth was so dry she had to pry her tongue from her teeth before she could speak again.

"Did she tell you she was pregnant when she called that time?"

"No. I asked why she was calling us if she had this Winnie to help her. She didn't like that at all. She said terrible things I won't repeat and hung up on me. The next time I heard from her she was so high she couldn't string two words together."

"Do you remember the year she claimed to be pregnant? Not when she was fourteen, but the second time."

"I don't understand why you need to know this."

Juno was losing her; she'd have to act fast.

"Because I think she really was pregnant."

Terry Russel was breathing heavily on the other end of the line, probably deciding whether or not Juno was crazy or credible.

"April 2007," she said finally. "She called asking for money. She was living in Oregon and said she was eight weeks pregnant and wanted to get back to Seattle."

"And then did you ever hear from her again? Or hear about a baby being born?"

Terry was quiet, and when she spoke again, there was a different tone, one that didn't sound quite as sure of itself.

"Yes. She called after she supposedly had it. I couldn't hear a baby in the background, though. So I asked her where the baby was."

"What did she say?" Juno asked, growing impatient.

"She said that Winnie had stolen him."

Juno felt herself get hot all over. For a moment her eyes closed and her head lolled back.

I need a minute, she thought, feeling woozy. But she didn't have one; Terry was waiting for her to say something on the other end of the line. She could see the reflection of her own face in Winnie's framed photographs across from her. A deep groove cut down the center of her forehead. It had been there since she was twenty-five. Kregger called it her Mariana Trench. *Try to come at this from Terry's angle*, she told herself.

She remembered the obituary: "Died unexpectedly." It wasn't a lie, just a cover-up. Terry was disappointed in the product she'd put out into the world and hardened her heart against her own flesh and blood. So did Juno really want to alert her to the possibility of a grandson? Well—yes, because if Sam was Josalyn's, telling Terry was the right thing to do. Sam was the one Juno cared about, and Sam deserved to know his real family.

"What?" Juno said.

"She was a very disturbed young woman. She thought a lot of things," Terry replied.

"I raised two children myself," Juno said. "You get what you get, and you try to help them as much as you can. They take the help or they don't."

Juno had finally poked the sore spot; Terry Russel began to cry. She could hear the muffled quality of it at first, and then she really let loose, gasping and sobbing into the receiver like it was her best friend's shoulder.

"I'm so sorry," Terry said after a minute, sniffing. Her voice lacked some of its refinement now that she had a stuffy nose. "You never stop grieving, but I suppose you know that, don't you?"

She knew all too well that no matter how fresh the day was, the rot of the grief permeated through it. No day was safe, no hour, no minute; grief came and went as it pleased.

"No, but you find new things to be hopeful about as you move forward. Terry..." she said, switching to the woman's first name without permission, "may I have your email address? I have something I want to share with you."

26

JUNO

After hanging up with Terry, Juno bustled straight to the computer. Her mouth was puckered into a little bud as she sat down and swiveled toward the keyboard. As she touched the mouse gingerly, her mind was still going over the conversation she'd had with Josalyn Russel's estranged mother.

Terry had been vague about the details of Josalyn's death, but Juno was a stranger. She'd been surprised that Terry had told her as much as she had. So why had it felt like snide gossip? This time, Juno typed in "missing teen Lima/Seattle dead" and found three pages of results. The first that she opened was enough: a short clip from the *Seattle Times*.

An unidentified female had been found in a landfill next to an incinerator in Tacoma, Washington, on February 10,

2008. She was between sixteen and twenty-five years old, 5'6" and 114 pounds, with faded dyed hair. She wore black bikini panties and a single ring, worn on her right hand. She had good muscle tone and, at one point in her life, had taken good care of her teeth. The victim had likely died on February 8.

Josalyn Rose Russel had been reported missing from her home in Lima, Ohio, in 2005, when she'd run away from her family home after an argument; that's what Juno gleaned online. According to an acquaintance, Josalyn had hitched a ride to California, after which she was not seen or heard from again.

Juno sat back, her mind tussling with this new information. So Josalyn had fled Ohio and, a year later, in 2006, ended up in Washington, a teen runaway under the care of Winnie Crouch. In 2007 she'd had a baby, and in 2008 she had been found dead. Winnie, she was sure, had had maternal feelings toward the girl. But why had Josalyn run away in the first place? Juno thought of the cold aloofness she'd heard in Terry Russel's voice. The denial mothers, that's what she'd called them in her therapist years; women who dragged their sullen, druggie kids into the office for her to fix. They didn't want anything to do with the actual therapy; there was a strong aversion to the truth.

"The denial is strong with that one," she'd say to her secretary, Naveen, who would take the outstretched file with a sad, knowing smile. But even if Terry had been a denial mother, she had every right to know that she had a grandson. *And he has every right to know about her,* Juno thought decidedly.

Josalyn had described Winnie to Terry as a friend. That meant the girl had trusted Winnie. Social workers often felt like friends to their patients, and it was easy for lines to become blurred. Fifteen years ago, Winnie would have been fresh out of grad school, young and energetic. The pictures were in every room and on every wall, Winnie posing with various landmarks and accomplishments: high school graduation, college graduation, engagement, wedding, grad school graduation…and then, Juno imagined, it was time for a baby. Winnie liked things to be orderly, and Juno supposed that at some point, she'd decided it was time and approached Nigel about it. But—plot twist—she couldn't get pregnant. Entitled, spoiled Winnie—it must have irked the hell out of her when she found out Josalyn the teenage homeless girl was pregnant and didn't even want to be when Winnie herself couldn't conceive. Juno felt a surge of disgust for Winnie—for Nigel, too, who'd known and who'd helped Winnie get what she wanted out of Josalyn.

Juno created a new Gmail account; it took her a minute to think of something suitable. She settled on Hum123@gmail.com and clicked to open a new message.

"Like riding a bike," she said to no one. All those years when she actually had a computer: one at home, one at work and one always in her bag, a sleek silver laptop. It made her laugh and feel sick at the same time.

Dear Terry, she typed. We had a conversation on the phone today. Thank you for speaking with me. I know that must have taken a tremendous toll on you emotionally. When I called to inquire about Josalyn and you told me that she claimed she had a baby in late 2007, I did some digging and stumbled upon a police report filed by a homeless woman in December of 2007, claiming her infant had been kidnapped.

Juno had not done some digging; she'd found both xeroxed police reports in Winnie's lockbox, along with the bloody scraps of cloth. One report had been made by an unnamed homeless woman in December 2007, claiming that her infant had been kidnapped. The report, filed by a Sergeant Morales, indicated that the woman had seemed under the influence of alcohol or drugs, perhaps both. And the other report concerned the body of a young woman found in February 2008. Neither the woman in the report nor the homeless woman who filed it were named. But one thing Juno knew firsthand was that the homeless were largely nameless to the general public, described in terms of their drug addiction and crimes instead of their names and personalities. And this was Josalyn, she knew it. One report was Josalyn claiming that her infant had been kidnapped, and the other one was Josalyn found dead. Had Winnie had something to do with Josalyn's death, too? Did that explain the bloody cloth in the lockbox?

Her fingers found the keys again and she began to type.

She never gave the police her name but I've included the case number from the report so you can look into it yourself. I may have lost you by now, Mrs. Russel, so let me just say one last thing: in the statement, the officer described her as having what appeared to be track marks on her arms as well as being disoriented with slurred speech. She wouldn't allow the officer to take her to the hospital to be examined, despite her claims that she'd just given birth and someone had stolen her baby, and became aggressive when he tried to coerce her into going for help, running across the street and almost being hit by an oncoming vehicle. The officer, Sgt. Morales, made a note on the report saying that he saw blood on the woman's pants, though he couldn't attest to where the blood was coming from. Nothing further was followed up on since the woman gave no name or address and refused to go to the hospital. There was, however, one detail I'd like you to look over. The officer mentioned a tattoo in the report and I was wondering if Josalyn had any. You'll see a short description of it in the last line. In the case that you can confirm that the tattoo belonged to your daughter I've included an address.

Juno paused, resting her hands in her lap as she considered how to word the next part. The next part was important.

Your grandson is in that house.

She hit send without bothering to sign her name. There. All she had to do now was wait. Wait for Terry, wait for atonement, wait for death.

27

WINNIE

On Winnie's last day at Illuminations for Mental Health, she'd had to turn in her work phone and laptop, which would then be assigned to whomever replaced her. She remembered feeling almost relieved as she set the two items in a box, along with her badge and access cards, and placed them on her superior's desk. She would no longer be tied to the things of the past. When she stepped out of the building for the last time, the sharp February air filling her lungs, she felt…free. That's what her therapist was helping her see: at the end of trauma was the road to a new beginning.

Winnie had felt like she didn't deserve a new anything—and then hope had come in the form of a missed period and a positive pregnancy test. After all the years of hoping, all six miscarriages she couldn't bring herself to let go of, despite the heartbreak they caused her. She'd even secretly kept scraps of the clothing she'd been wearing when she'd miscarried all those times, as morbid as that probably was.

Renewed, she felt that God had given her the forgiveness she had been begging for. She wasn't a terrible person; she was a good person who had made a bad decision. And for the rest of her life, Winnie planned on atoning for that decision, starting with her baby. He or she would be raised to be conscious of all life, tender, well rounded. Winnie would fix what she had done. She would raise such a wonderful child, so caring and aware. And she'd started by quitting her job so she could take care of this baby full time. She'd only gone back to work when he started kindergarten.

Sam was just going through a stage; all teenagers rebelled against their parents. How many times had she repeated that to herself over the last six months? If Winnie were honest, she'd be able to acknowledge that her current lust for another baby had been triggered by Samuel's snipping of the apron strings. Fill the hole, do a better job as a mother next time. It was a bold-faced lie she enjoyed telling herself. She could give birth to ten of her own babies and that one baby would still take the primary spot in her heart and mind. *Because you killed him*, Winnie told herself. And she would never, ever forget that day.

Winnie walked into the house just as the sky was waking up. She didn't remember getting back into the car or driving home, and now, as she fumbled with the lever on the kitchen sink, she opened it and bent her head to guzzle water straight from the tap This isn't happening, not really, it's just a very bad dream, *she told herself. There was a strange buzzing noise, interrupted by chirps. A phone. A phone was ringing somewhere. Her phone, she knew. She couldn't even bring herself to dig for it and look at the screen—she knew whose name she'd see there. She watched as the water washed down the sink. Nigel's voice was behind her, in the kitchen. It was louder than the awful noise—that god-awful buzzing.*

"What happened, what happened?" he said, over and over. She didn't know; this was a dream. No, it was real. The noise was her; Winnie realized that she was crying, mewling like a lost kitten.

"What happened?" he said again.

Winnie looked down at her sweatshirt, over the spot where her heart was. It was empty. She'd pulled his little body out and laid him on the passenger seat of her car.

"Winnie!" Nigel was shouting now, shaking her. His hand came up and hit her across the face, hard enough to stun her out of the nightmare.

So she told him. Nigel had stopped yelling and was staring at her, his eyes so wide. She'd never seen him look that afraid.

"It was so cold, Nigel, he was suffering... I just wanted to help him." She was trembling so hard her teeth knocked together. Nigel took a step away from her. "There was trash everywhere. I had to crawl to reach him—"

"Winnie... Winnie..." he said, breathless, interrupting her. "Is he dead? Is the baby dead?"

Her howls came from somewhere deep in her belly, raw and ugly, answering his question. Nigel grabbed his wife, pressed her face into his chest so that she would stop screaming.

"The car. It skidded on black ice. I had him in my sweatshirt." She held a fist to the spot; she could still feel his heat against her, his tiny vulnerable body cradled to her chest. "I thought I could keep him warm that way. I was taking him to the hospital. The car skidded... I hit the barrier." She raised three fingers to her hairline where her forehead had hit the steering wheel. There was blood, but only a trickle. "I think he died on impact, or I smothered him!" Her voice was hysterical.

Nigel grabbed her face, pinched it between his fingers and studied her with wild eyes.

"He's dead. Oh my God!" She tore at her face, her nails ripping, but she could barely feel it.

"Winnie!" He shook her hard so that her head snapped back. "Did anyone see you take him?"

She shook her head, lips pressed together. "No, Jos—she was alone."

"And the accident…?" His fingers bit into the flesh of her arms and she yelped.

"No one saw," she sobbed. "You're hurting me."

"How do you know?" She could hear her teeth crack together as he rattled her like a doll.

"It was snowing! There was no one on the road." She drew back, trying to pull herself from his hold, but he wouldn't let go. "The car was still on so I drove home."

"Where is it? Where is the body?"

"In the car." She reached for his face and he pulled back, disgusted. "You have to bury him. She gave birth to him in a tent. She was a drug addict!" She screamed this last part into his face, spit landing on his cheek. He stared at her in disbelief.

"And that makes what you did okay? Fuck!" He pulled at his hair, shaking his head. "It's not for us to decide. We have to go the proper route, tell the authorities…"

She could feel how labored his breathing was, could hear the thumping of his heart. Nigel was scared.

"No! Nigel, no. They'll arrest me… I'll lose my job. We can't— please."

Winnie clawed at his chest in panic. She never thought, not in a million years, that he would suggest turning herself in. She imagined herself in prison and let out a wail. Nigel grabbed her wrists, held them. She flailed, wanting to get away, but also wanting to be held until her hysteria passed.

"Stop it. Stop," he commanded. She thought he was going to slap her again, but he didn't.

"You killed it, Winnie. You stole a baby and you're responsible for what happened to it after that."

"It's not an it, Nigel. It's a baby boy."

"Was!" he screamed so loudly Winnie stepped back, knocking into the fridge.

Nigel breathed through his mouth.

"A baby boy who belonged to someone else, someone who might one day come back looking for him." In the pause that followed, Nigel dropped his eyes to the hollow at Winnie's neck. He wouldn't look at her. Turning away, she whimpered behind him, aware of the rejection.

"Nigel—please. I'm sorry."

He spun on her so fast she covered her face like she was almost afraid of him.

"You're sorry? You you killed a child tonight! Because of your foolishness. Because nothing is ever enough." And then he punched the wall beside her head, his hand beating through the plaster in one sharp jab. Winnie screamed and slid down the wall, her eyes closed and her hands flailing. She could see the hate in his eyes, feel it so profusely that in that moment she knew he'd never be able to come back from it.

"Please!" She grabbed the hem of his shirt, but he stepped away, ripping it from her hands. She gaped up at him, her mouth opening and closing, but no words coming out. For better or for worse, was he forgetting that? "Help me. I love you. Please help me…"

28

WINNIE

Nigel had left for a run, and he'd only been gone for a few minutes when the doorbell rang. Winnie was tidying up the kitchen, scooping the last of the crumbs into her palm and dropping them in the sink as the chimes sounded. She brushed her palms together and then headed for the door, glancing up the stairs as she passed them, wondering if Samuel was finished with his homework. She'd take him a snack in a few minutes, she decided. Before her husband had left, he'd given her a generous kiss on the mouth and when he pulled back he'd said, "You're wearing your face, slim."

"Oh...? And what face is that?"

He'd grinned knowingly, but Winnie already knew what he was talking about. Things weren't exactly good, but they were better. She'd stopped pulling away when he reached for her, and Nigel had resigned from his job so he'd be away from Dulce and they could try to keep their marriage alive. As always, Winnie was optimistic. He'd given her one last kiss and squeezed her right breast, saying "Later..." And now the prospect that he'd come home early to do "later" things excited her. Though why would he ring the doorbell? Had he forgotten his keys? She hadn't looked at her phone; maybe he'd been calling her.

Winnie did not gaze through the peephole as she normally did. She opened the door with a smile, ready for whatever quip Nigel would deliver.

At first she thought the woman was trying to sell her something. She was older, maybe in her sixties, with an expensive haircut, and had a determined look about her. Winnie mentally rolled her eyes; she had been meaning to get a No Soliciting sign to hang by the door. She straightened her face, trying not to look as put out as she felt. She had her own expensive haircut, and she felt confident as she gazed down at the woman.

"Can I help you...?" Obligatory words.

"My name is Terry," the woman said. She tilted her head to the side to examine Winnie, who felt affronted by the once-over she was being given.

And then Terry spoke rapidly, saying words that didn't fit inside Winnie's world: a therapist named Juno Holland had given her this address; did Winnie know where her grandson was? Stepping out onto the front step to join the obviously distressed grandmother, Winnie looked up and down the street to see if she could spot a lost boy. It was not fully dark yet, and she could make out several small figures across the street in the park. As a mother herself, she felt anxious for the woman; she'd lost Samuel once in Greenlake Park, and it had been the worst day of her life.

"Is he missing? Have you called the police?"

But the woman looked right past Winnie into the house. She was staring at the row of family photos that hung on the wall. She was staring at Samuel.

"Your grandson," Winnie said again. She had the urge to snap her fingers in the woman's face; make her focus. "Do you need to use my phone?"

The woman—Terry—looked back over her shoulder at the park, and then nodded. She was a nice-looking older woman, and as Winnie led her inside, she could feel hard muscle underneath her button-down shirt. Yoga, Pilates, a tennis trainer—she recognized the Hermes scarf tied around Terry's neck. A rich little boy was lost, she noted. In the foyer, she sat Terry down in the chair. "I'll be right back."

And then she dashed off to the kitchen for her cell phone, grabbing a bottle of water off the counter to take with her. When she rounded the corner, phone in hand, Terry was no longer in the chair. Her back to Winnie; she was studying Samuel's third grade class photo, but when she saw Winnie, she made no move toward the phone.

"Here," Winnie said, extending it to her. She'd taken the time to open it first, the keypad ready to dial 911.

"Ma'am…?" Winnie didn't like calling women "ma'am"; women of her mother's age especially hated it. "I'm sorry, Terry…"

"Your son, how old is he?"

"I'm sorry?" she said again. Suddenly, she felt like little fingers were lightly touching her spine—warning fingers. Winnie retracted the hand offering the phone and took a step away.

"My name is Terry Russel."

Terry Russel. That name landed in a loud *gong* in her head.

"I thought you said your grandson was missing. What do you want?"

Winnie held the phone tighter. She was the one in control here; she could call the police.

"You tell me." Terry Russel turned toward Winnie, a cold smile on her face, served with ice-blue eyes. She was walking on black kitten heels. It occurred to Winnie that no one would be walking in the park with their grandkid while wearing Prada kitten heels.

"Tell you what? I have no idea what you're talking about and if you don't get out of my house, I'm going to call the police."

At this Terry smiled, reseating herself on Winnie's foyer chair.

"I think you should," she said, crossing her legs. It looked like she was settling in for the night. "Tell them that Josalyn Russel's mother is here, and that she would like a DNA test done on that boy!" The woman pointed at Samuel's photo.

The fingers on her spine turned into a heat that exploded inside Winnie's chest. She heard herself stutter "Ja—joss—"

Terry looked triumphant. "Josalyn," she said, enunciating each syllable of the girl's name, her eyes drilling accusatory holes into Winnie's face. "My daughter."

Winnie didn't know what to do. The sound of the dead girl's name paralyzed her, and she stared at Terry Russel, feeling like her face had turned to plaster. How had Terry found her? Everything that had happened that night had felt like the sort of thing that would happen in the movies, the sort of mistakes a stupid character made that left you yelling "No!" at the TV.

Even though Winnie was in her own house, on her own turf, she took a step back, and that was obviously enough to solidify her guilt in Terry's mind. The older woman looked murderous.

"I know everything," she said. "I know exactly what you did."

"It was you!" Winnie said. "You sent me those articles and you somehow checked out a book on my library card! You've been stalking me!" She shook her head, openmouthed, so angry now that she missed the look of confusion on Terry's face. "You're crazy! I didn't do anything to your daughter. Get the hell out!" Winnie marched toward the front door, determined to get this madwoman out of her home before Samuel heard or Nigel came home. She tried not to let her fear show as she yanked open the door and stared expectantly at Terry. Winnie had learned that if you used confidence to command people, they were often compelled to listen.

She heard Samuel's bedroom door open at the same time Terry Russel turned to face the exit she clearly didn't plan on taking. She stared right at Winnie as she said, "I know that you worked for Illuminations, the supposed facility where Josalyn was receiving care."

Winnie's heart was racing. If either she or Terry called the police, there would be questions. Of course, there was no proof—nothing. Was there?

"I have the police report Josalyn made, reporting her kidnapped infant," Terry continued, and that's when Winnie's vision shook like there was an earthquake in her head. If she hadn't been holding on to the door, trying to usher Terry Russel out, she would have collapsed.

The police report. No one knew about that because the woman in it had not been named—she'd been a Jane Doe. Josalyn had somehow found Winnie's landline after she stopped picking up her cell—and left a message on the answering machine.

Winnie could still hear the girl's voice, thick with something she'd either drunk or smoked. When she said Winnie's name it came out "Wunnie…"

"Someone took my kid, my fucking kid. Please call me. I don't have a phone anymore, I'm calling from a payphone. I tried to go to the police and make a report, but fuck, they don't give a shit about me, they never did! Fuck you, Officer Morales!" She'd shouted the last part, like there was an officer standing in front of her. "They thought I was drunk, they wouldn't listen to me…!" And then the line had gone dead. She'd played the message once more and then deleted it. Within the hour, Winnie had disconnected the home phone with the company and put the cordless relic in the pile to take to Goodwill. She changed her cell number, too, and made sure the new one was unlisted. She'd replaced the landline later, when she wasn't so afraid, and Nigel asked why they got rid of it in the first place.

"I don't remember," she had lied.

For the next few weeks, she'd pored over articles online, trying to find a mention of Josalyn, though Winnie wasn't certain who to look for. A girl…? A homeless woman…? A prostitute…? She'd been all those things under Winnie's care, but she'd also been something else—a very vulnerable, likable girl. There was nothing in the news or online about any of the above, nor did the news report a missing infant. A child no one knew existed had simply ceased to exist. She could have let it go, but her need to know what happened to Josalyn was consuming. Eventually she'd done the only thing she could—asked Nigel for help.

"Why can't you leave it alone?"

"Don't you want to know so we can be—"

"What, Winnie?" He had a look of disgust on his face. "Better prepared to lie our way out of it?"

She'd seen red then; it was like he wanted her to go to prison. "Well, yes, Nigel," she'd snapped. "I don't want to go to prison. Do you want me to go to prison?" She'd placed both hands on her belly, which had swollen to the size of a melon. He'd caved. Nigel had no intention of raising a baby alone. Together, they'd decided that Nigel would go to Mike, Shelly's husband. Not only did Mike really like Nigel, he was of those "bros before hoes" types. If Nigel asked his cop brother-in-law to dig up some dirt on someone or look up police reports, he would. And if he asked him to keep it a secret, he'd do that, too—the more beers Nigel was able to get in him the better.

"No idea what you're talking about," she said firmly, masking her fear with her deep disdain for this woman who'd shown up on her doorstep to start a war.

"Of course you don't." Terry Russel smiled bitterly. "But I have it right here if you need to see it." She pulled a piece of folded paper from the side pocket of her handbag and held it out to Winnie. She stared down at the white square in horror. She had no intention of touching that thing. She shook her head, not taking her eyes from the woman's face. She didn't have to read it; she knew exactly what it said. How could this woman have it? And she didn't want Terry Russel thinking she was entertaining the garbage coming out of her mouth either. *But it's not garbage is it, Winnie?* said a voice from deep inside her.

She tried again. "I need you to leave right now." If the woman didn't get out of her home in twenty seconds, she was going to remove her herself. But Terry Russel looked as if her own spool of sanity was unraveling. Winnie had seen that look plenty—often in the mirror. With a sinking feeling in her belly, she realized that she wasn't going to get rid of Terry Russel that easily.

Terry, seeing something waver in Winnie's eyes, pulled back her upper lip and said from between her teeth, "Where is my daughter's baby? Where is Josalyn's son?"

Winnie's mouth was so dry she couldn't have said a word if she'd wanted to. Was this woman saying—did this woman think—she was still trying to piece together what was happening, that there was a stranger in her house accusing her loudly of something as her son was doing his homework upstairs. Samuel. Terry thought that Samuel—

"You took my daughter's child!" Terry Russel wasn't shouting, but her voice was so cold she didn't have to.

"He's...not her son!" Winnie gasped. "You crazy old bitch. Get out of my house!"

She hadn't called anyone a bitch since she was eighteen, and then it had been because her best friend had slept with her boyfriend. It flew out of her mouth with enough venom to stop Terry Russel in her kitten-heeled tracks. But then—oddly—Terry's head pivoted right, like she'd seen something outside the open door. Winnie thought that she was imagining the whites of Terry's eyes growing larger with each passing second, but then the woman's mouth opened and she let out a little gurgle of surprise.

And then it happened: the scene shifted, and the villains rearranged themselves into a new order. The whole thing couldn't have taken more than ten seconds to play out, but to Winnie, everything happened excruciatingly slowly.

A noise preceded her husband, a guttural, wet moaning that raised the hairs on Winnie's neck. He moved into view in slow, laborious steps, like he was pulling something behind him. Winnie saw his brow, then his nose, and then his shoulders struggled past the open door, heading straight for Terry, who seemed frozen, staring.

He was walking in a strange, zombie-like gait. What Winnie noticed first was that the white T-shirt he'd been wearing when he left to take his run was no longer white. A bloom of red started just under his shoulder, near his collarbone, dark in the center and bright scarlet on the edges. She just had time to register that her husband was injured—terribly so—before he fell directly into Terry Russel's arms. Winnie ran for Nigel at the same time as his weight pushed the older woman off her feet and onto the foyer floor with a hard thump. They went down in a tangle of legs. But before Winnie could reach them, Nigel had rolled off Terry Russel and was lying on his back on the floor, gasping.

Winnie dropped down next to him. He was rearing his head up, struggling to look out the door.

"Dakota..."

Winnie heard him but couldn't register his words. Her husband was busted like a cracked wine bottle, leaking on her hardwood. Winnie didn't even notice that Terry Russel had risen to her haunches and backed herself against the closet door, her mouth slack with horror.

She saw the blood on his shirt at the same time her brother walked through the front door holding a gun in one hand and a knife in the other.

29

WINNIE

"**D**akota...oh my God, call an ambulance!" Winnie's hands were slippery, and she didn't want to think about the color of the substance on them; the color was hurting her eyes and there was so, so much of it. She was trying to stop the blood that was easing out of Nigel's shoulder in a thick stream.

She had her phone a second ago; where was it? Her eyes scanned the floor around her as she tried to remember if she'd dropped it. Nigel moaned, the whites of his eyes flickering through the small gap of his eyelids. How was she supposed to stop the bleeding? Ripping off her sweater, she balled it up and pressed it to Nigel's shoulder. Her cream-colored sweater soaked his blood like a sponge and Winnie let out a cry. God, he was going to bleed to death. That horrible woman—Terry Russel—was slowly standing up, using the closet door as leverage so she could slide slowly up the wall. One of her kitten heels had come off and was lying on its side next to Nigel's head.

"Dakota!" Winnie cried again. She turned to Terry, her rage so large her words grated out of her throat. "You! Get out! Get out right now!" Then, back to her brother—

"Are you drunk, Dakota? Did you hear me? Nigel is hurt!"

"He knows that," Terry Russel said. Her voice was almost dry. "He's the one who did it."

Her voice summoned Dakota's gaze. He looked at Terry with little interest, and that was when Winnie really began to panic. Her gaze leveled on the knife held limply in his hand and she felt a quake of uncertainty, but then Nigel was squeezing her hand. What strength he had left was leaking out of his body alarmingly quickly. His face was a shade of gray that scared Winnie. People didn't turn that color unless something was very wrong. Nigel's eyes were open, and he was staring at Dakota, his mouth distended with terror.

Winnie connected the dots slower than she would have if it wasn't her husband who was dying in front of her. Terry Russel knew exactly what was going on, which was why she hadn't made a dash for the door: the object of her fear was blocking it. Dakota. She glanced back at Terry and saw the older woman's eyes scan the room and then, with a little flicker of hope, land on her handbag, the one she had so primly carried on her arm when she knocked on Winnie's door.

Dakota's face was expressionless, like he was zoned out watching TV rather than his brother-in-law bleeding out on the floor. He sheathed the knife in a holster on his belt, the holster she knew he used for hunting because she'd bought it for him. She was about to scream his name again, this time wake him up from whatever alcohol- or drug-induced trance he was in—when she *really* saw the gun, and Manda's words came rushing back to her: *He has it out for Nigel...*

"Dakota, what are you doing?"

He ignored the question—he ignored her altogether, in fact, and took a step toward Nigel, lifting the arm holding the gun.

"Dakota!" Winnie's scream was shrill, but the only indication he'd heard her was a slight sway his head made in her direction.

She looked down at Nigel, afraid to leave him and even more afraid to move him. But if her phone was trapped underneath his body... She needed to calm down, clear her head. She thought of Samuel, upstairs doing his homework—had she really heard his door open, or had she imagined it?—and mentally begged him to stay put. If he heard Dakota's voice he'd stay in his room, she thought. But Dakota had yet to say anything, and that was the strangest, scariest part.

Winnie tried to stand up, but something abruptly slammed her back to the floor. She felt pain explode in her knees and she fell forward over Nigel, the palm of her hand almost landing on his bleeding shoulder. Astonished, she looked over her shoulder at Dakota, who had been the one to shove her down. He wasn't looking at his sister; his eyes were now on Terry Russel—the thing that didn't belong in this situation. Winnie tried to stand up again with the same result: Dakota's heavy hand resting on her shoulder before slamming her back to her knees. This time, she managed to crawl across Nigel's legs and away from her brother.

"What is wrong with you?" she gasped, backpedaling farther from him. His only response was to raise the gun, the muzzle pointing at Nigel's chest, and to shoot it, once...twice. Winnie didn't scream; she was too stunned. Besides, if you knew you were dreaming it was stupid to scream, wasn't it?

Terry Russel screamed, however. It was an old woman's scream, deep and frail, and it didn't go very far. Nigel's body bucked only when the second bullet hit him. There was a faint curling of smoke above where the bullet entered his chest—or at least Winnie thought there was. The pops of the gun were so loud Winnie's vision seemed to tremble, and when the air settled, her husband was dead. Winnie was puzzling over the fact that her knees had hurt when Dakota shoved her down, hurt like it wasn't a dream. She could see a stream of red pooling underneath Nigel; his shirt had been white, hadn't it...? She reached to touch the blood; if it was warm, this wasn't a dream. You couldn't feel warm in a dream. Winnie opened her mouth to scream; in that moment her head suddenly exploded with pain and everything went black.

Her eyes opened gently, but what came after she opened them was the most painful moment of her life. Her head felt like someone had opened her skull and poured hot coals inside. Pressing the heel of her hand to her right eye, she struggled to sit up. When her vision cleared, the first thing she saw was Terry Russel, sitting across from her on the floor of the blue bedroom, the one in the apartment. She wasn't dreaming, and that meant that Nigel was dead.

Winnie felt the pain straight down her middle; it tore out of her mouth in what should have been a cry of anguish, but, muted by the gag in her mouth, came out as no more than a muffled sob. Her hands were bound behind her back with what felt like duct tape. She couldn't see; beneath her tears, her eyes strained to focus on anything other than Terry Russel. She moaned again, this time in frustration, and blinked furiously to clear her eyes. Where was Samuel? The panic drove her to her feet, which she was relieved to see were not bound. She wobbled unsteadily before rushing for the door.

Winnie couldn't reach the doorknob with her hands bound. She had no doubt it was locked from the other side, the house side. Nigel had insisted they put a solid lock on the door to the separate apartment in case they did decide to take on a renter; they could make sure the tenant couldn't get into the main house, he'd said, by dead-bolting the door from the Crouches' side. She looked around at the kitchenette and bathroom door. On the other side of the locked door was Nigel's den. She could picture the Lovesac, the ridiculously overpriced couch he loved so much. At the thought of her husband she bent over, pulling short breaths in through her nose. *Focus. Samuel... Samuel... Samuel... Focus.*

Her eyes were stinging as she considered the room.

This room—the addition—had its own entrance, the one her husband had insisted on. This entrance led to an alley behind the house.

Her eyes darted to that door at once, and she saw Terry Russel's head jerk in the direction. She didn't want to think about that awful woman right now; her brother had snapped, murdered Nigel in cold blood, and she needed to get to Samuel. If she could get out to the street, she could run to the neighbors for help. But Dakota had duct-taped her hands together so tightly behind her there was no give. How was she going to open the door? She had no idea what time it was or how long she'd been unconscious, though it was dark outside the windows. She could knock her head against the glass until someone on the street heard. But what were the actual chances of that? Dakota would hear her, if he was still in the house, or she'd give herself a concussion and then she wouldn't be able to help Samuel.

Terry was rocking back and forth, her eyes practically rolling around in their sockets. Her brother had used the woman's own scarf to gag her, and a portion of her hair had gone into her mouth with the gag. She was making absolutely no move to do anything helpful, just staring at Winnie with panicked eyes. Winnie started working on getting her hands free.

But Dakota walked into the room not two minutes later, the gun still in his hand. Winnie craned her neck to see if Samuel was with him, trying to call to him around her own gag.

"Where's Samuel, where's Samuel?"

But it sounded like nonsense, like "Wazazow…wazazow." Her eyesight blurred again with new tears. Grief and horror were cycling through her, and she bent at the waist as Nigel's death replayed behind her eyelids, the way his body had jerked when the bullet hit.

Dakota grabbed her roughly by the shoulders and pushed her onto the bed. Her legs flew up as she fell on her back, which was what he was counting on. He had her ankles tied before she could even try to struggle into a sitting position. She screamed at him through the gag, screamed until her throat was on fire, trying to get him to acknowledge her, but her brother's face was as vacant as a mannequin's.

30

JUNO

J uno was in Hems Corner when Dakota shot Nigel Crouch. She made a noise when the gun went off, but it was drowned out by guttural screaming, and then the screaming stopped abruptly. There was a thud as a body hit the floor, and then Juno wet her pants.

Terry Russel was remarkably quiet for a woman who'd stumbled right into a family tragedy and had seen a man murdered in front of her. Or had Dakota shot her, too? Juno had heard two shots and a scream. She could hear harsh breathing from the other side of the closet door, but she couldn't tell whose it was.

Juno had crept up to the door when she'd heard Terry's voice. She'd been waiting for Terry Russel to show up, counting on it. Nigel stumbling into the house minutes after with Dakota on his heels had been a complete shock to Juno. She'd expected Nigel to discover the two women at odds when he came back from his run, then shit would have really hit the fan. But now Nigel was dead—presumably—and that was not something Juno had ever wanted. She reached for the trapdoor. She'd crawl back down there and hide until this was over. The neighbors must have seen something—heard something—cops would be swarming the place before too long. But before she could open the trapdoor and crawl through, she heard voices. Terry Russel—she was alive!—was pleading. She was talking very quickly, as if Dakota might turn the gun on her next. Juno buried her face in the carpet, carpet that still smelled faintly of urine from the last time.

"My name is Terry Russel, I am here for my grandson, I have money. You can take all of my cards—here—"

Terry must have offered her handbag to Dakota because she followed up with a "—please take it. There's five hundred dollars in cash in the side pocket, and all my car— What are you doing? No!"

They struggled. Juno could hear banging on the outside of the closet door—an elbow or maybe a knee. There was a crash, and the song of broken glass as it shattered on the floor. She crept farther back, her heart thumping in her throat, and closed her eyes. Winnie was repeating something to Dakota over and over again: "What are you doing, what are you doing! Dakota…!" Juno held a hand over her own mouth to suffocate any sound that might betray her. *What is he doing? He's gone mad*, she thought. Afraid to make any noise that would alert them of her presence, Juno crawled over the trapdoor, pushing herself against the back wall as far as she could, the hems sweeping her face. She had to disappear from sight in case the door somehow opened. That was survival, disappearing when you needed to.

Dakota must have gotten Terry under control because she heard the older woman begging again—"Please don't hurt me"—as he dragged her away. It sounded like he was moving toward Nigel's den and the little apartment with its separate entrance. Juno scrambled out of her hiding place, only half-feeling the arthritis that was screaming loudly in her joints. When she opened the closet door, she saw Nigel first, lying on his back in a lake of blood. Winnie was crumpled on the floor beside him, and Juno knew that Dakota would be back for her any second. She darted around the corner and up the stairs, her fear so hot she could smell it rolling off her. *This is what animals must feel like when they're being hunted,* she thought. She grinned against the pain, pumping her legs harder as she neared the bend in the stairs. She should have taken a pill today, one of those glorious pills that muted out the pain. She heard Dakota discover her. She never saw it, she was already around the corner, hauling her stubborn body up by the bannister.

"You!" he called, as the last of her disappeared around the corner. "I told Manda I wasn't crazy, I knew there was a ghost!"

But he didn't come after her as she had thought he would. Juno was braced to hear his boots on the stairs, but the only sound in her ears was her own rasping breath. *He probably thinks he can deal with me later,* Juno thought as she ran for Sam's room, *or maybe he thinks I really am a ghost.* She threw open the door to find it empty. She stepped inside, half expecting to find him hiding, but he wasn't in the room. *Thank God, thank all the gods.* It was then that she saw the open window. Sam had gotten out. He would get the police. Her relief was immense, but now she could hear Dakota coming up the stairs. The heavy *donk, donk* of his work boots sounded on the floor. Juno knew where to hide; she always knew. She slipped quickly from Sam's room before Dakota rounded the bend in the staircase.

She heard him walking through the rooms quickly. She supposed he didn't have much time, considering the two women downstairs; it seemed like he was hardly looking. Juno was in the cabinet under the sink, the one where Winnie kept the fresh towels. She heard him walk into the bathroom, his shoes squeaking on the marble floor. She was shaking so hard her teeth were knocking together and she swore Dakota would hear, but a second later he left, and she heard him going down the stairs.

So he had seen her once before. She hadn't wanted to admit she'd been that careless, but he had. He'd been drunk, and Juno hadn't exactly known what he'd seen when she'd tiptoed from the bathroom as he was coming out of the kitchen. It was dark and she'd darted away just as he'd turned around, sensing something was behind him. She'd slipped back into the closet in a panic, fearing she wouldn't make it into the crawl space, but Dakota hadn't pursued her to her little hidey-hole.

Now, she pushed open the cabinet door, unfolding like a stiff metal toy. She stood on the bathroom mat, her eyes darting around like she was going to find a solution somewhere in this room. It was her fault that Terry Russel had come to the house; she'd put it in the woman's head that Josalyn's son was living with his kidnappers, and then she'd given the woman the Crouches' address. If Terry died here, it would be Juno's fault.

"Oh, God..." Juno mumbled softly. She stood on the bathroom rug and covered her ears with her hands, squeezing her eyes closed and swaying back and forth. She could feel a panic attack coming on. It was regression if she'd ever seen it. In prison, she'd resorted to the same method to control anxiety attacks, finding a corner and swaying like she was having a religious experience. They'd called her Hail Mary, and she hadn't cared because when she was crazy Hail Mary she couldn't hear or see any of them. But Juno didn't have women heckling her this time, just herself. She'd done it again, the thing that had rent her family right down the middle all those years ago—getting too involved in people's lives, taking it a step too far, crossing a line. And for what? Kregger had said she'd chosen psychology because she needed to be overly involved in people's lives. And she had, hadn't she? She'd been that way since she was a little girl at her mother's salon, eavesdropping on breakups and makeups, thinking about their stories as she lay in bed at night. Darla Hess, who was pregnant with her fifth and didn't want to be; Sarah O'Neil, who'd left her husband for the high school football coach, and then... Pattie and Pastor Paul.

But no. This time, it wasn't her fault. Winnie had stolen someone's baby and raised him as her own. Juno had merely stumbled upon the information and acted like any normal person would, doing the right thing. The same went for Terry, who had made the choice to come to the Crouch house rather than going to the authorities. There it was.

She opened her eyes, dropping her hands to her sides. She needed to get out of the house, get away from these poisonous people. She was no longer in prison, and she didn't have to stay here. She made it three steps when she thought of the open window in Sam's room. Casting a cautious glance toward the stairs, Juno slipped into Sam's room again. Her eyes scanned his desk for some sign of what had been happening in his head before he escaped. His backpack was gone. She opened his dresser drawer; she knew he kept his money rolled and secured with a rubber band. Juno had mused over it the first time she'd seen it, the way he stashed his cash.

What if he'd overheard what Terry Russel had said to Winnie? Could he have left the house before Dakota arrived? Her breath vacuumed in as she considered the possibility that Sam had run away instead of running for help. His roll of money was gone from its spot. That's when her heart really started hammering. Gone. She didn't care what happened to Winnie, and she didn't much care what happened to Terry Russel, either. Juno had chosen her side long ago. Sam was who mattered. Her feet started moving, shuffling at first and then running.

31

WINNIE

Once Winnie's ankles were tied, Dakota firmly seated her on the floor and turned toward Terry. She stared at the back of his head, wondering where her brother had gone, and if someone could just...change overnight. But it hadn't been overnight, though, had it? Dakota knelt in front of Terry, blocking Winnie's view of her terrified face for a moment. They'd known that Dakota had problems, and Manda had been warning them for years about how serious they'd become, but the family hadn't listened hard enough, had figured that Dakota was Manda's problem now. When Dakota stood up, the floral scarf was slung over his palm and Terry was licking her lips, staring up at him like a cornered animal.

"Who is your grandson?" he asked her. His voice was

rough, husky, like he'd just woken up from a nap. Winnie envisioned the first night he'd come to stay with them, how she'd found him sobbing like a baby on the couch. There was no trace of that man now.

She stopped struggling to listen.

Terry's eyes didn't waver when she said "Samuel."

Winnie could feel the sweat gathering between her breasts and on her forehead. Dakota gave a loud smack of his lips, before casting a glance over his shoulder at her. Winnie didn't like what she saw in his eyes—or maybe it was what she didn't see that frightened her, the absence of her brother.

"Samuel...?" he repeated. He said it with a slight sneer, like Terry might be the craziest person in the room.

"She stole another woman's baby and passed him off as her own," Terry said. "Go ahead, ask her."

Winnie screamed against her gag, her rage channeling a demon-like cry. They both turned to look at her. Her brother's face was impassive as he looked at her.

"That true, Win...? You steal someone's kid...?"

Winnie yelled around her gag until her throat was burning, but Dakota seemed to be done looking at her for now; he was focused again on Terry with rapt attention.

"That sounds like something you'd do, Win. Remember when we were little, and you stole the puppy from the neighbor's yard and brought it home?"

She stared at him, dumbfounded. That had happened over twenty-five years ago. The story had been told over and over by her siblings, each version painting Winnie like some sort of remorseless sociopath. She'd just been a kid, seen a puppy launching itself at the side of the fence to get to her, and had... taken it. She'd made a mistake. Dakota wasn't being serious, he couldn't be.

She tried to yell at him, but she couldn't form words. "The

kid's not here," Dakota said, still looking at Terry. "But even if he were, what would make me believe a wild story like that, even if it does sound like Winnie?" His voice had the tone of a man speaking to a misbehaving child. The hairs on the back of Winnie's neck stood at attention. That didn't sound like Dakota *at all*.

Over Dakota's shoulder, she could see Terry's eyes ticking back and forth like a metronome. She was working on an angle, Winnie realized, and before she could blink a second time, Terry was spinning it.

"Did you ever see her pregnant? Your...sister?"

Winnie froze. When Terry continued, she sounded breathless, winded by her lies.

"She wanted a baby very much, didn't she? She was probably jealous when everyone else her age started having them."

Dakota stood up suddenly, towering over Terry Russel and rolling his neck from side to side like he had the world's largest crick. He considered her for a moment and then said, "Now that you mention it..."

Terry's face transformed from hopeful to triumphant, while Winnie's tears began a slow leak down her face. Her throat was raw from screaming against the gag, and there was an ache in her chest that was paralyzing in its enormity. Terry told Dakota her story in a clear, calm voice, painting herself as the distraught, concerned mother whose daughter had gotten involved with the wrong crowd, the crowd that had eventually swept her away from Akron, Ohio, toward greener grass in Washington. Her sweet Josalyn had landed pregnant and destitute in Seattle. Enter Winnie.

Winnie herself, who no longer had the energy to hold her head up, sat slouched against the wall, her face dangling above her own crotch. When Terry Russel said her name, she didn't bother looking up. She had pieced together the story and had spun a narrative that suited her. And she'd done her research.

"She was working at Illuminations for Mental Health at the time Josalyn sought care there," Terry said. "I spoke with the head doctor at the facility, and he confirmed that your sister was Josalyn's counselor. In fact, after your sister left her job—" she paused "—Josalyn contacted Illuminations several times, asking for contact information for Winifred Crouch. She even once told the receptionist that Winnie stole her baby."

Winnie watched the back of her brother's head, wondering if he was buying this. Even six months ago, she'd have known the answer to that. She thought she knew everything about her brother, but now, she realized that she knew only what she wanted to know, what it suited her to know.

Terry Russel was asking Dakota to look at the police report in her handbag. He did, the gun still dangling from his hand, tossing aside Terry's wallet, which he briefly opened to check her license.

"She's who she says she is," he said, turning to Winnie. His eyebrows were raised in mock surprise. Winnie could do nothing but blink. She was fiercely thirsty. She kept expecting Nigel to walk through the door; he'd help her get out of this. But her own brother had murdered him. Murdered. The word was foreign to Winnie. She'd never once worried that someone she loved would be murdered, never had to.

She looked at Terry, who was smiling coldly at her, a challenge. Josalyn had said that her stepfather molested her and that her mother had chosen not to see it. Looking at Terry Russel, Winnie wondered if it was true. And how had she come to find Winnie? Juno Holland, who was that? Another of her husband's whores, she thought. As if Dulce Tucker hadn't been enough. And it was mostly anger that filled Winnie after that: Nigel had told someone, and that someone had sent this woman to her doorstep.

"Your grandson is dead!" she screamed through her gag. But she could tell they hadn't understood her words.

Terry licked her lips again, keeping her eyes trained on Dakota like she was trying to hypnotize him.

"I'll take him and go. I won't tell anyone what happened. I only want my grandson. Please."

Dakota took a few seconds to process what she'd said before he started to laugh. The shocked look on her face indicated that Terry had thought her negotiations were going well.

"You don't want to hurt him, he's just a boy."

Winnie stared between them desperately. Terry Russel was trying to save her son from whatever Dakota had planned, but only so she could kidnap him. It was like looking at the speeding car coming toward you and knowing you were going to be killed by lightning before it arrived. "The kid's not here," Dakota had said. Samuel had to be hiding somewhere in the house, terrified. Could he have managed to get out...? Jumped out his window...?

"Just a kid," he repeated, nodding slowly. But his voice was flat and emotionless, like he was reading off of a script. "No one cares about my kids. No one cares that they won't have a father." She read the alarm in Terry's eyes, saw her blinking rapidly.

"You can be their father. You can. Leave right now and—"

But Dakota was crying, his shoulders shaking. That felt more normal, Winnie thought, and silently, she urged her brother to come to his senses.

"Nigel," he gasped, "took my family from me." He spun away from Terry, walking toward Winnie with so much determination she was sure he was going to kill her right then and there. He knelt so that he was directly in front of her face.

"Manda won't take me back and Nigel turned you against me, too." He jerked toward Winnie on the last word, and she braced herself for impact. But Dakota didn't hit her. He was looking at her like he couldn't decide what to do with her.

"You're not my family," he said. "You stopped being my family the day you took that pig's side and kicked your own flesh and blood out of your house." His words sounded wet and slushy, like he was talking through a mouthful of water. Winnie began to moan. She knew these stories; she'd worked with the mentally ill for years.

Dakota didn't seem to see either of them as he stood up and turned toward the window, staring into the darkness, his head tilted. He'd snapped; it didn't matter why or how, and now her brother was going to kill them like he'd killed Nigel. He'd needed someone to blame for the pisswork he'd made of his life, and with Manda filing the divorce papers...

"What do you have to say for yourself, sister?"

But Winnie couldn't answer; the gag stopped her words.

Dakota tottered around for several seconds, off balance, like he didn't know where he was, then he strode toward Terry Russel, lifting the gun as he went.

"Pow, pow," he said. Then he shot her. Two bullets, just like Nigel. Winnie screamed. She was crying so hard now she could barely breathe, tears flying off her face as she shook her head in disbelief. She gagged as Dakota stared in fascination at Terry Russel's body.

Winnie moaned again; she wasn't going to die a victim of her brother's anger, she was going to choke to death on her own vomit. Dakota turned, and his dead eyes found her as she keeled over on the carpet. He watched her for what felt like an eternity, and then he knelt in front of her and yanked the gag out of her mouth. Winnie rolled to her side, gasping for air. She could smell the stink of vomit and now there was another smell—blood. She could see it on the wall, sprayed like a Rorschach test, Terry slumped below.

"Come to think of it,' sis, I didn't see you pregnant."

Chills ran across her limbs like insects.

"I—we didn't tell anyone, remember? After the miscarriages, we kept it to ourselves until the last trimester. And you lived in Tacoma then. That's why we didn't see each other."

Please God, let him accept the truth. Her voice sounded like it was grating over gravel; she didn't know how much of it she had left to use.

He shook his head like she had it all wrong. "You didn't even have the baby shower until after he was born. That's kind of strange, isn't it? I remember having to drive Manda there because she was nine months pregnant and couldn't reach the steering wheel around her belly. I walked her in and there you were, all slim and put-together like you'd never been pregnant." He smiled dully. "Manda even leaned over and whispered in my ear about how good you looked for having just given birth."

Winnie was balanced on her knees. A trickle of saliva hung from her chin, but she made no move to wipe it away. Her twin brother was lifting the gun. She couldn't think clear thoughts; she was still trying to understand what had happened that had led up to this.

"This isn't you," she said, before her throat closed in panic and she started to cough. "This isn't my brother. Dakota, please—"

32

JUNO

Juno leaned over Nigel, for once not feeling the cracking pain pinching into her back like talons, and focused on reaching her stiff fingers into the pockets of his running shorts. They were empty except for his headphones. He'd either dropped his phone outside or Dakota had taken it along with Winnie's, which was as missing as Dakota's mind. She heard shouting coming from the apartment, saw Nigel's blood swimming around her feet. Her vision shook like Jell-O, and Juno thought she was going to keel over. The Crouch family portraits stared at her from the wall. She felt her survival instincts kick in.

Slow but steady, she thought, taking a step toward the front door. Sam was safe—or safer than he would be in the house; he was the only person she cared about, anyway.

Except Terry wouldn't be here if it weren't for her. *You have to decide, Juno, are you the hero or do you creep back to your hidey-hole?* She rubbed the spot behind her ear.

She could walk out the door right now, save her own skin. She stepped over Nigel. She thought she could hear Terry Russel's voice. This was none of her business. She heard a car drive by, the radio churning out rap music. Outside was so close; just a few steps and she'd fall right into the cool night. But what about Winnie...? She tried to kick the thought, think around it.

She might hear the story on the news from the women's shelter if she got there in time to get a cot, tomorrow, maybe, but no one would ever know she'd been here. The story wouldn't be about her this time, and she wouldn't be the one to go to prison. The thought of prison sent panic skittering through her limbs. She was dying, and she was not going to yield up her soul in some shit cinder-block prison cell while her roommate masturbated in the bunk above her. Her hand reached for the dead bolt.

Then she heard another gunshot, her terror so blinding she moved on instinct. She was going to have to move quickly—and quickly cost her a great deal of pain. The keypad to the alarm system was in front of her. But in her haste, her shaking fingers hit the emergency button, and instantly a terrifying wailing began to scream through the house. She fumbled with the lock, risking a glance over her shoulder, and saw Dakota lumbering through the kitchen toward her. Her attention now focused on her hands, she managed to flip the dead bolt. Then the door was open and cool air was on her face and filling her open mouth. She made it to the edge of the concrete where the walk dipped into the grass and then the sidewalk. It was dark, the street outside deserted.

Juno ran, despite her aching body, pumping her legs harder

than she ever had since she'd run with her boys at the park all those years ago. But everything was wrong; she wasn't getting anywhere. And then she felt a hand yanking her back, grabbing her before she could even reach the sidewalk. With the alarm wailing in her head, and her arms and legs flapping like those inflatable waving men that stores used to advertise, Dakota dragged her back inside the house.

By the time Juno found her voice, way back in her belly where it was hiding, Dakota was closing the door behind them, disarming the alarm. Of course he would know the code—he'd stayed here more than once, after all. He tossed her away from him, and Juno's shoulder blade struck the closet door. Even with the breath knocked out of her, she still hadn't screamed. Dakota, seeing his mistake in shoving her away, reached for her again, but Nigel's body was in the way and he tripped over it, sprawling. Juno had a split second to consider her options: the front door was out of the question; she wouldn't get two feet before he grabbed her. That left the apartment beyond the kitchen, but that door had its own dead bolt, and beyond that was the gate with the latch and the alley. And who knew what she would find in that apartment. Two dead women?

She was up the stairs before he was on his feet. She didn't hear his footfalls behind her. That was good; she had time. As she cleared the stairs and ran for Samuel's bedroom window, she heard him yelling something. Her lungs were almost in as much pain as her joints as she gasped for air. If he wasn't coming up the stairs after her, maybe it meant that one of the women was alive, and she bet it was Winnie. She reached Sam's window at the same time she noticed the house had fallen eerily silent.

Her finger found the place behind her ear, but she pulled her hand back, shaking. He'd come up here next; he was probably already on his way up the stairs. She cast a glance over her shoulder, to the window Sam had climbed out of not twenty minutes ago. She'd probably break her neck falling from the roof.

But at least Dakota won't break your neck. Don't you want to die on your own terms? But she'd been wrong about all of it. Samuel—Sam—he'd lost Nigel tonight, and maybe he didn't even know it yet; could she die in peace knowing she was responsible for him losing his mother, as well? She didn't look at the window again, the window that would no doubt save her life. She left it open and hid instead, returning to the spot under the en suite sink.

Nigel had taken most of his toiletries to the downstairs bathroom and had yet to bring them back up. This had cleared out a space where she curled in a tight ball. Dakota stood nearby as Juno held her breath, her back curled against the space. Then she heard him close the window in a whoosh, and the snap of the lock. He did a quick tour of Sam's room, the bathroom, the closet, and then his footsteps receded to the lower level. There was some commotion downstairs; she heard things slamming around. She braced herself to hear another gunshot, but none came. When Dakota's clangs and bangs sounded far enough away, she pushed open the cabinet door and peered around nervously.

She had to stop him from killing Winnie; she was the only mother Sam had, even if she wasn't Sam's biological mother. She'd made a mistake in getting involved; she'd done the wrong thing, and now she had to do the right thing. Juno unfolded herself with the grace of her former years and the pain of her latter. She didn't hesitate. She headed for the stairs with a rough plan forming in her mind.

Downstairs, Dakota was barricading the doors like he was preparing for some type of siege. When Juno reached the bottom of the stairs, she saw that he'd pushed the foyer chair in front of the door and had reactivated the alarm, the red light glaring like an eye.

He didn't want anyone else getting out. But where was he now?

Juno ducked around the corner, grateful for the hundredth time that Sam wasn't here, and headed for the kitchen. As her feet crept over the black-and-white-checkered floor, she heard Winnie's guttural scream from the apartment. "What are you doing? You killed her! Dakota…!"

She could hear them struggling as she reached the junk drawer, yanking it open and sticking her hand all the way to the back. She found what she was looking for. As her hand closed around it, and she tucked it into the back of her pants, she heard Dakota howling like a wounded animal, followed by an incredulous "You bit me!"

Even in the midst of everything, Juno found that ludicrous. *How dare you bite me after I shot and killed your husband!* What she also found more than ludicrous was that none of the neighbors had called the cops. How was that possible? Where was Mr. Nevins? Something thumped heavily, and Juno ran toward the sound. He was going to shoot Winnie, she was certain of it. He didn't just want to hurt the elusive Manda, who had wounded his pride by not taking him back, he wanted to show his family what would happen when they didn't prioritize him. Juno realized something else as well: he was going to kill himself. She could see now that Dakota had planned this out; she'd seen his truck circling the house and had thought nothing of it. And for Dakota's final act of power, he needed to hurt everyone who'd hurt him.

She took a resigned peace in her final evaluation as a therapist—even one who had lost her license—as she moved toward her destination, the mantel. Winnie's garish decorating provided five-pound weights; the busts and the statue of David Juno hated were expensively heavy. The orange one was dead center—the one that reminded her of Joe and his orange juice. She ran for it, darting past the open door of the den and grabbing it by the neck. Beyond the den, in the apartment, Dakota was pulling his twin to her feet. She had a brief glimpse of Winnie's back, and then the fireplace was in front of her. Juno wasn't sure if he'd seen her. The weight of orange David made her knees dip; as she straightened up, she moved out of sight, hiding behind the open door to Nigel's den.

Juno closed her eyes and said a silent prayer, her heart hammering so hard it hurt.

Dakota stepped out with Winnie held against his front, walking slowly, the gun to her head. Her hands were bound and the gag was back in her mouth. But as soon as Dakota stepped across the threshold and into Juno's sight line, it was already too late for him. Juno, concealed behind the open door, was already behind him. She stepped forward from behind the door and swung the base in an arc like she was holding a baseball bat. The orange David hit Dakota's head with a dull thud, and she dropped it as pain exploded down her arm from the impact. Dakota let go of Winnie, who looked like she was barely conscious, and lurched forward. Winnie fell face-first onto the carpet and stayed there; Juno didn't know if she'd passed out or was playing dead. Both were an excellent idea on her part. Juno stared at Dakota, who had fallen onto his knees, roaring in pain, an ugly grimace on his face. She didn't wait to see what he'd do next. Juno ran again.

She held her arm cradled to her chest, legs pumping with the last of her adrenaline. When she got to the front door, she saw again the heavy chair Dakota had pushed under the door handle. The time it would take her to move it... If she went back now and ran for the kitchen, she'd most likely run directly into him. She managed to unlock the deadbolt before she heard him in the hallway behind her, but she couldn't open the door without moving the chair, and Nigel's body was between it and the door. God, Dakota wasn't as dumb as he looked. She ran for the closet instead, opening the door and closing it behind her; she hauled up the trapdoor with her good hand. She was so distracted by the thought of Dakota finding her at any minute that she didn't move her face out of the way; the corner of the trapdoor whacked her above her left eye, slicing through her eyebrow. Juno felt the sting and then the warm flow of blood. She didn't wait for her vision to clear—as the closet door opened, she slipped into her cave.

Juno knew deep down that she should have left this house when she had the chance. Now here she was, going deeper into the shit rather than out of it. But wasn't that the story of her life? Out on parole but in a different type of prison. *But the crawl space is safe*, she told herself. She knew it well, and Dakota had never been in it before, so she had the advantage, even if her body was screaming.

She dropped onto her hands and knees and immediately began crawling. She didn't need light to know where she was going, but Dakota would. She heard him swearing behind her and then the thud of his feet as he hit the floor. He was big, that would slow him down some, but he also had the gun. As her hands slid over dirt and gravel, she thought of Winnie, tied up and facedown on the floor, still oblivious to Juno's existence, still confused about what was happening to her brother. That woman would be clueless until the day she died, and for Sam's sake, Juno would do her best to make sure that day would be a long way away. She thought of Samuel— Sam—and their short interactions, which had meant so much to her. And she thought of Nigel; he was dead. As she crawled forward, a piece of broken glass sliced her palm, but she left it where it was, hoping it would have at Dakota, too. She didn't remember breaking anything—had the glass been here all along?

She couldn't pause to wipe the blood that was running from the cut above her eyebrow, so she was completely blind in one eye and her hand was stinging.

And then the pop came: a loud bang, and pressure on her shoulder. She fell flat on her face, breathing dirt up her nose and gasping for air. Something had hit her, but not a bullet, a rock maybe; the bullet had hit the ground and sent debris flying. *He shot at me,* Juno thought incredulously. *That bumbling idiot shot at me.* But the bumbling idiot was still coming after her; she could hear his grunts and his hands slapping at the ground. She crawled faster still, toward the dirt pile she rarely ventured past. The back end of the space still creeped her out. She felt something hit her in the back of the head, but she didn't stop. And then a hand was on her ankle, yanking her backward. Her sweatshirt rode up as he pulled her along the uneven ground, and Juno felt something sharp stick into her breast. She yelled, she screamed and kicked, and, clawing on the ground, she wriggled away from him. She scooted a few feet ahead when she heard him curse. She scrambled over a ledge of dirt that rose so high to the ceiling of the crawl space she had to shimmy past it on her belly. He couldn't follow her back here, could he? And then she was rolling down the incline, dirt coating the blood on her face like a mask. She didn't have far to roll. She came to a stop at the bottom, lying on her stomach and spitting mud out of her mouth. She lay suddenly still, listening, deciding how far away Dakota's grunts were. "You're so fucking slow!" she called out. "No wonder your wife left you."

That did it. "Who are you, you fucking bitch?" But she

could hear the wobble of fear in his voice. Men always called names when they were scared.

"What were you going to do, Dakota? Kill your twin sister and then yourself?"

There was a shocked silence, during which she could hear him hammering out breaths. He was moving faster now, and if she wanted to stay alive, at least for a little while longer, she'd have to move.

She began scooting forward on her belly, using her elbows to pull herself along. She was almost there, to the little gravesite. She'd come back here only once, and that had been enough. She didn't remember what she'd been doing back there, maybe boredom, but she'd found the remains, obviously of an animal. It was just a scattering of small bones, but it had creeped her out enough to never return. The earth dipped down and circled around the mound, but Dakota wouldn't know that. He was almost to the rise now; he'd be able to look into the valley Juno had rolled into, but he wouldn't be able to see her in the dark. *He'll probably still shoot*, she thought. Once her feet were pulled to safety she reached into her pocket and pulled out what she'd taken from the kitchen drawer; then, she began moving quietly forward. Juno rounded the corner as Dakota pulled back from the rise. She knew she wasn't where he thought she'd be. He'd need to turn around if he wanted to keep looking for her. She eyed the gun, which was in his right hand, pressed to the dirt as he grunted in surprise at not seeing her. He'd be able to turn around any second, and he'd see her there. If she didn't act, she would die as Terry Russel had, at the hands of a sick, angry man. Juno didn't like those terms.

She didn't wait: lunging forward, she fired the Taser she'd swiped from the kitchen drawer into his neck. The two-pronged barbs penetrated the skin near Dakota's pulse, delivering a kick of voltage that made him convulse. In the small space Juno wasn't able to move in time; Dakota's left arm swung out and Juno saw stars for a second or two as it made contact with her head. She righted herself, her vision swimming. She felt frantically along the ground for the gun, her fingers scraping at dirt. Juno had used a Taser before, she knew what happened next. He was strong; he'd recover fast. She figured she had less than five seconds to find the gun and shoot Dakota if she didn't want to die. He roared as he lunged for her, but Juno didn't shrink back; her hands swept the dirt in frantic arcs. Then her fingertips touched the cool tip of the barrel, and relief briefly found its place in her mind. Before she could get a good grip, Dakota grabbed her arm and yanked her toward him, dragging her body painfully over the ground. He tried to get to his feet while holding onto Juno's arm, but his head connected with the roof of the crawl space with a sickening crack. Dakota was temporarily stunned, loosened his hold on her arm. She rolled because it was the only thing she could do, and she'd seen alligators subdue their prey that way. She barely heard his cry of pain over the roaring panic in her own head. Her right hand found the gun. Juno wrapped her fingers around the barrel, pulling it toward her chest. She had just enough time to roll onto her back and point the gun upward. She pulled the trigger.

3 3

WINNIE

Winnie woke to the sound of sirens. Her first thought was of Samuel. Where was Samuel? He was buried in the crawl space! She bolted upright and the room righted itself, but her head didn't. No. Samuel was alive. He wasn't the one buried in the crawl space. He was her baby. Hers. She pressed her palms to her face, pain shooting through the backs of her eyes and landing in the base of her skull. And then the realization: her hands were free. She remembered lying on the floor, still gagged, one of her knickknacks smashed to pieces, orange shards of porcelain that looked like mandarin peels flecking the rug. She saw blood on her clothes next, and in a rush the last hours rose into her memory, choking her with shock.

Dakota had shot Nigel. Nigel was dead. She hauled herself

to her feet, closing her eyes against the pain chewing at her brain. Strips of severed duct tape clung to her clothes and she brushed them off. Had Dakota cut her free? When she was upright, she took a few tentative steps forward until she had a clear view into the apartment. Terry Russel was no figment of her imagination; the old woman lay sideways with her back to Winnie. A groan came from somewhere deep in Winnie's throat where she tasted blood and bile. Where was her brother—why would Dakota do this? The nausea unfolded and Winnie doubled over, thinking she was going to be sick. Had he cut her hands free? No. She didn't have time to be sick. Straightening up, Winnie started to stumble forward. She had to find Samuel—her miracle baby, *her* baby—not Josalyn's. She'd prayed to God for a child, like Hannah had in the Bible, even though she'd not felt worthy to be a mother after what she'd done. And then, when she'd found out she was pregnant shortly after that horrible night, it was like God had forgiven her, he'd trusted her with her own baby. She'd done a terrible thing to Josalyn Russel, and she'd been too much of a coward to make herself accountable for what she'd done, but Samuel was hers alone. She reached the foyer, stepping over Nigel, refusing to look at him. She didn't want to think about Josalyn right now. The front door was wide open, furniture scattered and shoved in corners like someone had kicked it around in a hurry. From outside came the sounds of sirens gusting into the house along with cold, fresh air. Gasping at the feel of it on her skin, Winnie stepped across the threshold, waving her arms at the help that was finally pulling up from every direction. Mr. Nevins stood at the edge of the lawn, arms hanging limply at his sides, his face washed of color. She broke eye contact with him to watch as the police ran across her lawn, their weapons drawn.

"Please, please help my son! Please!" she screamed, even

as they yelled at her to get down. Winnie looked back at the house as police officers swarmed around and past her, through her open front door. Would they find her brother inside or had he run out before her?

Everything that followed was a blur of voices and faces until the medics tried to load her into an ambulance. She screamed Samuel's name until one of the paramedics, a Black woman with close-cropped white hair, spoke so firmly to Winnie she stopped struggling.

"You can't be anyone's mother if you're dead. Are you hearing me right now?"

Winnie stilled to watch the woman attach a blood pressure cuff to her arm. "Good, you're listening. You have a concussion, and we're taking you to the hospital so none of that slapping. You got me in the face and that made me angry because I'm trying to help you."

"My son..."

"Yes, Samuel, I know, you've been screaming his name for the last ten minutes. The police are looking for him. Maybe he left. All we can do right now is take care of his mother. Lie back."

Winnie did as she was told, thinking of the open door. Yes, maybe he'd gotten out, had run before Dakota could catch him. And that was the last thing she remembered.

When she woke up again she was in the hospital, attached to what seemed like a thousand wires. Right away, she knew. There was no moment of not remembering this time, though she would have preferred that. Her eyes looked for someone to tell her about her son, but the room was empty.

"He—ey," she said. "Hey... I'm here."

A nurse came in a moment later, and she smiled at Winnie before hitting a button on the wall. "Paging Dr. Willis, the patient is awake."

The patient, Winnie thought. That was her; and the nurse didn't even have to say her name or room number. The fear of what that meant made Winnie close her eyes.

The nurse carried over a plastic cup and inserted the straw between Winnie's lips.

"Just a little, I know your throat must be a mess."

Winnie drank a few sips and then opened her mouth to start her barrage of questions, but the nurse cut her off.

"Dr. Willis will be here in a moment. Save your throat and ask them when he gets here." She didn't say it unkindly, and Winnie thought she was probably right; even the attempt at speaking had left a burning in her throat. Dr. Willis came in a few minutes later; he was youngish, with ginger hair and an aww-shucks air about him.

"Mrs. Crouch," he said, coming to stand by the bed. "We're very happy to see you awake. You had a pretty serious concussion."

Winnie gathered his words and sorted them in her mind, her eyes closed. Everything was taking too long to understand.

"How long…?"

"Eleven days." He tilted his head to the side when he said it, and for some reason that made Winnie cry.

"Where is my son? Where is my son?" She started coughing after that, and it took several minutes for her body to calm down enough to hear Dr. Willis speak.

"He's fine. He's with your sister."

The relief rode through her body with such force that she tried to sit up. The wires yanked, the machine beeped and the nurse was at her side, pushing her back down gently as the doctor watched.

"Police found him in Greenlake Park a few hours after you

were taken to the hospital. He had no idea what was happening at home, and his intention had been to run away." He paused, and the weight of that hit Winnie in the gut. He knew now, dear God, he knew his father had been murdered by his uncle. Dr. Willis, seeing the look on Winnie's face, gave her a moment to process. "There is a detective here that would like to talk to you. You don't need to if you don't feel up to it, but they've been haunting the halls and annoying my nurses. Do you want to talk to them, Mrs. Crouch?" Winnie didn't hesitate before nodding. She very much wanted to talk to them and get more details about Samuel.

The police detective introduced himself as Detective Rey Abbot. He pulled a chair up to Winnie's bed and looked at her with genuinely sympathetic eyes when he asked her how she was.

"I'm worried about my son. I'm confused about what happened." He nodded like he understood all of this and offered Winnie the box of tissues when she started to cry.

"Your sister-in-law, Amanda Straub, said that your brother Dakota and your husband had issues for some time." He paused, and Winnie shook her head in confusion.

"Issues? My husband wasn't overly fond of my brother. Dakota is—erratic, but Nigel also let him move into our house when his wife kicked him out."

"Mrs. Crouch, we have reason to believe that it was a little more serious than that. That their relationship may have declined over recent months."

"I don't understand why you're saying any of this. Nigel is dead and Dakota killed him. I saw it with my own eyes."

"Your brother and Nigel argued a short distance away from the house, just across the street at the park. An eyewitness says they saw a man run across the street in the direction of your house, and then another followed behind shortly after.

Your brother stabbed Nigel here…" he pointed to a spot on his own chest and Winnie remembered the flow of blood she'd tried to stop by pressing down…the blood had slipped through her fingers regardless. She was lost in that moment, the memory of the blood on her hands, as the detective discussed her husband's murder in his quiet, matter-of-fact tone.

"—he then tied up both you and a woman named Terry Russel. Mrs. Russel was found tied up, dead from a gunshot wound to her head…in the apartment in your home. When police arrived at the scene, you were running out of the house. Records from the alarm company confirmed that someone disarmed the alarm from inside the house shortly before we arrived."

He watched her face carefully. Winnie was unable to hide what she was feeling.

"My brother must have disarmed it before he ran out. The door was wide open. He must have cut me free, too." She couldn't breathe, the memories were fresh pain. She clawed at her neck, searching the detective's face for help. What was happening? Had Dakota changed his mind about killing her at the last minute? Or maybe he never intended to hurt her or Sam, only Nigel.

"Get out." The nurse took one look at Winnie, casting a disdainful look at Detective Abbot. He started to say something but clearly thought better of it, glancing at Winnie before heading out of the room. Winnie reached for the nurse, unable to catch her breath, her hands grabbing at air.

"She's having a panic attack," she heard someone say. And then there were more people, and then there was nothing. When Winnie woke, her sister was sitting in the chair the detective had occupied.

"Shelly," she said, struggling to sit up. "How's Samuel?"

Shelly looked ten years older than the last time Winnie had

seen her. Her mouth was curved in an ugly line, and the rest of her looked almost loose at the seams.

"He's worried about you, but other than that, he's doing as well as you can expect."

Winnie relaxed back into her pillow. There were a dozen questions cueing up in her brain and she was too foggy to organize them. "Dakota..." she said.

Shelly's pinched features twitched and then her mouth sagged open to release the rest of the story. Winnie tried to piece it together between her sister's sobs.

"Wait... Shelly...are you saying they haven't caught him?" Winnie felt like her stomach was about to pay a visit to her throat.

"N-n-no..." Shelly was dry-heaving now. "He killed that woman and then, and then he...ran."

"Ran where...? Did he cut me free?" Winnie was starting to cry now. "He killed Nigel. Where is he, Shelly?"

Shelly stood up and came to sit on the edge of the bed, taking Winnie's hands in her own. They cried together for a few minutes, just holding hands, before her sister said, "They don't know, Pooh Bear. When the police arrived, he was already gone, the front door was wide open like he ran out pretty fast..."

"But the neighbors... Mr. Nevins must have seen him..."

"Your neighbor—" Winnie could hear the distaste in Shelly's voice when she said those two words "—heard the gunshots, the ones that killed Nigel and the Russel woman. Initially he thought it was fireworks from kids in the park. He called the police and I guess he made a noise complaint to them about it. Then he went about his business."

To Winnie that sounded exactly like Mr. Nevins; the nosy, self-righteous busybody. Shelly was put off by the fact that he didn't follow the first call with an investigation. That's what she would have done.

"Apparently, he heard the sound again, another shot, around twenty minutes later. Only *then* did he decide to investigate. He walked out of his house and toward the park, where he claims to have stood for a good five minutes before turning around to go home." As an afterthought Shelly added, "And that's when he saw your front door open and called the police for the second time."

"What other shot?" Winnie said. But Shelly was shaking her head.

"They don't know. There's something else, Winnie." She wasn't meeting Winnie's eyes this time. "There were footprints in the blood." Shelly wiped her nose with the back of her hand and looked down at the sheet. "They weren't yours or Nigel's or that woman's." She shot Winnie a look. "They were small."

"A child's? What do you mean?"

"They weren't Sam's. And he had no trace of blood on his person or clothes," Shelly said quickly. "But that's why that detective was here wanting to talk to you."

"About footprints?" She was so confused. She had no idea what these footprints were about, but how long until they made the connection between her and Josalyn Russel?

"I don't understand what you're saying, Shelly."

"Look, I don't know, either. They've questioned the Russel woman's family, and they have no idea what she was doing in Washington. She was from Ohio, Winnie." Shelly leaned closer, her eyes so bloodshot Winnie flinched. "Why was she at your house?"

Winnie could smell the coffee on her sister's breath. She suddenly felt the lack of air creeping up on her and closed her eyes. Her son was safe, her son was safe.

When she opened her eyes, Shelly was staring at her intently. Winnie found this incredibly annoying. Whatever lecture there was she didn't want to hear it; her twin brother had murdered her husband and was on the loose somewhere. Winnie braced herself for a fight. She wasn't going to lose Samuel, not for some nutjob like Terry Russel.

"The Russel woman had a bunch of stuff in her bag...papers, an email. There was even a police report about a Jane Doe..." Shelly glanced toward the door and Winnie wanted to scream her impatience. "The email is what I have to tell you about. Someone was writing to this woman and telling her things about Sam." Winnie felt light-headed. She gripped the rail of the bed and stared hard at her sister. She didn't have the energy to respond in the way that Shelly wanted. "What things...?"

"That Sam was her dead daughter's son. And that you had stolen him from her."

Winnie didn't have to feign shock; the look of panic on her face made Shelly squirm in her seat. "Police think she was trying to kidnap Sam."

Winnie tried to sort through her questions before someone came in. Her head wasn't right; she needed to remember this later. "Who sent the email?" Winnie asked.

Shelly shook her head, but for a moment Winnie saw doubt in her sister's eyes. "I just know what Mike tells me." Winnie didn't particularly like her brother-in-law Mike Stallwart, but he didn't know that. She'd asked him for a few favors over the years, and he'd been nice enough to never mention it to anyone in the family. This time it involved more than just Winnie so of course Mike was telling them everything.

Winnie ignored the question. "Was she married...? What about the husband?"

"She was. He told the police that she'd been depressed on

and off since her daughter's death and had even contacted a medium…" Shelly paused to let that sink in. "Her daughter was homeless, and last she heard from her she was in Seattle and pregnant in early 2007."

Winnie nodded slowly but her hands were shaking even as they were locked in an embrace. "So why would she think Sam was her daughter's kid? Sam was born in 2008."

Shelly shrugged. "Terry obviously didn't know that when she showed up."

"So Samuel knows I'm his mom, right?"

"Of course," Shelly said. "They're saying it was a terrible coincidence that Terry came on the same night Dakota…" Winnie shook her head vigorously. She didn't want to hear any more about Dakota.

"Anyway," Shelly said quietly. "They're investigating. I'm sure they'll do what police do."

Winnie didn't want to know what that meant. Whoever that person was, they'd known enough to get Terry Russel involved. She shifted the subject to Manda, wanting to think more on that later. Shelly's face soured at the mention of Dakota's wife.

"She's angry. She's blaming us—all of us," she added, glancing at Winnie. "She says he's always been mentally ill and we knew it and enabled him." Shelly spat this out with laughter in her voice, and Winnie felt herself get so hot under the thin hospital sheet she had to close her eyes to keep from yelling. "Dakota was normal until he met her. She's the one who—"

"My God, stop it. I was there, Shelly. What Manda is saying is true. It may not be solely our fault, but we ignored what was right in front of our faces. I bought pot from him, for God's sake."

Shelly's head jerked up at that. "Marijuana doesn't make someone a murderer," she said tightly.

"No, it doesn't, but the fact that he hid everything from his wife and children, the fact that he shot Nigel and tried to kill me—I think that all points to the fucking fact that he was sick!"

"Stop," she hissed, glancing around nervously. "They'll find him. But when they do, your brother is going to prison for life. Do you understand that? Your twin brother, Winnie."

All she could do was gape at her sister. Was Shelly asking her to feel bad for Dakota in this moment, excuse him?

"I understand that he deserves to go to prison for killing my husband."

Her sister rose from her seat with the sort of lofty air Winnie had always respected, but now made her rageful.

"He's family. Excuse me if I can't hate my brother."

"You'd hate him if it were you. Go home, Shelly. I want to be alone."

"You've always been the biggest hypocrite in the family," she said, moving toward the door. "Sam told us that Nigel hid liquor bottles from you. So I wouldn't be so quick to point fingers."

Winnie blinked at her sister with something like revulsion on her face. Was she really comparing a bottle of Jack Daniel's to murder? Winnie wouldn't even dignify that with a response. Shelly went for one more blow before she left. "Mom is brokenhearted. First her husband dies, and now her son is gone."

Winnie was released from the hospital three days later. Nigel's mother, Nancy, picked her and Sam up and took them to her town house, where they would stay until they found something else. Sam—he'd firmly asked to be called Sam—was glued to her side. Nigel's mother already had him in therapy, and Winnie was glad of it. She wasn't sure how to make decisions for them yet, so they burrowed down in her mother-in-law's spare room for the time being. Detective Abbot came by every week to check on them and update her on the case. It had been six weeks, and they still hadn't found Dakota. He'd left his truck a few blocks away, parked on the street and unlocked, his wallet inside the glove box. Winnie, who'd always felt connected to her twin, felt nothing at all. If he was out there, what he'd done had severed any tie they had. As for Josalyn, they'd made the connection eventually and Detective Abbot had come to talk to Winnie at her mother-in-law's town house.

"Josalyn was your patient, so we believe Terry Russel chose to take the death of her daughter out on you. It happened very quickly on her end. She received the email and had booked a flight to Washington within an hour."

"Who sent the email? Could it have been Dakota?" But Winnie knew the answer before it was given. Dakota wasn't calculated enough to pull off some grand scheme; he was all impulse and anger. And besides—how could he have known about Josalyn? And when Terry had told him her story in the back rooms of the house, it was clear he was hearing it for the first time.

"Did you know that Dakota and Nigel had words the night before he came to your house with the gun?"

Winnie shook her head. She wished she could fast-forward through this part; he was going to say things to make her hate both her husband and her brother.

"Your cousin, Amber, she told Dakota that Nigel was cheating on you. Do you remember having that conversation with her?"

Winnie nodded. "Yes, but Amber didn't tell me she'd told Dakota."

"Your brother threatened Nigel in the parking lot of his

work. They shoved each other around before the security guard broke it up."

"That's absurd. He would have told me if that happened."

"Are you sure…?"

She didn't like the look on his face.

"Okay…" Winnie said cautiously. "What are you saying? That Dakota came to my house and killed my husband because he was cheating on me? Then why did he tie me up and almost shoot me, too?"

"We think that when you didn't appreciate what he was doing for you—"

"Come on!"

Detective Abbot held up his hand. "Give me a minute. To Dakota, it didn't matter that you didn't know about his scuffle with Nigel. He was the brave and chivalrous brother and you were ungrateful."

"No. I don't believe that." She looked out the window to where a seagull sat briefly on the railing outside before flying away.

"Did you know that your brother had schizophrenic episodes?"

"No! Well, I didn't want to believe it." Winnie was horrified. Manda had been telling the truth. She'd known there was something bigger going on with Dakota, but none of the family had bothered to listen. The detective pulled a sheet of paper from a cream folder he was holding. "Dakota held a piece of broken glass to a guy's neck at a football game, saying the guy had messed around with his girlfriend."

"Listen, Detective, that was years ago. But I know my brother is sick. I'm not arguing with you. I just want to know that my son is safe and that Dakota is not going to come after us."

"We're actively working to find him. But we're still working on two separate cases here. You know that the emails

Terry Russel received were sent from an IP address in your home, and we have the phone records saying calls were placed to her home from your house line."

"Detective Abbot, with all due respect, I am done talking about Nigel being involved in sending that woman to my house. My husband is dead and can't answer for himself."

A small smile turned up the corners of his mouth, though it didn't reach his eyes, Winnie noticed. Could he hear her heart?

"I have one more thing, Mrs. Crouch, and then I'll be out of your hair." She highly doubted that, but she tried to arrange her face into something pleasant as she waited for him to speak. "The third set of footprints in the blood we found around Nigel—"

"Oh, this again? Are you serious right now? I was there, the whole time. There was no one else. You made out one tiny footprint in the corner of the room and now you think my psychotic brother had a child accomplice?"

"You weren't *conscious* the whole time, though, were you?" He touched his fingertip to the center of his forehead as if he were pressing a button. Winnie sat as still as she could so nothing would betray the noise inside her own head.

"All right...all right," he said, but his eyes continued to evaluate her. "Well, you know the drill."

"I know it well. If I think of anything else, I'll call you. You remember where the door is, I assume."

Winnie made herself a cup of tea after the detective left and sat in the recliner by the window so she could see the water. Sam was at school; Nancy had gone back to work a few days ago. Winnie got it: busy was the easiest way to be right now. They'd given Winnie extended leave at work, which sometimes proved to be a bad thing, like today. She had too much time to think, and Abbot's visit had unsettled her. She was trying to cope with her own grief while steering Sam through his, analyzing every moment of that night had nearly driven her mad the first weeks. And now it felt like a luxury with everything she had going on.

She thought again about the tiny footprint. She had heard another voice in the house, a female voice, or so she thought. But things had been confusing, and the memory of her brother chasing after someone was punctuated by Winnie floating in and out of consciousness. She'd entertained the crazy idea that it had been Josalyn's ghost come to help her, but even in death, Josalyn would never help Winnie after what she'd done. Winnie put the voice to rest because it seemed like the only thing she could do.

She'd put the Turlin Street house on the market the week before, and there was already an offer on it. Not that she was getting market value for the house—the gruesome things that had happened there made it a tough sell, though not tough enough for someone not to take advantage of a discounted house on Greenlake Park, it seemed. As soon as the sale went through, she planned on moving to Portland with Sam—a fresh scene for healing. She was barely talking to anyone in her family anymore. They'd made it abundantly clear that it was Manda and Winnie who'd driven Dakota to what he'd done. They didn't dare blame Nigel; the dead couldn't defend themselves.

As for Terry Russel, Winnie supposed she'd never know why Nigel had sent Terry Russel the information that brought her to the Crouches' doorstep. How could he? Nigel had helped her that night, as she clung to him crying, her arms wrapped around his waist. He'd gone to the car and taken the baby's body out, put it somewhere no one would ever find it. That's what he promised her: *No one will ever find him. I put him somewhere safe.* He'd put her in the shower, scooping her bloody clothes from the bathroom floor as he went, and come back a few minutes later with a sleeping pill and glass of water. Winnie had let him dress her and put her to bed all in a semicatatonic state. How could he help her this way and then bring Terry to her doorstep? And how could he do it without implicating himself? Though what other possibility could there be? Abbot had said that the emails had come from the IP address in their own home.

The morning after the baby had died, she'd woken up and gone downstairs to find Nigel drinking coffee in the kitchen, freshly showered. When he looked up and their eyes met, she saw something different inside them, something…gone. She knew she had ruined their lives that day. Had it been enough for Nigel to finally snap and incriminate them both, after all these years?

She'd been so distraught at everything that had happened, she'd almost talked herself into confessing to the crime she'd committed fourteen years ago. In the end, she'd decided she couldn't help that little boy anymore, but she could help her own son by being around. *Let the dead deal with the dead,* Winnie thought. And that's the last she thought about it for a while.

EPILOGUE

They'd been living in the new house for a month before they smelled it. It was terrible, wet and rotting. When George caught onto it, he'd gone around the house, sniffing, crawling on his hands and knees in the kitchen at one point, sure he'd find a dead rat behind the fridge. But there wasn't a dead rat, just the permeating smell of death.

"It's an animal, it's died in the house...oh my God, what if it had babies in the walls?"

His wife was always the negative Nelly, but George had heard weird noises at night, and at night was when the sneaky animals came out. *She may not be wrong*, he thought.

The smell was thicker on the main level; it was a sizable animal, he decided. He grabbed a handful of thick, industrial garbage bags from under the sink. He wished he had a mask to put over his mouth and nose—wherever that smell was coming from, it was only going to get worse as he got closer. There was a mask shortage, go figure, some virus people were shitting their pants about. George found a bandanna from his wife's accessory drawer and wrapped it around his nose and mouth, and then he went downstairs to the foyer, wearing the gloves he used for yard work.

The entrance to the crawl space was in the front closet, the left one, if you were facing the front door. He'd had to pull the plans out to find the entrance to the thing, but he knew old houses like this one had them. He yanked open the closet door, eyeing the floor carefully. It was carpeted. New-looking, from what he could see. He might even have to pull the whole thing up. He dropped to his knees, looking for a seam, and found it: a trapdoor lay beneath a rectangle of carpet. George held his makeshift mask tighter across his face. Yep, that's where it was coming from. The door was an original fucking piece of wood, if ever he'd seen one. It was easier pulling it up than he expected, and as soon as he did, a gust of god-awful drifted up and George gagged. *Too far to turn back now*, he thought.

He lowered his flashlight into the hole, hoping to God something wasn't going to jump out of the darkness and eat his face. *Rat babies*, he thought. No—bigger—possum babies, maybe. But as the beam from his flashlight spun around the darkness in quick, manic jerks, he saw no obvious movement. The bottom wasn't far off, so he lowered himself down, landing in a crouch. Here he could see that some parts of the dirt floor were uneven, making the space a roller coaster of high and low spaces. Like caves. He chose a direction at random and got to searching.

This place was creeping him the fuck out. He'd only crawled a little ways when he saw what he thought was garbage piled in a mass, in a far corner. It reeked. *How the hell…?* George thought. He was starting to have a very, very bad feeling. The hairs prickled on the back of his neck. In one corner, cans, bags, wrappers, and plastic gallon bottles were stacked against a wall in a neat row. Garbage enough to fill more than a dumpster. That's when, in a panic, he began searching the ground, pausing occasionally to vomit his lunch, and then continuing on. The smell was getting stronger away from the rubbish pile, and his hand hit something wet and sticky; he kept going, though, his knees surely bleeding at this point from the little stones rolling under his palms.

The real estate agent who had sold them this house, a real hard-ass originally from New York, had said something about the former owners. George didn't care for women's gossip, but his wife had latched on, asking a dozen follow-up questions. They were new to the area. Was it possible it wasn't safe? How many families were there on the street? She'd driven the hard-ass from New York to exhaustion with her questions, but at least it gave George a break. Amber had been her name; she'd said the previous owners had moved to Portland after a family tragedy, but there was something else he was trying to remember, something important that had stood out at the time.

He yelped when something cut his knee, stabbing sharply into the soft flesh on top of his kneecap. Glass. He pulled it out, tossing it aside. He was going too far; he should definitely fucking turn back. Turn back. The father had died, along with a woman, that's what had happened. Killed by his brother-in-law, who then disappeared. George had seen the stories on the news, but the juicy details of people's lives were his wife's specialty. He'd not thought anything of that until—*fuck*—he could see something now. Sweatpants…hair… George panted, head hanging toward the dirt. He'd sweat through his shirt, and he could smell his own ripe smell on top of the stench.

A thin line of spit hung from his mouth, swinging toward the dirt. Where had his wife's bandanna gone? He lifted his eyes again, more slowly this time, reluctant to look but unable not to.

There were two feet, small, like a child's. George had to know; he hadn't suffered all this way just to go back now. He crawled around the body so he could get a look at the face. The ground rose around the corpse in a cradle; George had to crawl upward and hold his flashlight between his teeth, pushing forward on his belly. It had a beanie on its head, pulled down low, but in the shaking light of his flashlight George saw strands of long gray hair stuck to a mottled gray face. Not a child, the opposite. In the yellow glow of the flashlight she looked almost peaceful. Where had that thought come from…? Someone dead in a crawl space—*his* crawl space—and they did not die *peacefully*. His mouth dropped open, and the flashlight rolled into the cradle with the body. George could not see to get back without it. He reached in toward the light, being careful not to touch anything—to touch *it*. But as he pulled the flashlight away, something came with it, roused in the dirt.

He picked it up, horrified to be doing so and yet unable to stop himself. It was small, like a piece of chalk. George held it up to his face, panting, sweat running into his ass crack. A bone. He was sure it was the hip bone of something very small. *Fuuuck!* He dropped it, shaking his hand. *It's human*, he thought, and very quickly unthought it. It was *not* human; it couldn't be. It was too small. The shock was still present as George began his long crawl back to the trapdoor. What was he going to tell his wife? This house had been his idea of a new start for them, even with its grisly history, but the minute she found out about this—*and what was "this"?* George thought. He'd almost reached the front of the trapdoor again, and he shone his light back and forth as he went, scared something was going to jump out at him. And then the beam of his flashlight illuminated something else and he jumped, hitting his head on a beam and then falling backward onto his ass. But he still had his flashlight. He swept it over the darkness, panting softly. *You've already seen one dead body, idiot*, he thought. But George did not want to see another dead body, even though he was pretty sure now that there were two back there. He wanted to be sick again.

And there it was: just five feet behind the trapdoor, lying sideways among the garbage like a bloated, gray cabbage; how had he missed it on the way in? George screamed. Dust swept into his mouth as it yawed open, and then he was coughing and crying. He sounded like a fucking dying racoon. Someone had decorated the dead man's body with garbage, piling it around him like a tomb. There was a cardboard sign with writing propped near the feet of the corpse, and there was something wedged in his mouth between two gummy, grotesque lips.

George shone his flashlight toward the mouth that would give him nightmares for years to come and saw the metal barrel of a gun. Someone had rammed the weapon, backward, into the dead man's mouth so it stared with a single eye at George. His eyes went back to the sign, the writing slanting off the cardboard in a drunken scrawl. He wondered what the man had done to deserve having a gun rammed down his throat the wrong way. And who had been angry enough to do the ramming? He lunged for the trapdoor, getting one last, horrified look at the face he would later find out was the missing man, the murderer. Someone, probably the someone rotting in the ditch back there, had left a message.

I'm sorry. I was wrong. I just wanted to do the right thing.

★ ★ ★ ★ ★

ACKNOWLEDGMENTS

Thank you to my agent, Jane Dystel, of whom I am a complete fangirl. You are a woman to be reckoned with *and* you have great cheekbones. I am so grateful for you.

My editor, Brittany Lavery, who offered so much patience and flexibility as I wrote this book and came up with Juno's last words. You're a class act, Brittany! My team at Graydon House, who I'm genuinely excited to be a part of—Ana, Pam, Susan, Roxanne. And at HarperCollins Canada—Karen, Leo, Cory, Jaclyn, Kaiti. Thank you for being my dream team. You make me feel so lucky. Thanks to Sean Kapitain for the great cover.

Shannon Wylie for working through the plot with me in the early days of writing the book.

Serena and Luke Knautz for always being available and willing to do for others. What you've done for me and my career could never be repaid. I love you guys. And to Sophia and Cash, who let me borrow their mom every day—thanks, guys! She's the best.

Traci Finlay, to whom this book is dedicated. You were my first writing partner and first best friend. I don't know anyone with sharper eyes for plot. Thank you for always dropping everything to help me.

Erica Rusikoff of Erica Edits, Christine Estevez from Wildfire Marketing. Thanks to the bloggers who have included my stories in their passion to share books.

To the PLNs who have supported me through every phase of my writing and life, I attribute much of my joy and success to you. Thank you for being a loud voice for my art. You will always be my favorites. Heathens. I hate croutons.

Willow Aster for being my daily support, love, and mental health stabilizer. Colleen Hoover, I'm sick of loving you but I can't stop. Kathleen Tucker, Dina Silver, Claire Contreras, Christine Brae, Cait Norman. Holly for moving to come help me when I needed it most. Bertha, I love you so, thank you for helping me keep my everyday life together. My early readers, Dez, Tobi, Amy, Lindsey, Tasara, Jaime. To the lovely Tess Callahan, who wrote one of my favorite books, *April & Oliver*. Andrea Dunlop for your valuable insight. Shanora Williams for your friendship. James Reynolds for your friendship and sharp ideas.

My perfect babies, Scarlet and Ryder, who ate a lot of takeout while I wrote this book, thanks for all the babysitting hours you guys put in and for coming to hang out with me in my office for all those months I made it my crawl space. And to Avett, who ripped up my notebook outlining *The Wrong Family*: thanks for reminding me to be a pantser, Avett.

Thanks, Mom, for being my forever supporter and never telling me to get a real job. You told me I could do this and I believed you. Jeff for always supporting and feeding me.

To my husband, Joshua, who sat for hours with me in the dark while I wrote, bringing drinks and snacks and falling asleep on my office floor so I wouldn't be in there alone. You're all the romance I'll ever need.

And finally, to my aunt Marlene Groenewald, who told me a version of this story twenty years ago. I think of you every day. This book would not exist without you. I love you so much and I miss you. Tell Dad I said hi.

THE
WRONG
FAMILY

TARRYN FISHER

Reader's Guide

GRAYDON
HOUSE

1. Motherhood is a theme that runs through this whole book: Winnie's relationship to Sam, Juno's relationship with her own estranged sons, Juno's relationship to Sam, and, of course, Josalyn's role as a mother and Winnie's interference in that. As a society, how do we judge mothers who we perceive have made mistakes, and how does the role of motherhood in this book reflect that?

2. Winnie is a complicated character who doesn't always behave well or do the right thing. Did you feel sympathy for Winnie, even after you discovered the full truth about her? Why or why not?

3. How does Winnie's need to control things around her, especially her family life, backfire on her?

4. Nigel is clearly unhappy in his marriage. Why do you think he stays?

5. While Juno isn't perfect, her situation is created by a lot of systemic inequality regarding mental health, physical health, housing needs, and the prison system. How do you think real people are disenfranchised by these systems? Do you think

everyone who might be disempowered by these systems is disempowered in the same ways? How difficult would it be for someone like Juno to get back on her feet?

6. Why do you think the Straub family denied to themselves that Dakota needed some serious mental health assistance? Why do you think that this kind of issue goes undiagnosed? What advantages does Dakota have that others who struggle with mental health might not have? Discuss the mental health struggles that Dakota, Juno, and Josalyn have, respectively. How differently did their situations turn out, and why do you think that is?

7. Juno has some definitive thoughts about Winnie and the Crouches' marriage. Do you agree with the opinions she has formed? Why or why not?

8. Why do you think Juno chooses to stay in the crawl space? What options do you think she has, if any?

9. Discuss the ways in which privilege functions for the characters in this novel.

10. In many ways, Winnie is performing the perfect family life she wants to have, even though her performance is designed to hide a terrible secret. In what ways do we perform in our own lives, and in what ways does society pressure and prompt us to do that?

What was your inspiration for *The Wrong Family*? Did it start with the idea of a troubled marriage, or did it start with the crawl space?

When I was fifteen, my aunt Marlene, who was visiting from South Africa at the time, told me a story about a couple in her city. In short: they'd found a squatter living in their closet, and the squatter had been there for months. I was less mortified than I was intrigued. What a great idea! Sneak into someone's house and live there without them knowing! I wanted to be the squatter; I wanted to spy on the couple. I wanted to know what she saw and how involved she was in their lives. The story stuck with me and over the next twenty years I'd find myself revisiting the couple and their squatter until I decided to sit down and meet them. I did so in my mind, and I did not get what I was expecting.

What draws you to write about a complicated—maybe even doomed—marriage? Or family dynamics more generally?

I'm an introspective person. When I began writing seriously in my early twenties, I was exploring myself and my personality in a fictional world. I took my issues and my questions and my trauma to stories where I dressed them in characters and scenes. When I ran out of personal issues to write about, I began exploring human issues in general. Why do we do the things we do? Some authors write to beautify the world; I write to expose things in the crumbling of it.

How did you develop the character of Juno?

When I first moved to Seattle, I'd often write in coffee shops downtown. I befriended a handful of homeless men in the area who'd come sit at my table and chat with me. I met a homeless engineer, a homeless mechanic, a homeless musician, and a homeless vet during the three years I spent in the area. Their stories were told with painful remorse as they would recount the one mistake that derailed their lives. Juno mostly developed herself from those stories. I could hear those men in my head as I wrote about her. I knew she had to be desperate and I knew she wanted to make things right.

Juno's and Winnie's voices are so different, and yet they struggle with some of the same issues. Did one of them come more easily to you? Was one more of a challenge? What similarities do you see between Winnie and Juno? Might we say that they represent two directions stemming from the same forked path?

Winnie and Juno: different voices, same issues. They were separated by age and economics and yet they shared so many similarities. Juno was hiding in a crawl space; Winnie was hiding in her pretty house. One wanted to make amends for what she'd done and the other one wanted to forget what she'd done entirely. In the end, both were seeking peace, and they were both too dishonest about themselves to ever find it.

What comes first for you—the overall idea for the book or a character?

I ask what-if questions about myself and then seek to answer them. What if your husband had two other wives...? What if you were homeless...? What if you snapped and became a serial killer...? What if someone kidnapped you and locked you in a cabin? I've written all those stories because I wanted to read them. The characters show up at their leisure and I don't always like them. But I always listen and tell their truth.

One of the great ironies of this story is that Winnie works in mental health but can't see how deep her own brother's struggles are, and Juno also worked in mental health but can't see her own diagnosis. Was that irony deliberate, something you wove in from the beginning, or was it something that developed organically and perhaps even unconsciously as you wrote?

I think that it is a human issue. We see what we are comfortable seeing and shade our eyes to the rest. Winnie and Juno are both very selfish and self-involved individuals. They might work in an occupation that aids people, but they look to help themselves first. I think they're both addicted to how doing good makes them feel, but in the end it's still about their feelings.

A similar question: this book touches on a lot of important and deeply relevant social issues. Mental health, homelessness, incarceration—the book shows us how someone can be affected by any or all these things, and that people's situations are rarely simple. Was it your intent to write about those things, or did the characters and the story reveal themselves to you as you went?

I worked in mental health and those experiences definitely shaped me as a writer. What I've found about people in general is that they rarely try to understand their personal antagonist. When you put a face and a past and a trauma on your enemy, you are given understanding which is a powerful avenue for growth. So I want to write about the complicated things that we do to each other and give insight into why we do them.

What other writers are you loving lately? Any thriller writers you're into or any other genres?

I've been reading BIPOC authors this year. I was blown away by the compact art in My Sister, the Serial Killer by Oyinkan Braithwaite. I still think about that book every day. I could not accomplish what Oyinkan did in that book; she told a complex story with few words and it was powerful. Mexican Gothic by Silvia Moreno-Garcia was a favorite this year—let's go, women who write horror! And I would highly, highly recommend The Girl with the Louding Voice by Abi Daré. I'm not sure there's been another book in my lifetime that has made me feel so many things.

Do you have any must-have routines or rituals as a writer that help you focus?

There are things I can't have: obligations. Obligations crush any desire to create. If I know I have to be somewhere or do something, I can't focus. I need to be able to wander in and out of my office at leisure to type a hundred words here or there, and I need to know I don't have anywhere else to be. So when I dive into a book, I become largely unsocial and unresponsive to friends and events. I guess that's how writers end up alone.

Can you tell us anything about what you're working on next?

Yes, it's going to be another unique story line, but this one is less cerebral than The Wives and The Wrong Family. It's instinctive and fast-paced—visceral.

I'm writing about a hunted woman who is hiding in plain sight. If you hunt a woman for long enough, she will evolve to be the stronger thing. My new character is the badass we need right now.

If you loved this book and you haven't read Tarryn Fisher's
runaway bestseller The Wives, *keep reading for a special excerpt.*
You won't be able to put it down!

1

He comes over on Thursday every week. That's my day, I'm Thursday. It's a hopeful day, lost in the middle of the more important days; not the beginning or the end, but a stop. An appetizer to the weekend. Sometimes I wonder about the other days and if they wonder about me. That's how women are, right? Always wondering about each other—curiosity and spite curdling together in little emotional puddles. Little good that does; if you wonder too hard, you'll get everything wrong.

I set the table for two. I'm a little buzzed as I lay out the silverware, pausing to consider the etiquette of what goes where. I run my tongue along my teeth and shake my head. I'm being silly; it's just me and Seth tonight—an at-home date. Not that there's anything else—we don't do regular dates very often at the risk of being seen. Imagine that…not wanting to be seen with your husband. Or your husband not wanting to be seen with you. The vodka I sipped earlier has warmed me, made my limbs loose and careless. I almost knock over the vase of flowers as I place a fork next to a plate: a bouquet of the palest pink roses. I chose them for their sexual innuendo because when you're in a position like mine, being on top of your sexual game is of the utmost importance. *Look at these delicate, pink petals. Do they make you think of my clit? Good!*

To the right of the vaginal flowers sit two white candles in silver candlestick holders. My mother once told me that under the flickering light of a candle flame, a woman can almost look ten years younger. My mother cared about those things. Every six weeks a doctor slid a needle into her forehead, pumping thirty cc's of Botox into her dermis. She had a subscription to every glossy fashion magazine you could name and collected books on how to keep your husband. No one tries that hard to keep their husband unless they've already lost him. I used to think her shallow, back when my ideals were untainted by reality. I had big plans to be anything but my mother: to be loved, to be successful, to make beautiful children. But the truth is that the heart's desire is a mere current against the tide of nurture and nature. You can spend your whole life swimming against it and eventually you'll get tired and the current of genes and upbringing will pull you under. I became a lot like her and a little bit like me.

I roll the wheel of the lighter with my thumb and hold the flame above the wick. The lighter is a Zippo, the worn remnants of a Union Jack flag on the casing. The flickering tongue reminds me of my brief stint with smoking. To look cool, mostly—I never inhaled, but I lived to see that glowing cherry at my fingertips. My parents bought the candleholders for me as a housewarming gift after I saw them in a Tiffany's catalog. I found them to be predictably classy. When you're newly married, you see a pair of candlestick holders and imagine a lifetime of roast dinners that will go along with them. Dinners much like the one we're having tonight. My life is almost perfect.

I glance out the bay window as I fold the napkins, the view of the park spread out beneath me. It's gray outside, typical of Seattle. The view of the park is why I chose this particular unit instead of the much larger, nicer unit overlooking Elliott Bay. While most people would have chosen the view of the water, I prefer a view of people's lives. A silver-haired couple sits on a bench, staring out at the pathway where cyclists and joggers pass every few minutes. They're not touching, though their heads move in unison whenever someone goes by. I wonder if that will be Seth and me one day, and then my cheeks warm as I think of the others. Imagining what the future holds proves difficult when factoring in two other women who share your husband.

I set out the bottle of pinot grigio that I chose from the market earlier today. The label is boring, not something that catches the eye, but the austere-looking man who sold it to me had described its taste in great detail, rubbing his fingers together as he spoke. I can't recall what he'd said, even though it was only a few hours ago. I'd been distracted, focused on the task of collecting ingredients. Cooking, my mother taught me, is the only good way to be a wife.

Standing back, I examine my work. Overall, it's an impressive table, but I am queen of presentation, after all. Everything is just right, the way he likes it, and thus, the way I like it. It's not that I don't have a personality; it's just that everything I am is reserved for him. As it should be.

At six o'clock sharp, I hear the key turn in the lock and then the whistle of the door opening. I hear the click as it closes, and his keys hitting the table in the entryway. Seth is never late, and when you live a life as complicated as his, order is important. I smooth down the hair I so painstakingly curled and step from the kitchen into the hallway to greet him. He's looking down at the mail in his hand, raindrops clinging to the tips of his hair.

"You got the mail! Thank you." I'm embarrassed by the enthusiasm in my voice. It's just the mail, for God's sake.

He sets the pile down on the little marble table in the entryway, next to his keys, and smiles. There is a tilt in my belly, heat and a flurry of excitement. I step into the breadth of him, inhaling his scent, and burying my face in his neck. It's a nice neck, tan and wide. It holds up a very good head of hair and a face that is traditionally handsome with the tiniest bit of roguish scruff. I nestle into him. Five days is a long time to go without the man you love. In my youth, I considered love a burden. How could you get anything done when you had to consider someone else every second of the day? When I met Seth, that all went out the window. I became my mother: doting, yielding, spread-eagle emotionally and sexually. It both thrilled and revolted me.

"I missed you," I tell him.

I kiss the underside of his chin, then the tender spot beneath his ear, and then stand on my tiptoes to reach his mouth. I am thirsty for his attention and my kiss is aggressive and deep. He moans from the back of his throat, and his briefcase drops to the floor with a thud. He wraps his arms around me.

"That was a nice hello," he says. Two of his fingers play the knobs of my spine like a saxophone. He massages them gently until I squirm closer.

"I'd give you a better one, but dinner is ready."

His eyes become smoky, and I silently thrill. I turned him on in under two minutes. I want to say, *Beat that*, but to whom? Something uncoils in my stomach, a ribbon unrolling, unrolling. I try to catch it before it goes too far. Why do I always have to think of them? The key to making this work is not thinking of them.

"What did you make?" He unravels the scarf from his neck and loops it around mine, pulling me close and kissing me once more. His voice is warm against my cold trance, and I push my feelings aside, determined not to ruin our night together.

"Smells good."

I smile and sashay into the dining room—a little hip to go with his dinner. I pause in the doorway to note his reaction to the table.

"You make everything beautiful." He reaches for me, his strong, tanned hands tracked with veins, but I dance away, teasing. Behind him, the window is rinsed with rain. I glance over his shoulder—the couple on the bench are gone. What did they go home to? Chinese takeout...canned soup...?

I move on to the kitchen, making sure Seth's eyes are on me. Experience has taught me that you can drag a man's eyes if you move the right way.

"A rack of lamb," I call over my shoulder. "Couscous..."

He plucks the bottle of wine from the table, holding it by the neck and tilting it down to study the label. "This is a good wine." Seth is not supposed to drink wine; he doesn't with the others. Religious reasons. He makes an exception for me and I chalk it up to another one of my small victories. I have lured him into deep red, merlots and crisp chardonnays. We've kissed, and laughed, and fucked drunk. Only with me; he hasn't done that with them.

Silly, I know. I chose this life and it's not about competing, it's about providing, but one can't help but keep a tally when other women are involved.

When I return from the kitchen with dinner clutched between two dishtowels, he has poured the wine and is staring out the window while he sips. Beneath the twelfth-floor window, the city hums her nightly rhythm. A busy street cuts a path in front of the park. To the right of the park and just out of view is the Sound, dotted with sailboats and ferries in the summer, and masked with fog in the winter. From our bedroom window, you can see it—a wide expanse of standing and falling water. The perfect Seattle view.

"I don't care about dinner," he says. "I want you now." His voice is commanding; Seth leaves little room for questions. It's a trait that has served him well in all areas of his life.

I set the platters on the table, my appetite for one thing gone and replaced by another. I watch as he blows out the candles, never taking his eyes from me, and then I walk to the bedroom, reaching around and unzipping my dress as I go. I do it slowly so he can watch, peeling off the layer of silk. I feel him behind me: the large presence, the warmth, the anticipation of what's to come. My perfect dinner cools on the table, the fat of the lamb congealing around the edges of the serving dish in oranges and creams as I slip out of the dress and bend at the waist, letting my hands sink into the bed. I'm wrist-deep in the down comforter when his fingers graze my hips and hook in the elastic waist of my panties. He pulls them down, and when they flutter around my ankles, I kick free of them.

The *tink* of metal and then the *zzzweeep* of his belt. He doesn't undress—there's just the muted sound of his pants falling to his ankles.

After, I warm our dinner in the microwave, wrapped in my robe. There is a throbbing between my legs, a trickle of semen on my thigh; I am sore in the best possible way. I carry his plate to where he is lying shirtless on the couch, one arm thrown over his head—an image of exhaustion. I cannot remove the grin from my lips, though I try. It's a break in my usual facade, this grinning like a schoolgirl.

"You're beautiful," he says when he sees me. His voice is gruff like it always is postsex. "You felt so good." He reaches up to rub my thigh as he takes his plate. "Do you remember that vacation we talked about taking? Where do you want to go?" This is the essence of postcoital conversation with Seth: he likes to talk about the future after he comes.

Do I remember? Of course I remember. I rearrange my face so that it looks surprised.

He's been promising a vacation for a year. Just the two of us. My heart beats faster. I've been waiting for this. I didn't want to push it since he's been so busy, but here it is—my year. I've imagined all the places we can go. I've narrowed it down to a beach. White sands and lapis lazuli water, long walks along the water's edge holding hands in public. *In public.*

"I was thinking somewhere warm," I say. I don't make eye contact—I don't want him to see how eager I am to have him to myself. I am needy, and jealous, and petty. I let my robe fall open as I bend to set his wine on the coffee table. He reaches inside and cups my breast like I knew he would. He is predictable in some ways.

"Turks and Caicos?" he suggests. "Trinidad?"

Yes and yes!

Lowering myself into the armchair that faces the sofa, I cross my legs so that my robe slips open and reveals my thigh.

"You choose," I say. "You've been more places than I have." I know he likes that, to make the decisions. And what do I care where we go? So long as I get him for a week, uninterrupted, unshared. For that week, he will be only mine. A fantasy. Now comes the time I both dread and live for.

"Seth, tell me about your week."

He sets his plate down and rubs the tips of his fingers together. They are glistening from the grease of the meat. I want to go over and put his fingers in my mouth, suck them clean.

"Monday is sick, the baby…"

"Oh, no," I say. "She's still in her first trimester, so it will be that way for a few more weeks."

He nods, a small smile playing on his lips. "She's very excited, despite the sickness. I bought her one of those baby name books. She highlights the names she likes and then we look through them when I see her."

I feel a spike of jealousy and push it aside immediately. This is the highlight of my week, hearing about the others. I don't want to ruin it with petty feelings.

"That's so exciting," I say. "Does she want a boy or a girl?"

He laughs as he walks over to the kitchen to set his plate in the sink. I hear the water running and then the lid of the trash can as he throws his paper towel away.

"She wants a boy. With dark hair, like mine. But I think whatever we have will have blond hair, like hers."

I picture Monday in my mind—long, pin-straight blond hair, a surfer's tan. She's lean and muscular with perfect white teeth. She laughs a lot—mostly at the things he says—and is youthfully in love. He told me once that she is twenty-five but looks like a college girl. Normally, I'd judge a man for that, the cliché way men want younger women, but it isn't true of him. Seth likes the connection.

"You'll let me know as soon as you know what you're having?"

"It's a ways off, but yes." He smiles, the corner of his mouth moving up. "We have a doctor's appointment next week. I'll have to head straight over on Monday morning." He winks at me and I am not skilled enough to hide my flush. My legs are crossed and my foot bounces up and down as warmth fills my belly. He has the same effect on me now as he had on the first day we met.

"Can I make you a drink?" I ask, standing up.

I walk over to the bar and hit Play on the stereo. Of course he wants a drink, he always wants a drink on the evenings when we're together. He told me that he secretly keeps a bottle of scotch at the office now, and I mentally gloat at my bad influence. Tom Waits begins to sing and I reach for the decanter of vodka.

I used to ask about Tuesday, but Seth is more hesitant to talk about her. I've always chalked it up to her being in a position of authority as first wife. The first wife, the first woman he loved. It's daunting in a way to know I'm only his second choice. I've consoled myself with the fact that I am Seth's legal wife, that even though they're still together, he had to divorce her to marry me. I don't like Tuesday. She's selfish; her career takes the most dominant role in her life—the space I reserve for Seth. And while I disapprove, I can't entirely blame her, either. He's gone five days of the week. We have one rotating day that we take turns with, but it's our job to fill the week with things that aren't him: stupid things for me—pottery making, romance novels and Netflix; but for Tuesday, it's her career. I root around in the pocket of my robe, searching for my ChapStick. We have entire lives outside of our marriage. It's the only way to stay sane.

Pizza for dinner again? I used to ask. He'd admitted to me once that Tuesday was a takeout-ordering girl rather than a cooking girl.

Always so judgmental about other people's cooking skills, he'd tease.

I set up two glasses and fill them with ice. I can hear Seth moving behind me, getting up from the couch. The soda bottle hisses as I twist off the cap and top off the glasses. Before I'm finished making our drinks, he's behind me, kissing my neck. I dip my head to the side to give him better access. He takes his drink from me and walks over to the window while I sit.

I look over from my spot on the couch, my glass sweaty against my palm.

Seth lowers himself next to me on the couch, setting his drink on the coffee table. He reaches to rub my neck while he laughs.

His eyes are dancing, flirtatious. I fell in love with those eyes and the way they always seemed to be laughing. I lift one corner of my mouth in a smile and lean back into him, enjoying the solid feel of his body against my back. His fingers trail up and down my arm.

What's left to discuss? I want to make sure I'm familiar with all areas of his life. "The business...?"

"Alex..." He pauses. I watch as he runs the pad of his thumb across his bottom lip, a habit I'm endeared to.

What has he done now?

"I caught him in another lie," he says.

Alex is Seth's business partner; they started the company together. For as long as I can remember, Alex has been the face of the business: meeting with clients and securing the jobs, while Seth is the one who manages the actual building of the homes, dealing with things like the contractors and inspections. Seth has told me that the very first time they butted heads was over the name of the company: Alex wanted his last name to be incorporated into the name of the business, while Seth wanted it to include the Pacific Northwest. They'd fought it out and settled on Emerald City Development. Over the last years their attention to detail and the sheer beauty of the homes they build has secured them several high-profile clients. I have never met Alex; he doesn't know I exist. He thinks Seth's wife is Tuesday. When Seth and Tuesday were first married, they'd go on vacations with Alex and his wife— once to Hawaii and another time on a ski holiday to Banff. I've seen Alex in photos. He's an inch shorter than his wife,

Barbara, who is a former Miss Utah. Squat and balding, he has a close-lipped smugness about him.

There are so many people I haven't met. Seth's parents, for example, and his childhood friends. As second wife, I may never have the chance.

"Oh?" I say. "What's up?"

My existence is exhausting, all of the games I play. This is a woman's curse. Be direct, but not too direct. Be strong, but not too strong. Ask questions, but not too many. I take a sip of my drink and sit on the couch next to him.

"Do you enjoy this?" he asks. "It's sort of strange, you asking about—"

"I enjoy you." I smile. "Knowing your world, what you feel and experience when you aren't with me." It's true, isn't it? I love my husband, but I'm not the only one. There are others. My only power is my knowledge. I can thwart, one-up, fuck his brains out and feign an aloof detached interest, all with a few well-timed questions.

Seth sighs, rubbing his eyes with the heels of his hands. "Let's go to bed," he says.

I study his face. For tonight, he's done talking about them. He holds out a hand to help me up and I take it, letting him pull me to my feet.

We make love this time, kissing deeply as I wrap my legs around him. I shouldn't wonder, but I do. How does a man love so many women? A different woman almost every other day. And where do I fall in the category of favor?

He falls asleep quickly, but I do not. Thursday is the day I don't sleep.

Need to know what happens next? Pick up your copy of
The Wives *wherever you buy your books!*

Copyright © 2019 by Tarryn Fisher

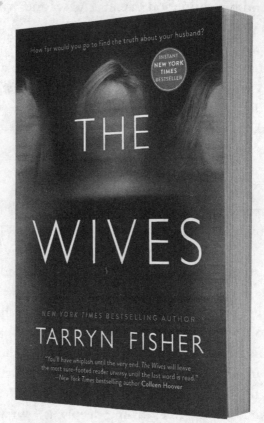